Christmas Recollections
at Grace Chapel Inn

Tales from Grace Chapel Inn

Christmas Recollections at Grace Chapel Inn

Melody Carlson,
Beth Adams &
Anne Marie Rodgers

Guideposts

DANBURY, CONNECTICUT

Christmas Recollections at Grace Chapel Inn

Published by Guideposts Books & Inspirational Media
100 Reserve Road, Suite E200
Danbury, CT 06810
Guideposts.org

"Alice Remembers..." was written by Melody Carlson.
"Louise Remembers..." was written by Beth Adams.
"Jane Remembers..." was written by Anne Marie Rodgers.

Cover and interior design by Müllerhaus
Cover illustration by Bob Kayganich, represented by Deborah Wolfe, LTD.
Typeset by Aptara, Inc.

Printed and bound in the United States of America
10 9 8 7 6 5 4 3 2 1

Grace Chapel Inn

A place where one can be
refreshed and encouraged,
a place of hope and healing,
a place where God is at home.

Prologue

The delectable aroma of vanilla cookies drew not just Alice but Louise as well to the cozy but well-equipped kitchen. "I didn't think it would take long for you two to join me." Jane grinned as she removed a sheet of shaped cookies from the oven.

"Holiday baking already?" Louise's pale brows arched. "Christmas is more than three weeks away, Jane."

"I like to get ahead of the game." Jane set a plate of slightly misshapen cookies on the table. "These are the rejects. Help yourselves, girls."

"Thanks." Alice chuckled as she reached for what looked like a humpbacked snowman. "And we won't take the reject part personally."

Louise picked up a lopsided star. "What about those other cookies?" She nodded to the marble countertop lined with perfectly shaped cookies. "Won't they get stale?"

"I'll freeze them to be frosted later. Maybe some of our holiday guests might want to join in the fun." Jane set three teacups on the table.

"Holiday guests?" Louise sounded dismal. "I just can't understand what's happening. We're usually full for Christmas week, but with two cancellations today, we only have one room reserved now."

"Don't worry," Alice reassured her. "We've been down this road before. We'll be booked full soon. Just wait and see."

Jane set the teapot on the table. "Yes, we always get last-minute reservations before the holidays. It's just that life can be complicated at Christmas. Plans change, and people don't know what to do about it." She picked up a one-winged angel shape. "And that's when we get guests kind of like these cookies."

"You mean the rejects?" Louise's tone was wry.

Alice laughed. "Not rejects, Louise. Just people with problems . . . people who need an extra portion of patience and love at Christmastime."

"People who go home happier than they came." Jane smiled as she filled Alice's teacup.

"Yes, you're both right." Louise stirred her tea. "Some of my best Christmas memories at the inn involve those very people."

"The ones who drive you certifiably nuts at first"—Jane sipped her tea—"and then you tear up when they leave."

"Like Mr. Grover." Alice sighed. "Remember him?"

"And his little dog too?" Jane laughed.

"How could we forget them?" Louise shook her head and chuckled.

And suddenly they were all reminiscing and laughing so hard they were crying, trying to determine which Christmas guest had been the crankiest—and then the sweetest—to visit Grace Chapel Inn. It was hard to decide!

Alice Remembers...

By Melody Carlson

Chapter One

While sweeping powdered snow from the front-porch steps, Alice Howard paused to adjust the red velvet bow on the windblown Christmas wreath when something caught her eye. She watched with interest as a lone figure slowly moved down the sidewalk. Walking with a slight limp, his head bent low against the blustering snow, the man didn't seem familiar. Alice shuddered, pulling her flapping fleece jacket tighter around herself. *Not a fit day for man or beast*, she could imagine her father saying. And certainly not a good day for an afternoon stroll.

As the stranger came nearer, she noticed how his rumpled overcoat appeared lopsided, misbuttoned perhaps, and his shabby felt hat drooped over his ears. His hunched head and shoulders, thoroughly draped in snow, only seemed to add to the overall forlorn impression. Who was he, and where was he going? Her curiosity increased as the man turned onto the inn's footpath, which was already in need of shoveling again. Was this poor fellow lost? Yet the tilt of his chin seemed determined—as if he knew where he was going and wanted to get there.

She called out a friendly greeting as he reached the steps. The man looked up in surprise, and Alice could see he was elderly and that he seemed to be clutching something in his arms. Tufts of brown fur suggested a small animal of some sort, tucked underneath his raggedy overcoat.

Alice smiled at him. "Can I help you?"

"Is this Grace Chapel Inn?" he demanded in a stern, gravelly voice.

"Yes, yes, that's right." Alice's smile remained fixed, but she felt a wave of concern mixed with sympathy. Was this poor old man destitute? Perhaps he'd assumed Grace Chapel Inn was a homeless shelter—that had happened before. Even though Acorn Hill was a bit off the beaten path for indigents, they occasionally passed through. Not so much in wintertime though.

"Doesn't look much like an inn to me." He scowled up at the tall Victorian house.

"We're more of a bed-and-breakfast," she clarified. "Although we do serve other meals during holidays or for special occasions." She wondered if this fellow was hungry. She could offer him a bite to eat and some bus fare then send him on his way before the other guests came back.

"Humph." Leaning against the porch railing, he placed a snow-encrusted shoe on the first step.

"Can I help you, sir?" she asked for the second time.

"You can let me get out of this blizzard." He frowned at her. "If that's not too much trouble."

"Yes, of course. Let me lend a hand." She stepped down, reaching for his elbow as he hobbled up the steps.

"I'm fine," he growled. "Don't need your help."

"Please, do come in." She opened the front door, waiting for him to enter the spacious foyer. "But I should warn you, sir, if you're looking for a room, we have no vacancies at the moment."

"What do you mean, *no vacancies?*" He stooped down and, extracting a scruffy little dog from under his coat, he set it on the Persian area rug. "Did I misunderstand you? This *is* Grace Chapel Inn, isn't it?"

"Yes, it is. But our inn is booked through the holidays." Alice moved behind the reception desk, wishing that Louise would pop in and confirm that they were indeed full. But her older sister was at the church, playing piano for the children who were practicing for this weekend's Christmas pageant. "Is there some other way I can be of assistance? Perhaps I can call someone for you?"

"You can show me to my room," he declared. "I'm cold and tired and in need of some rest."

"But I'm trying to explain to you." Her tone was gentle but firm. "We are fully booked just now. But perhaps I can call—"

"Are you saying you gave away my room?" he demanded. "Of all the demented, confounded—"

"I'm sorry. You don't seem to understand." She pointed to the reservation book with frustration. "Our rooms are all full. Or about to be." She read Louise's Post-it note on the front of the book. "We do have one unoccupied room, but it's reserved for a couple." She knew she was babbling now, but she didn't know what else to do. "You see, we expected them to arrive last night, but they didn't show. It's possible they might cancel due to the weather. We haven't heard from them yet. But Mrs. Grover paid in advance, and we can't just give up—"

"I am *Mr.* Grover."

"Oh…really?" She grimaced. Despite not liking to be suspicious of anyone, Alice knew better than to give in this easily. Louise would throw a fit if the Grovers' room was handed over to a homeless man and his scruffy dog. Even if it was Christmas.

"Isobel—that's my wife," the man gruffly declared. "She booked us a room here for the holidays."

Alice blinked in confusion. That all sounded right. "I'm terribly sorry, sir. I didn't realize that. My sister usually handles this." She looked toward the door, wondering why he'd come on foot and why he looked so shabby. "But where is Mrs. Grover?"

"She's not here." He fumbled to extract a worn wallet from his inside coat pocket and opened it, holding it out for her to see the driver's license encased in a plastic sleeve. "Look at my ID if you don't believe me. And I should have the confirmation information here somewhere too. Isobel made the reservation last January. And she paid in advance."

Alice nodded nervously. "Yes, yes, that's right. My sister mentioned that last night. She was worried about why you weren't here. And she tried to call you." She peered at his out-of-state driver's license just to make sure he truly was Robert Grover—and not a crook. How many times had Louise reminded them to do this with new guests? "Thank you." She smiled.

"Now, please, may I go to my room?"

"Yes, of course. But what about your bags and your—"

"The car broke down yesterday. I had to spend the night in Pittsburgh. Lousy noisy hotel, never slept a wink. This morning, thanks to Triple A, I got the car towed to a garage right here in Acorn Hill." He pocketed his wallet. "Bags are still in my car. The mechanic promised to drop them here after work—after five, he said."

"Oh yes." Alice nodded. "I'm sure you must be worn out, Mr. Grover. But what about your—"

"I am *exhausted*." He glared at her. "I'd like to go to my room. *Now.*"

"Yes, of course." Alice reached for the brass room key, but as she stepped out from behind the desk, she still felt uncertain. *Where is his wife?* And what about that dog? Had Louise been aware they were bringing a pet? She hadn't mentioned it. There would be an extra cleaning fee—should Alice mention that to him now? She wished Jane was here to help. More assertive than Alice, her younger sister was great at resolving prickly situations. But Jane was off getting groceries at the moment.

"Right this way." Alice handed him a Grace Chapel Inn brochure that listed their various amenities and helpful information. "You'll be staying upstairs. In the Sunset Room."

"*Sunset* Room?" He groaned as he stooped to pick up his dog. "Is that where you put all your elderly guests? For the sunset of their lives?"

"Oh no, it's not like that at all. It's just that the room faces westward. And it's decorated in sunset colors. It's quite popular in the wintertime for the afternoon sunshine it usually gets." She paused by the staircase. "Can you manage these stairs okay?"

"Yes, of course," he snapped. "Just takes me longer."

"Would you like me to carry your dog for you?" she offered. "So your hands can be free to hold the banister?"

"I suppose that's wise." He held the little dog out toward her. "Don't want to fall down and break my good leg."

Alice tried not to wrinkle her nose at the strong canine aroma—such a big smell for such a little dog. "And what's your name?" she murmured to the brown pup.

"*Mr. Grover!*" the man growled at her.

"No, no." Alice attempted a laugh. "I meant your dog."

"Oh well. That's Suzie Q. Silly name, I know. But I didn't name her."

"Nice to meet you, Suzie Q." Alice tried to hold her breath as she scurried up the stairs ahead of the cantankerous guest. The sooner she got him settled into his room, the happier they'd all be. She unlocked the door for him then handed him the key. "I assume you've read our pet policy and—"

"Yes, yes, my wife handled all that. And don't worry. Suzie Q is house-trained and never barks." He removed his soggy hat. "You don't need to concern yourself." He glanced at the door, as if to hint it was time for Alice to make herself scarce.

She moved to the doorway then paused. "So, when do you expect your wife will be arriving?"

"I don't," he snapped. "Now if you'll excuse me, I'd like to get some rest." He reached for the doorknob and, before she could say another word, firmly closed the door—practically in her face.

Alice slowly shook her head as she walked back down the stairs. Unless she was mistaken, Mr. Grover was going to be difficult—precisely what they did not need during the holidays. And what about his mysteriously missing wife? Where was Mrs. Grover? Surely, he hadn't left the poor woman in Pittsburgh. Perhaps she was still in town. Maybe she'd gotten weary of his grumpy attitude and made up an excuse to linger there. She might be doing some last-minute Christmas shopping, and he'd come on ahead to secure their room. But why wouldn't he have simply explained that? And why had he said he didn't expect her at all? Maybe that was just his way of telling Alice to mind her own business. Whatever the case, Mr. Grover made no sense to her. No sense at all.

Chapter Two

A lice had just begun to inform Jane about their latest guest's arrival when Aunt Ethel burst into the kitchen. "Oh my!" Their elderly aunt shook snow off the woolen shawl she'd worn to make the short trek from the carriage house to the inn. "The snow's coming down hard and fast." She stomped her snow boots on the tiled kitchen floor. "We're supposed to get another fourteen inches by tomorrow. I'll be buried by then!"

"Our handyman is shoveling our front walk right now. He just finished at the church, and I'm sure he'll get the walk and drive to the carriage house when he's done." Jane turned her attention back to Alice. "So what's this about the Grover couple?"

"Just Mr. Grover." Alice described their cantankerous guest in more detail, including his disheveled appearance and the smelly little dog. "At first I thought he was a homeless man. And his wife isn't with him. I wasn't sure what to make of him."

"And you're certain he's really Mr. Grover?" Jane unloaded groceries onto the island.

"He showed me his ID." Alice emptied a bag of sweet yellow onions into the proper bin.

"So no problem then." Jane set a carton of milk in the fridge.

"I don't know. Identity theft is on the rise." Aunt Ethel helped herself to a recently made cookie. "I just saw a news show about the problem. They target older people."

"He is older, Auntie." Alice picked up a bag of nice-looking honey crisp apples. "And I really don't think he's an imposter. He's just an elderly man. I'm guessing close to eighty."

Aunt Ethel patted her titian-red hair, which looked as if her roots had been recently retouched. "Careful about who you call elderly, Alice. Age is just a number."

"Well, he's not like you, dear auntie. He *acts* elderly. He's a bit of a curmudgeon, and he's got a bad leg too."

"So we've established that he is Mr. Grover." Jane directed this to Alice. "But where is his wife? Louise was concerned they weren't here yesterday. She said Mrs. Grover made the reservation a full year ago. Louise remembered that she really wanted to be here for Christmas. It was her husband who was dragging his heels. Louise seemed eager to meet her."

"Maybe the poor woman got fed up with her cranky old husband and stayed home," Aunt Ethel suggested.

"And sent him here without her?" Jane chuckled. "So she could have peace and quiet by herself?"

"And so you girls could deal with the old grump." Aunt Ethel reached for a second cookie. "And his stinky dog too."

"Or maybe she's passed on," Alice said quietly. "I think we've all been wondering that in the back of our minds but didn't want to think too hard about that sad possibility."

"Then why would he come here by himself?" Jane asked. "Especially since he didn't want to come in the first place."

"Yes…and he didn't seem too pleased to be here now." Alice considered this.

"And if his wife has passed on, why wouldn't he just say so?" Aunt Ethel challenged.

"I don't know." Alice washed and dried the apples. "It's confusing."

"But what if he's *not* Mr. Grover?" Aunt Ethel persisted dramatically.

"Why would he *pretend* to be Mr. Grover?" Jane set a bunch of bananas in a basket with a skeptical expression. "Good grief, Auntie. What's his motive?"

"And how would he know all the information he shared with me?" Alice asked a bit defensively. Why was Aunt Ethel getting so carried away?

"Because he's *stolen* the Grovers' identity," Aunt Ethel declared. Suddenly she was telling them about a gruesome case she'd seen on TV about a man who'd murdered an elderly couple in order to steal their identity. "Apparently they had no family around to notice. The dirty rotten scoundrel sold off all their possessions and their home, and then he emptied their bank accounts and left the country with their credit cards that he maxed out down in Mexico."

"Well, this man isn't leaving the country," Alice told her. "He's napping upstairs. And how would he know about the reservation here? Or that Mrs. Grover had paid in advance?"

"And why would he waste time coming here?" Jane folded her reusable shopping bag. "Wouldn't he be busy selling off their home and booking the next flight to Cabo?"

Alice remembered something. "Yes, and I forgot to mention that he offered to show me the confirmation for the room."

"Did you *see* it?" Aunt Ethel's pale brows arched.

"Well, no…" Alice carefully arranged the shiny apples in the big wooden bowl. "Really, you're blowing this out of proportion. He is Mr. Grover." Why had she even told them about the old man?

"I'd love to be around when Louise hears this news." Aunt Ethel chuckled as she reached for her shawl. "But I need to be off. I only came through the inn to wait for Lloyd. It's our bridge club night, and I told him to pick me up here since the driveway to the carriage house hasn't been cleared of snow yet."

"Isn't it too early for your bridge club?" Alice asked.

"Lloyd needs me to check his costume before we play. You know, he's Santa for the pageant again this year." Aunt Ethel checked her watch. "In fact, he should be here by now."

"Have fun," Alice called as their aunt bustled on out.

"Watch out for murderers and identity thieves," Jane teased.

"Oh Jane." Alice chuckled.

"So do you think it's wrong for me to envy my elderly aunt's social life?" Jane set a large pot of water on the big gas range.

Alice laughed again. "You have a great social life."

"Not compared to our vivacious aunt." Jane turned on the burner.

"You wouldn't want to participate in half the things Aunt Ethel's involved with—and you don't even like bridge. Plus you and our dear mayor usually end up in an argument."

"That's true. Lloyd Tynan brings out the worst in me sometimes—or maybe it's the other way around." Jane pushed a long brunette strand of hair away from her face and then winked. "And unless you want to be on KP right now, you should probably go make sure the water's hot and the tea things are set up for our guests."

"Speaking of guests, where is everyone?" Alice picked up the apple bowl. "I know the Bernard sisters are helping Louise with pageant practice and they should be back soon, but what about Mr. and Mrs. Downey and—"

"The Downeys have asked us to call them Myron and Katie," Jane reminded her. "And they won't be back until after five. Beverly took Dylan to Bethlehem to see the Christmas village and railroad museum, and they plan to be back before dark."

"Dylan will love the railroad museum. It's so perfect for a nine-year old." Alice carried the apple bowl out to the dining room buffet, making sure the electric water kettle was turned on and that teacups and saucers were set out, then returned to the kitchen.

"And, because of the snow forecast, I promised Dylan we'd have cocoa available today." Jane pointed to an attractive tray she'd arranged. A large mason jar with her special cocoa mix encompassed by some cute Santa mugs, complete with candy canes for stirring sticks. "I know Dylan's thrilled about this snow. I just hope Beverly is comfortable driving in it."

"She told me she grew up in Minnesota." Alice picked up the cocoa tray. "I'll bet she'll be just fine." Even so, as she made room for the tray on the buffet, Alice said a silent prayer for the mother and son driving back to Acorn Hill. It wasn't unusual for Alice to pray for their guests. But the guest who needed the most prayer right now seemed to be Mr. Grover—*if he really was Mr. Grover.*

Alice wondered if the old man would come down for tea. Or perhaps he hadn't taken time to read the brochure she'd given him. But if he did make an appearance, how would he interact with the other guests? Would he growl at them like he'd growled at her? Hopefully, his presence wouldn't put a damper on the holidays for everyone.

As she returned to the kitchen, Alice reassured herself—the weary old man was probably sound asleep by now. And maybe Mrs. Grover would be here after all. Maybe she'd simply been waylaid somehow. Surely his wife would know how to smooth things out with him and their dog. Well, unless the couple was having some sort of domestic difficulties. That could happen....

"Are you okay?" Jane peered curiously at Alice. "You look sort of dazed."

"I guess I'm still trying to figure out the Mr. Grover dilemma." Alice sighed. "I wish we knew more about his wife. Do you think she could be shopping in town and he just didn't want to say so?"

"So you're not buying Auntie's morbid theory?" Jane teased.

"Oh Jane." Alice shuddered.

"Sorry. But I don't see why you're so concerned."

"I'm just worried about Mr. Grover. I hope he's okay."

"Well, our big sister will get to the bottom of this." Jane nodded to the platter of festive Christmas cookies on the counter. "Go ahead and put those out for teatime too. I told Dylan they'd be here today."

"They're almost too pretty to eat."

"Aunt Ethel didn't think so." Jane chuckled as she chopped an onion in half. "And don't worry, I've got plenty more where they came from."

"Of course you do." Alice smiled as she picked up the platter. "You're such a wonder in the kitchen, Jane. I'm afraid we take you for granted sometimes, but I hope you know this inn wouldn't be nearly as successful without your culinary talents."

"Well, I think we three sisters make a pretty good team." Jane reached for a garlic clove and gave it a solid whack with the side of her chef's knife.

Alice paused by the swinging door. "Well, you're certainly the queen of the kitchen. And Louise is a whiz at the business end of things. But sometimes I wonder how much I really contribute."

Jane looked up from mincing the garlic. "Alice, you can't possibly be serious. Sometimes it feels like you're the glue that holds this whole place together. You always offer kindness to everyone or some unexpected words of wisdom—just like Father did when he was alive. Trust me, sweet sister, you definitely contribute—much more than you realize."

Alice thanked her, but as she returned to the dining room, she felt unsure. Her "contribution" for today might've been to allow a criminal into their beloved inn. Oh, she didn't really think Mr. Grover was any kind of criminal or identity thief. Alice didn't like to judge anyone, but something about this old man felt off. And his cantankerous attitude didn't help.

After she turned on the Christmas tree lights and then the exterior Christmas lights, she paused to gaze out on the snowy front yard. Nothing beautified a dreary winter landscape like freshly fallen snow. They would have a true white Christmas—perhaps not terribly convenient for travelers, but how perfectly lovely.

She suddenly remembered the image of Mr. Grover as he limped up the walkway toward her. Therein lay her answer! That little dog tucked into his misbuttoned overcoat, protected and warm against the snowstorm…really, how could a man so tender toward a poor helpless animal possibly be a criminal?

Chapter Three

L ouise hung up the kitchen phone with a creased brow. "I was just informed that Isobel Grover's cell phone number is no longer in service," she grimly declared.

"Maybe she got a new phone." Jane hung a copper pan on the pot rack with a loud clang.

Alice sighed. "And maybe we're making a mountain out of a molehill."

"Maybe, but Aunt Ethel sure sounded concerned when she came home just now."

Alice cringed to recall how their aunt had gone on about Lloyd having seen a strange character wandering through town with a little dog this afternoon.

"Auntie said that Lloyd told her the poor fellow seemed disoriented—and looked homeless," Jane said.

"I had the same thought," Alice confessed. "It's why I asked him into the inn. I thought maybe we could help."

"So you didn't know he was a guest?" Louise asked.

"Not at first. But then he told me his name, and it all made sense. Well, sort of."

Louise adjusted her glasses, staring down at the registration book where the Grovers' information was listed. "Well,

Lloyd and Aunt Ethel probably just enjoy the drama of a mysterious guest. But I'll admit, the missing wife has aroused my curiosity. At the very least I'd like to speak to Mr. Grover about paying his pet deposit. I'd hoped to do that after dinner."

"I was a little surprised he didn't come down to eat," Alice said quietly. "He seemed so tired and weary when he arrived. I would've expected he'd be hungry too."

"Well, I won't take it personally." Jane turned on the dishwasher. "The other guests seemed to enjoy it."

"I'm guessing Mr. Grover slept through dinner. I tapped on his door when I set his bags up there, but it was quiet," Alice told them.

"Yes, and we don't want to disturb his rest." Louise frowned. "I'd just like to know why he showed up alone. His wife sounded so eager to spend Christmas here." She turned to Alice. "You're sure that you carefully checked Mr. Grover's ID?"

Alice reconfirmed this. "And I spoke to the fellow from the garage—the one who brought the bags," she confided. "I probably sounded nosy, but I asked about Mrs. Grover."

"Did you learn anything?" Louise asked eagerly.

Alice shook her head. "He never saw a woman with him."

"Where on earth is Isobel Grover?" Louise demanded.

"Maybe they traveled separately," Jane suggested. "She might've had business to attend to and is coming later."

"Yes, I suppose it could be something like that." Louise pursed her lips. "I don't know why I'm so concerned. Except that it doesn't make sense."

Alice glanced at the kitchen clock. "It's past nine, ladies. And it sounds like the other guests have already called it a night."

"Well, I'm ready to turn in." Jane stretched then winked at Alice. "Unless I can't sleep worrying about our mysterious Mr. Grover."

Alice forced a smile. "Like I already said, if you'd witnessed how protective Mr. Grover was toward that dog—little Suzie Q—well, I'm sure you'd both sleep better."

"Yes, yes, that's reassuring." Jane patted Alice's shoulder. "I shouldn't tease like that."

"Especially if you'd seen the poor man. He looked so down-and-out, Jane. Now I wish I'd thought to set some food up there with his bags." Alice frowned.

"And I wish I'd searched through his bags before you took them upstairs," Louise mumbled.

"Oh Louise. Not seriously." Alice stared at her sister in disbelief. "Isn't that illegal, or at the very least, unethical?"

"Probably. Although if I'd found anything questionable, I could've called the police department in the Grovers' hometown...you know, to find out if there's anything suspicious going on there. See if there are any missing person reports."

"You'd really do that?" Alice was stunned.

"You're sounding like Aunt Ethel." Jane shook a warning finger at Louise.

"Yes, you're probably right." Louise looked embarrassed.

"Well, I think we're all perfectly safe," Alice assured her. "I'm sure you're worn out after your long day of rehearsing with the kids. You should go to bed, Louise. I'll stay down here for a while, just in case Mr. Grover wakes up and wants something to eat."

"As long as you promise to call 911 if you have any concerns about our rather mysterious guest."

"Oh Louise, you do sound like Aunt Ethel." Alice sighed.

"Yes. Please, spare us the melodrama." Jane hung up her apron.

"I'm not trying to be melodramatic, just sensible. Even if this fellow truly is Mr. Grover like he claims, it's possible that he's not all right *upstairs.*" Louise tapped the side of her head with arched brows.

Alice exchanged glances with Jane. "Well, maybe when you see him with his little dog, you'll reconsider that theory."

"I might. Just the same, I'll be locking my bedroom door tonight. I hope you'll do the same." Louise picked up the registration book with a resolved expression. "And mark my words, we will get to the bottom of this tomorrow."

After Louise and Jane left, Alice poured herself one last cup of tea, took it into the living room, and sat down across from the majestic Christmas tree. Thanks to Jane's artistic abilities, everything in this room—and the entire inn—looked festively attractive. Elegant white electric candles graced the mantel, along with very realistic-looking artificial evergreen boughs—all fireproof—and glittering crystal snowflakes. Every nook and cranny had an unexpected touch of Christmas— from nutcrackers to snow globes to figurines. But none of it looked cheesy. All was done with taste, creativity, and beauty. And all the guests appreciated it. Well, maybe not *all* the guests.

Alice glanced to the foyer and the stairway banister, which was draped with a garland of artificial evergreen and tiny white lights and burgundy bows. A part of her wished that Mr. Grover were coming down right now, but another part of her cringed at the thought of meeting him alone down here. Oh, she didn't really think he was dangerous. Not truly. But it was unsettling.

Although she wouldn't be surprised to see him. After all, the poor man must be hungry. She sipped the last of her tea then returned to the kitchen where, after rinsing her cup, she made a generous roast beef sandwich and set it on a dinner plate along with some veggie sticks and a couple of Christmas cookies. She covered the plate with plastic wrap, got a bottle of water, and even snagged one of the honey crisp apples on her way out.

When she reached the second-floor landing, she could see Mr. Grover's bags right where she'd set them. And so she set the provisions on top. Hopefully, he'd find them before too long. She was about to start up the next flight of stairs when she heard the sound of a doorknob click. Trying not to act startled, Alice turned around to see the door to the Sunset Room slowly opening. From the light in the room, Alice could see Mr. Grover's silhouette. In his arms was the little dog.

"Good evening," she said quietly.

"Oh?" He jumped in surprise and scowled. "Are you always lurking about?"

"I was on my way to bed." She pointed to the food on his bags. "I thought you might be hungry."

His fuzzy brows arched then he nodded. "I haven't eaten since breakfast," he grumbled. "But I must take Suzie Q outside first."

"Want me to do that for you? You know, because of the stairs."

His brow creased as if he was confused.

"I don't mind. And I can take her out back. There's an area where the snow's been removed."

"All right." He handed the dog to her.

For the second time that day, Alice took the small dog and tried to hold her breath. Suzie Q needed a bath. She hurried back downstairs and, once outside, waited while Suzie Q took care of business. Thankfully, it didn't take long. Both she and Suzie Q were shivering as she hurried back up the stairs. Relieved that Mr. Grover's bags had been moved, Alice tapped on his door, bracing herself for more abrasive interaction.

"Thank you," he said gruffly as she handed him the dog. Before she could say "You're welcome," he shut the door.

Alice didn't know what to think as she went up the second flight of stairs. Perhaps Louise was right about Mr. Grover's mental state. Although that still didn't explain his missing wife...or maybe it did. At the third-floor landing, an area only occupied by the three sisters, Alice paused to say another prayer for Mr. Grover—as well as petition for the safety and well-being of everyone in the inn—and that all would enjoy a blessed and happy Christmas. Then, feeling very tired, she went into her bedroom. And despite her assurances to Louise that Mr. Grover was no threat to anyone, Alice locked her door.

Chapter Four

Alice got up early the next morning. She didn't plan to mention anything to her sisters, but she hadn't slept well. Something woke her in the middle of the night. At first she thought she'd heard something but then decided it was simply a bad dream. And this morning she'd felt certain her disrupted sleep was her own doing. Had she been mistaken to allow Mr. Grover into the Sunset Room yesterday? Really, she needed to be more assertive. Like both her sisters. Either of them would've handled the situation much differently. Good grief, Louise had been ready to go through the man's luggage.

The house was quiet as Alice went down the stairs, but when she stepped into the foyer, a scampering sound caught her attention. Something brown whipped past her, heading straight for the living room area. Alice glanced up the stairs to see Mr. Grover. Wearing an unbuttoned shirt, wrinkled trousers, and in his bare feet, he was starting down the stairs.

"I'll take Suzie Q out," Alice said. "You stay there."

He just nodded, but unless she imagined it, there seemed to be a flicker of gratitude in his eyes. "Come on, Suzie Q," she said to the little brown dog. "You know the way." As they went through the kitchen, Alice got a baggie and followed the dog through the laundry room and outside where once again Suzie Q did her business.

"You need a bath," Alice told the dog as they went back inside. "Do you think your master will object?" Suzie Q retraced her steps, going directly to the Sunset Room and waiting by the door as Alice knocked. As soon as Mr. Grover opened the door, Alice stated her intentions—her attempt at assertiveness. "I'm going to give Suzie Q a bath." She picked up the dog. "I'll bring her back when I'm done."

Mr. Grover said nothing but at least nodded his head before he shut the door. Alice told herself this might be progress as she carried Suzie Q back down to the laundry room. She set the dog down on the floor and got busy filling the big laundry sink with warm water. Suzie Q would be fine to sniff around the laundry room while she went to gather a few supplies. Alice soon returned with a couple of towels, a plastic cup, and lavender-scented shampoo and conditioner, as well as an old comb retrieved from the lost-and-found basket.

"Here goes nothing." She picked up the dog, hoping that Suzie Q had no aversions to water, and carefully set her in the sink. To Alice's relief, Suzie Q's little tail eagerly wagged.

"I thought you might enjoy this," Alice said as she dipped the plastic cup into the water, gently pouring it over the dog. Suzie Q couldn't have been more cooperative as Alice shampooed and rinsed then did it again. Finally she put on a little conditioner, massaging it into the matted fur before she rinsed it out.

"What on earth are you doing?" Louise demanded as she entered the laundry room.

"Welcome to my new doggy beauty parlor." Alice chuck-led as she lifted a now sweet-smelling Suzie Q from the sink, wrapping her in a towel.

"Since when did we start offering dog grooming services at the inn?" Louise adjusted her glasses to get a better look at the dog. "Is that a Yorkshire Terrier?"

"I honestly don't know, but this is Suzie Q."

"I just discussed Suzie Q with Mr. Grover."

"Oh?" Alice continued to towel-dry the dog. "How did that go?"

"Not very well." Louise scowled. "I began the conversation by pointing out that he hasn't paid a pet deposit. He insisted he did. And, well, it went downhill from there."

"Oh dear." Alice could imagine.

"That beastly man is an old curmudgeon." Louise removed a stack of linens from a shelf. "Just what we need at Christmastime."

"Did you ask about his wife?"

"He didn't give me the chance. He went back to his room—and slammed his door." Louise nodded toward Suzie Q. "Perhaps you'll have better luck when you return his dog to him."

Alice promised to do her best, but as she went upstairs she didn't feel hopeful. And when she tapped on the door and got no response, she felt even more worried. She knocked a bit louder, calling out Mr. Grover's name. "I've got Suzie Q here."

The door finally opened. Mr. Grover reached for his dog with a disgruntled expression. But before relinquishing Suzie Q, Alice put her foot in the doorway. "First we need to talk," she said in a gentle but firm tone.

"I don't want to talk," he growled back. "I just want some peace and quiet."

"I understand," she said quietly. "But I'd like to talk to you first." She glanced over his shoulder to where the empty plate from last night was sitting on a table. "And I'm happy to take that plate back to the kitchen for you."

He grumbled something but went to get the plate. "Here." He held it out to her.

Still holding on to the dog, with her foot blocking the door, Alice continued. "I'm afraid my sister Louise may have offended you. But we do have a pet policy. They're only allowed under permitted circumstances and always with a deposit."

"My wife took care of that."

Alice sighed. "It doesn't seem to be in Louise's records. Do you know when Mrs. Grover paid the deposit? Do you have a—"

"Like I said, my wife handled that. The dog was her responsibility." He frowned. "I wasn't in favor of a dog, but Isobel found this one at a shelter last winter."

"I see." Alice nodded. "So this is your wife's dog?"

"It was."

"Was?"

Mr. Grover looked directly into Alice's eyes. "My wife has passed away."

"Oh?" Alice suddenly remembered Aunt Ethel's horror stories but really didn't believe this was anything like that. "I, uh, I'm very sorry, Mr. Grover. Was it recently?"

He rubbed his hand through his hair, and his eyes grew misty. "She died last March. History of heart trouble. Finally it gave out."

"Oh, I'm so sorry for your loss." Alice handed him the dog, taking the plate from him as she did.

"Well, I'm not looking for anyone's pity." His tone grew gruff again. "Just a little peace and quiet is all I want."

"Have you had your breakfast?"

"I was on my way down to get some when I was accosted by your sister."

"I'm sorry about that. Louise can be, well, rather forceful. But it's only because she was confused. We were all confused. We thought your wife was coming too…. We didn't know."

"Yes, well, I suppose that's my fault too." His brows drew together. "But I figure if I mind my own business, everyone else will mind theirs. I'm sure it was a mistake to come here in the first place. Especially after my car broke down. But the room was paid for and, well, until my car's fixed, I guess you're just stuck with me." He looked down at the dog. "Thank you for bathing Suzie Q. My wife always took care of that."

"Will you come down for breakfast now?" Alice asked hopefully.

"I don't want to." He attempted to close the door, but it stopped at Alice's foot.

"Is it because of Louise?"

"Maybe. I'm no good around people. You probably surmised as much."

"I have an idea," she said suddenly. "I'll fix us both a plate and we can eat in the library—and you can bring Suzie Q too."

"I don't want to be trouble." His tone softened. "But I am hungry."

Alice told him how to find the library and promised to meet him there in twenty minutes. Then she hurried downstairs, explained the situation to Jane, and got breakfast for two set up on the card table in the library.

Alice met Mr. Grover at the door. "Come in," she told him, closing the door behind him. "Have a seat." She nodded to the small table.

"Thank you," he mumbled as he set Suzie Q on the floor.

As they ate, Alice made quiet conversation. Nothing that required too much of him but simply telling him a bit about Acorn Hill, their family's role in Grace Chapel Church, and how she and her sisters started the inn. Mostly, she just hoped to make him comfortable. By the time they finished breakfast and she'd refilled his coffee cup, he seemed to actually relax some.

"You've been very patient with me," he said quietly. "I'm afraid I'm not an easy person to be around. I have a short temper that seems to get shorter each day. Isobel was always warning me about it. Her favorite saying was *If you can't say anything nice*...well, you know how it goes."

"Your wife sounds like very a sweet person."

"Yes...she was. Kind and good. She was naturally congenial—and probably the only reason we had any friends. Of course, my excuse was that I spent forty years teaching high school science. You have to be tough to last that long."

Alice smiled. "I'm sure you do."

"I'm not trying to defend my bad behavior—something Isobel didn't approve of—but the past week has just about driven me over the brink."

"How so?"

"I shouldn't dump my troubles onto you."

"That's okay. I don't mind." She sipped her tea.

"Well, we had an unexpected hard freeze about a week ago. The pipes in my condo unit froze and broke. Water everywhere. I slipped on my wet kitchen floor and wrenched my knee. Nothing broken, but that's why I'm limping. Even though the condo maintenance cleaned up the water mess, the pipes still weren't fixed, so no running water. Let me tell you, that gets old fast."

"What a terrible week you've had."

"So I was going through my office, looking for my home insurance policy, when I saw the paperwork for this inn. I'd completely forgotten that Isobel had set this up. So I thought, why not come out here and get away from the unnatural disaster at home? Seemed to make sense."

"Yes, a perfect solution."

"Except that my car broke down in Pittsburgh. And then a sleepless night in that cheap motel. And riding in that drafty bone-jarring tow truck. Then finding out my car needs serious work. Finally, trudging through that snow yesterday. My feet were like ice. At one point I hoped for hypothermia—my ticket to meet up with Isobel."

"Oh dear."

"And now it seems I shouldn't have brought the dog without permission and—"

"I'm so sorry, Mr. Grover. No wonder you were grumpy. And, please, don't worry about Suzie Q. I'll straighten that out with Louise. It'll be fine."

His eyes brightened ever so slightly. "I appreciate that." Then he turned grim again. "But I really don't think I should be here. Especially during the holidays. It was a bad idea. I assumed this inn was like a hotel and that I could just hide out until my car and my broken pipes are repaired. But I read your brochure last night, and I can see that your inn is much more personal—'like a family experience' I think the brochure called it. Isobel would've loved it. But I'm not good at this sort of thing."

"I think you should give us a second chance, Mr. Grover. We started out on the wrong foot, but maybe we can rectify that. A lot of people come here in search of peace and quiet. There's no reason you can't do the same. I can let everyone know you don't want to be disturbed. We can even bring meals to your room if you'd like. Don't give up on us yet."

He sighed. "You're a kind soul. Thank you."

"So, please, just take it easy for the next few days. And don't feel compelled to interact with anyone if you don't care to." Alice smiled. "I have a feeling that Isobel booked this visit just for you. She's probably relieved that you're here right now. I promise we'll do our best to take care of you."

Mr. Grover didn't say anything, but as he swallowed and nodded, Alice could see tears glisten in his eyes. Despite his gruff demeanor yesterday, she knew he desperately needed some nurturing. And normally, Grace Chapel Inn was a good place for that. But Christmastime could get rather hectic. Boisterous guests could sometimes be noisy in their celebrations. She hoped she'd be able to keep her promise to Mr. Grover. Even if her sisters were too busy and distracted, Alice was determined to do her best to care for the old man.

Chapter Five

As the sisters grew busier with Christmas preparations, holiday festivities, and the usual responsibilities of running a fully booked inn, Alice did all she could to make sure that Mr. Grover got the peace and quiet she knew he needed. Meals were either served in his room or the library. Sometimes Alice joined him in the library, but if she was busy, he dined alone. She also did what she could to help with caring for Suzie Q since she knew Mr. Grover had difficulty on the stairs. Alice also explained to her sisters and aunt that they were not harboring a dangerous criminal but instead a weary and grieving widower. And she assured Louise she'd cover Suzie Q's missing pet deposit. She felt sure the little dog would do no damage.

In his own curmudgeonly way, Mr. Grover seemed appreciative of her efforts. Even so, it was impossible to prevent random run-ins with the various guests. For starters, the gregarious Bernard sisters had made a mission of "drawing the lonely widower out." Kay and May Bernard, the "spinster twins" as they called themselves, were only a bit younger than Mr. Grover and determined to establish some sort of friendship.

Mr. Grover didn't bother to hide his aggravation when they cornered him in the foyer on his third evening there, trying to coax him out to see the living Nativity in town. But his harsh rebuffs didn't even faze them, because the very next morning, they were urging him to go shopping with them in town. Even the Downeys, who mostly kept to themselves, seemed to irritate Mr. Grover. Myron and Katie Downey, middle-aged newlyweds, were rather vocal in working some kinks out of their marital differences.

"Good grief, you're *adults*," he'd growled at them when they'd crossed paths on the second-floor landing yesterday afternoon. "Can't you resolve your childish bickering elsewhere?"

Of all the inn's guests, it seemed that young Dylan had made the best connection with the retired science teacher. Thanks to Dylan's fascination with the solar system and space travel, Alice had sent him to the inn's library to search out a book she knew was there. Of course, she also knew Mr. Grover was there, having his lunch. A risky move, but to Alice's delight, the "serendipitous" start of a friendship, like a well-planned space journey, was launched. Not only did they share an interest in space, Dylan fell in love with Suzie Q.

As Alice set the dining room table for dinner, she felt encouraged that Mr. Grover and Dylan had moved to the living room. Louise was playing quiet Christmas songs on the piano, and several guests were out there, waiting for dinner to be served. Above the piano music, Alice could overhear Mr. Grover patiently explaining the speed of light to Dylan. His tone was that of an experienced teacher and, based on Dylan's questions, the lesson was being well absorbed and appreciated.

Alice, feeling hopeful that Mr. Grover might join the others for dinner for a change, set an extra plate. But as she filled the water goblets, she could hear the Bernard sisters interrupting the astronomy lesson.

"Do you have children, Mr. Grover?" May Bernard asked in her high-pitched voice. The main way Alice could tell the twins apart was their voices. May's was shrill and loud, and Kay's was low and booming. Both of them were "blessed" with the gift of gab. Even when they were furiously knitting or crocheting—their favorite hobbies—they could still talk and talk.

"No children," he mumbled gruffly.

"But you seem such a natural with children," Kay said. "One would think you'd have some of your own."

"I told you, I have no children," he answered abruptly.

"Well, I simply thought that—"

"Want me to take Suzie Q outside?" Dylan asked. "She might want to go out before dinner."

"Thank you, Dylan." Mr. Grover's tone softened. "I'm sure she'd appreciate that."

As Dylan left, Alice heard Beverly speak to Mr. Grover. "Thank you for spending time with Dylan. But I hope my boy doesn't bother you with all his questions."

"Nothing wrong with an inquisitive mind."

"Dylan doesn't have many men in his life." Beverly explained how Dylan's father had died in Afghanistan. "And then my father passed away just last year."

"I'm sorry for Dylan's and your loss." Mr. Grover's regret sounded genuine.

"Thank you. Dylan was quite young when his father died, but losing his grandpa is still pretty fresh."

Alice could hear Dylan and the dog coming back inside, and Beverly instantly changed the subject to Dylan's obsession with outer space and his dream to attend a space camp in Orlando. "My mother lives in Florida and promised to look into it for me."

"Yeah. I really want to go this summer," Dylan said brightly. "You get to do all kinds of cool stuff. Spacewalk, robotics, Mars habitation—"

"You don't actually go to Mars?" May Bernard exclaimed.

"Not for real," Dylan explained. "It's a simulation. They have all kinds of simulations that feel just like the real thing."

Their conversation was interrupted by Jane's announcement of dinnertime. Dylan seemed to assume Mr. Grover would eat in the dining room tonight, because he was asking him to sit next to him. As Alice set the water pitcher on the sideboard, she silently prayed that Mr. Grover would accept the boy's invitation.

"All right, Dylan," Mr. Grover declared. "I'll sit by you tonight. But only if you take Suzie Q up to my room first."

Dylan eagerly agreed. Then in an effort to insulate Mr. Grover from the Bernard sisters, Alice spontaneously "assigned" some seating, making sure that Beverly and Dylan would occupy either side of Mr. Grover on one side of the table, with the Bernard sisters on the other. Both Louise and Jane seemed sensitive that this was Mr. Grover's first time to dine with the others. Louise sat with the Bernards, chatting with the gregarious sisters, and Jane joined the Downeys, asking them about what they'd done today. To Alice's relief, dinner went relatively smoothly.

"Do you play chess?" Alice asked Mr. Grover as they were finishing dessert.

He nodded. "I do."

"So do I." Alice smiled as she stood.

"Is that a challenge?" It almost seemed that his eyes twinkled.

"It could be." Alice began clearing plates.

"Can I watch?" Dylan asked eagerly. "I want to learn to play chess."

"Let's meet up in the library," Alice told them. "Give me a few minutes to help in the kitchen and—"

"You go ahead," Louise told her. "It's my turn."

Before long, Alice and Mr. Grover were setting up the chessboard, explaining to Dylan the names of the pieces. "It's a lot to take in all at once," Alice told him. "But if you pay attention, you might figure a few things out."

"The best way to learn is by playing." Mr. Grover set his last piece in place.

"That's right." Alice almost said that her father taught her to play but suddenly remembered Dylan didn't have a dad.

Dylan was surprisingly patient for the first fifteen minutes, but as he began to get antsy, Alice could tell he was bored. "Don't feel you have to stay for the whole game," she told him as Mr. Grover captured her knight. "You can have another lesson tomorrow."

"Okay." Dylan stood. "Can I take Suzie Q with me? I think she wants to play."

"She'd probably enjoy some exercise before bedtime," Mr. Grover told him. "Thank you."

After Dylan left, Mr. Grover commented on what a well-mannered boy he was. "His mother must be raising him right."

"Beverly seems like a sweet woman," Alice agreed. "I heard her say that Dylan lost his father."

"Yes...very sad."

"Beverly mentioned that her mother paid for their visit to the inn because they couldn't get together this year. She didn't want Beverly and Dylan to spend Christmas alone."

"Yes, that's why Isobel wanted to come here too." He moved his bishop. "Check."

As she moved out of check, Alice explained that many of their holiday guests came to the inn to establish pseudo-family connections. She chuckled. "And, just like with real family members, you never know what you'll get."

"I've never had much real family." He moved his queen.

"Then perhaps you're in the right place." She countered his queen.

He cleared his throat then swiped his rook across the board, cornering her king. "Checkmate."

"Well done." She held up her hands. "I didn't see that coming. I guess I'm a little rusty."

"You were better than I expected." He began returning his pieces to their squares.

"I used to play with my father. But he passed away a few years ago."

"My father taught me to play too." He leaned back in the chair. "Do you think Dylan is too young to learn the game?"

"I don't know. I was nine when my father taught me to play. And Dylan seems quite bright."

"Yes, he's got a sharp mind."

"It was good of you to sit with him at dinner. I know he enjoyed it."

"He's a good boy." He sighed. "Isobel and I never had children."

Alice nodded and placed her last piece back on the board.

"She wanted children. Well, I did too. But her heart condition…it just didn't seem prudent."

"I understand. But there are other ways to have children. You were a teacher. In a way you've probably had a lot of children."

"I suppose. But I wouldn't have wanted most of them. Isobel was much better with children. She always had neighbor kids coming by for one thing or another. Of course, that doesn't happen anymore."

"Well, Dylan certainly seems to have taken to you." Alice smiled. "That's nice."

"Perhaps I'll see if he wants another chess lesson tomorrow." He slowly stood. "I'm ready to turn in now. This is the most social activity I've had in…well, since losing Isobel. I'm worn out."

Alice bid him a good night then went to find Dylan and Suzie Q, out in the backyard. She told Dylan that Mr. Grover was headed for bed then followed him inside. She watched from the foyer as Dylan, carrying the dog, accompanied Mr. Grover up the stairs, cheerfully telling him about the constellations he'd seen in the sky just now. "I spotted Orion. And maybe Gemini, but I'm not sure."

"Maybe I can help you do some star searching tomorrow night."

"That'd be great."

Mr. Grover thanked Dylan for exercising the dog.

"I can take her out in the morning for you," Dylan told him. "Right before breakfast. You're coming down to breakfast, aren't you?"

Mr. Grover confirmed this then said good night. Alice smiled. She didn't think it was her imagination. She could definitely hear a slight trace of cheer in the elderly man's voice. Dylan was good medicine. Maybe Mr. Grover wouldn't play the Christmas Grinch after all.

Chapter Six

The next morning, while helping with breakfast, Alice described Mr. Grover's progress to Jane. "Dylan really seems to be bringing him out."

"Dylan is a darling." Jane handed Alice a platter of sausage and bacon. "Go ahead and put this out there now. The first batch of pancakes will be ready in a minute."

As Alice set the platter on the buffet and adjusted a few other things, she could hear Aunt Ethel's voice in the kitchen. Judging by the shrill intensity, something was wrong. Alice hurried back to find out. "What's happened?" she asked her aunt.

"It's Lloyd." Aunt Ethel wrung her hands. "He fell on his icy front steps last night—he broke his leg."

"Oh dear. Poor Lloyd."

"Fortunately for Lloyd, his neighbor just happened to be outside right then. He heard Lloyd yelling for help. Otherwise Lloyd might've died of exposure."

"Goodness." Alice shook her head. "How is he now?"

"He's in the hospital. In traction. He'll be there the rest of the week."

"He won't have much of a Christmas." Jane piled a plate high with pancakes. "We'll have to take him some—"

"But that's not all." Aunt Ethel moaned. "Don't forget that Lloyd was our Santa Claus. And the pageant is tonight. I don't know what we're going to do without him."

"Find someone else." Jane handed Alice the plate of pancakes.

"Easier said than done." Aunt Ethel sniffed the air. "Breakfast certainly smells good this morning."

"Why don't you join us?" Alice suggested.

"Thank you." Aunt Ethel sighed. "I could use something nourishing to soothe my nerves."

By the time the guests, including Mr. Grover, were seated at the breakfast table, Aunt Ethel had informed everyone about the mayor's unfortunate accident. "Our problem is that Lloyd was going to play Santa Claus, and now we need a new—" Aunt Ethel covered her mouth with her hand, looking at Dylan with arched brows, as if she'd just let the cat out of the bag. "Oh dear, I'm sorry."

"Don't worry," Dylan said in an adult-like tone. "I've known for ages that Santa isn't for real."

"Oh well, I didn't want to spoil anything." Aunt Ethel smiled meekly at Beverly.

"Dylan figured all that out when he was about five or six." Beverly winked at her son. "But that doesn't stop him from expecting something from Santa just the same."

"I do it to make Mom happy," Dylan said with a twinkle in his eyes.

"That's too bad about not having a Santa." Katie poked her tall, thin husband. "How about you, Myron?"

"No way." Myron shook his head. "I played Santa at work once, and the kids were not fans. Besides complaining about my bony knees, they pulled my beard and made fun of my pathetic attempts at 'Ho ho ho.' It was more like 'Ho ho hum.'"

Everyone laughed. Except Aunt Ethel. She still looked worried. "I've already called several candidates, and no one is willing to step in."

"What about Jack Lewis?" Louise suggested. "He even looks like a Santa."

"I already called," Aunt Ethel told her. "He's got the flu."

"What about Vernon Myers?" Alice asked.

"Vernon and Marian are on a cruise."

"What about Mr. Grover?" Dylan asked suddenly.

"*What?*" Mr. Grover's eyes grew wide with alarm.

"You actually kinda look like a Santa." Dylan grinned at him.

"Really?" Mr. Grover's brow creased.

"No offense." Dylan looked uncertain. "But you've got that nice fluffy white hair and blue eyes. Kind of like the Santa pictures, you know. And you're such a nice guy, Mr. Grover, why don't you do it?"

"Oh yes, that's a wonderful idea," Aunt Ethel gushed. "You really would make a terrific Santa. Perhaps even better than Lloyd."

"And that's saying a lot," Alice told him.

"He's about the same size as Lloyd," Louise said to Aunt Ethel.

"Yes." Aunt Ethel nodded. "I'm absolutely certain the costume will fit. It's such a nice costume too. Heavy red velvet, and I just freshened it up with a new white fur collar and cuffs."

"I can imagine you with a white beard," Louise said to Mr. Grover. Suddenly, everyone was confirming that he would make a perfect Santa. But Mr. Grover was clearly not on board with this unexpected idea.

"I know—I know!" Dylan declared with excitement. "Suzie Q could be your elf. She could wear an elf hat and everything. Don't you think the little kids would love that?"

"You could be an elf too," Alice told Dylan. "With that curly hair you'd make a terrific elf. And you could help Mr. Grover with the gifts. Santa always presents all the children at the pageant with small gifts. The ANGELs have been busily wrapping them for the past two weeks."

"Angels?" May Bernard's brows arched.

"The ANGELs are Alice's youth group," Jane explained. "Kind of like Girl Scouts. Only better. Right, Alice?"

"Well, we do have fun." Alice smiled.

"And the ANGELs are participating in the pageant too," Louise told everyone. "They'll be wearing their wings and singing two lovely carols. Brittany Powers has a beautiful voice and will be doing a solo."

"But back to Santa and his elves," Aunt Ethel redirected. "I think the idea of Mr. Grover having a pair of elves, a boy and a dog, is just fabulous."

"What do you think?" Beverly asked her son.

Dylan shrugged with a shy smile. "I guess I wouldn't mind being an elf. It might be kinda fun—I mean, if Mr. Grover does it too. I could help him give out gifts."

"That's just wonderful," Aunt Ethel declared. "And I have everything I need to put together elf outfits for Dylan and the little dog. But I'll have to get busy." She stood and laid her napkin on her plate. "The pageant isn't until seven o'clock. I just hope I can have something ready by then."

"I can help you," Alice offered.

Aunt Ethel turned to Mr. Grover. "Don't you worry. Santa really doesn't have all that much to do. Just follow the director's directions. Be ready for your cue when the narrator starts talking about how Jesus is God's greatest gift to us and that inspires us to give to each other. Basically, you just make a big entrance and say 'Ho ho ho.' And then, of course, you'll give out the gifts to the children. Dylan will help you with that."

"I, uh, I don't really think this is such a good idea." Mr. Grover shook his head. "I'm no good at this sort of thing. I'm just not—"

"You'd be perfect," Dylan assured him. "I know you can do it, Mr. Grover."

Once again, everyone chimed in, and finally Mr. Grover agreed—perhaps with reluctance, but he did say yes. "Just don't blame me if the whole business falls to pieces," he told everyone as he stood. "I really don't have the Santa Claus temperament. To be fair, I'd probably do better playing Ebenezer Scrooge or that Dr. Seuss creature that ruined Christmas."

"You mean the Grinch who stole Christmas." Dylan laughed. "No, no, Mr. Grover, you're nothing like the Grinch. You're nice."

"Harrumph." Mr. Grover scowled at him, but it wasn't convincing.

"Besides that, we'll be pretending," Dylan reminded him. "Just playacting. I know you can do this, Mr. Grover. We'll practice together today."

And so it was settled. Their curmudgeonly guest was going to save the day by playing Santa at the Christmas pageant. Alice just hoped—and prayed—he wouldn't let them down.

Chapter Seven

After Alice took Dylan's measurements in the kitchen, she pointed out the carriage house where Aunt Ethel lived. "Come on over there a little before lunchtime—and bring Suzie Q with you," she told him. "And we should be ready to do a first fitting."

"Does Mr. G need to come too?" Dylan chuckled. "He told me it was okay to call him that."

"Let's not trouble, uh, *Mr. G* with the fitting," Alice said. "My aunt is pretty sure the Santa costume will work just fine."

"And if it doesn't, you've always got pillows to make it fit." Jane removed a sheet of molasses cookies from the oven.

"That's right." Dylan grinned. "Santa's supposed to be fat."

"Fat and *happy*." Jane slid a cookie onto the wire rack. "Let's hope he doesn't scare the children tonight. What if he growls?"

"Oh Jane, he won't growl." Alice sighed. "But I do hope he smiles a bit more."

"Maybe you should make him a Grinch costume," Jane teased. "I'll bet the kids would get a kick out of that."

"Mr. G isn't a Grinch," Dylan said defensively.

"No, he's not," Alice agreed.

"But he could be a bit more jolly," Jane said.

"I'll try to get him more excited about being Santa," Dylan offered. "Maybe we can practice together. I mean, when we're not playing chess. He's going to teach me how this morning. And then he's going to teach me more about the constellations. I don't see why everyone thinks Mr. G is grumpy. I think he's great."

"He thinks you're great too," Alice told him.

Jane held out a small plate of molasses cookies. "Maybe you can sweeten him up with these while you're playing chess," she told Dylan.

"Yeah." He nodded eagerly. "Good idea." He promised to bring Suzie Q over to Aunt Ethel's before lunch then took off in search of his chess instructor.

"Well, if anyone can get *Mr. G* to be more cheerful, my money's on that boy." Jane put the last cookie on the rack. "Although I have to give you credit too, Alice. Mr. G is a lot more congenial when you're around."

"He's carrying a lot of grief, Jane. He doesn't say much, but I can tell it's hard for him to talk about his wife. She was pretty much all he had. No kids. And it doesn't sound like they had much other family either. Being a grump has probably been kind of like wearing armor. He probably thinks it protects him from more pain."

"Do you really think he can do it? What if Santa has a meltdown tonight?" Jane got busy boxing up some of the cooled cookies. "Besides disappointing the kids, you know almost the whole town will be there. It could get awkward if Santa messes up. Or refuses to go out when the time comes."

"To be honest, I'm a little worried." Alice grimaced. "I've even imagined putting on the costume myself if we get in a pinch. Do you think I could pull it off?"

Jane laughed. "I don't know, but I wouldn't mind seeing you try."

"I'm pinning my hopes on Dylan. I can't imagine Mr. Grover letting him down. And I'll remind him of that very thing if I have to."

"Sort of guilt him into it?" Jane closed the box then tied it with a red ribbon. "These are for Lloyd Tynan. I know he and I don't always see eye to eye, but he's nuts over my molasses cookies. Want to take them over to Aunt Ethel's for me? I know she plans to pay him a visit today."

Alice gave her sister a sideways hug. "You're a sweetheart to think of this, Jane. I know Lloyd will love them." She pulled on her parka and snow boots and then, with her sewing basket and Lloyd's cookies in hand, she trudged over to the carriage house.

Aunt Ethel already had out a good selection of red and green felt fabric, some white faux-fur trim, and even some jingle bells. Aunt Ethel had always been handy with a needle and had taught Alice to sew as a young girl. Before long, with the measurements marked out on the felt, they were cutting and sewing.

"I thought maybe you'd want to drive me over to the hospital," Aunt Ethel said as she held up a small pair of short pants made from red felt and trimmed with green. "Perhaps you could come in with me and help cheer up Lloyd."

"Sure." Alice tied off a thread. "I'm happy to do that. If Jane doesn't mind, maybe I can fix a cookie plate to take to the nurses' station. I'd love to say hello to my old fellow coworkers."

"Good idea, Alice. Perhaps you can offer Lloyd some professional condolences. When I spoke to him on the phone this morning, he complained that the medical staff wasn't up to standards."

"Whose standards?" Alice sewed a red button onto the green vest.

"Well, I suppose Lloyd has high expectations. And you can't really blame him. After all, the mayor should get treated with respect, don't you think?"

Alice smiled to herself. Some nurses tended to resent those patients who felt they deserved special privileges because of their perceived social status. Consequently, some nurses weren't always as patient with their demanding patients as they were with those who seemed to appreciate the smallest kindnesses.

It was around eleven thirty when Dylan and Suzie Q showed up at the carriage house. "How was the chess lesson?" Alice asked as she led Dylan to their sewing area.

"Okay, I think. But I keep mixing up the bishop and the rook. I mean, the way they move. But Mr. G says I'm doing good."

"Speaking of Mr. Grover"—Aunt Ethel removed pins from her lips—"how is our Santa doing?"

"I'm not sure." Dylan set the dog down so Alice could fit it with the little vest she'd made.

"Still dragging his heels?" Aunt Ethel set the nearly finished green pointed cap on Dylan's curly head.

"I couldn't get him to say 'Ho ho ho.'" Dylan frowned. "Not even once."

"Oh dear. I hope he hasn't changed his mind."

"Me too." Dylan held out his arms for Aunt Ethel to slip the green vest on him.

"Oh my—you're an adorable elf," she said, going on about how great the green hat looked with his curly red hair.

Of course, Dylan didn't look overly thrilled to hear this. Alice hoped Mr. Grover's negativity wasn't rubbing off on the boy. "Look at Suzie Q," she said in an effort to distract Dylan from Aunt Ethel's gushing. "Isn't she cute?"

Dylan smiled. "She looks great. But how will you keep the hat from falling off?"

"I'll put a little elastic strap on it," Alice told him. "To wear under her chin."

After a few minutes and a few adjustments, they let Dylan take the dog back to the house. "I better go too," Alice told her aunt. "I need to set the table for lunch."

"And afterward, we'll go visit Lloyd?" Aunt Ethel asked hopefully.

"How about one thirty?" Alice pulled on her boots and coat.

"I'll bring over the elf costumes then." Aunt Ethel pointed to a plastic garment bag hanging by the front door. "Do you want to take that with you now? It's the Santa suit— for Mr. Grover."

"Oh, okay." Alice looped the garment bag over her arm.

"Maybe he'll want to try things on this afternoon. Sort of a practice run."

"Good idea." Alice hoped it was a good idea, but she wasn't too sure.

Aunt Ethel handed her a large shopping bag. "The boots and other accessories are in here. They're not real boots, so the size doesn't matter. They just slip over his shoes."

Carrying the bags, Alice hurried back to the inn, wondering how she'd get Mr. Grover to try on the costume. She had barely removed her parka when Jane informed her that Mr. Grover was not coming down to lunch. "He asked if it could be brought up to him."

"Oh dear. I hope he's not stressed about the pageant."

"He might be." Jane pointed to a plate she'd already prepared. "Do you mind taking that to him?"

"Okay. Hopefully, I can find out how he's feeling about his Santa debut tonight." With the costume bags over one arm, Alice picked up the plate.

"I have a feeling he's not going to make it, Alice." Jane's expression was sober as she held the door open. "Aunt Ethel should probably make a backup plan."

"I was afraid of that." Alice paused in the dining room.

"Or are you the understudy?" Jane winked. "You know, with the big white beard and Father's old wire-rimmed glasses. We could make your cheeks and nose nice and rosy. You just might be able to pull it off."

As Alice carried things upstairs, she wondered. Could she really play a convincing Santa? It would be sad if the little children saw through her. Hopefully, it wouldn't come to that. She tapped on the door and, calling out to Mr. Grover, she braced herself.

"Oh, it's you." He took the plate from her then frowned at the bags. "What's all that for?"

"Your Santa costume," she said brightly. "We thought you might want to try it on this afternoon. It's really quite nice and well made, I think—"

"I don't want to try it on." He was about to close the door, but she stuck out her foot.

"Then I'll just leave it with you." She walked into his room and hung the garment bag on the closet door, setting the bag right next to it.

"I don't think I'll be needing—"

"And there's Suzie Q's outfit too. I'll ask Dylan to bring it up to you," she said quickly. "Maybe he'll want to try his own outfit on. Perhaps you could help him with it. And help him to feel more confident about playing your helper." She was backing out the door. "Enjoy your lunch. Bye." Before he could respond or object, she closed the door and hurried back down the stairs.

After lunch, Alice told Dylan the plan. "Aunt Ethel will bring the elf costumes over in a few minutes. You can take

Suzie Q's up to Mr. G's room. Maybe try it on her again, just to be sure it's all right. And so Mr. Grover can see how cute she looks."

He nodded. "Okay."

"And you should show him your outfit too," she said hopefully. "That might encourage him. Maybe he'll even show you the Santa suit. It's really very nice."

Dylan brightened. "Yeah, I'd like to see it. And the beard too."

"Great."

As she drove Aunt Ethel to the hospital, Alice tried to put concerns about Santa's upcoming appearance at the pageant behind her. Worrying didn't help anything. But as they rode up the elevator, she still felt anxious. She prayed a silent prayer, asking for God's help with what was feeling like mission impossible. Whether it was getting Mr. Grover to dress and act like Santa or playing a convincing role of old Saint Nick herself, it was beginning to feel like climbing a mountain.

"You go on ahead to Lloyd's room," she told Aunt Ethel. "I'm going to drop these cookies at the nurses' station and visit a bit."

As they parted ways, Alice was looking forward to seeing some of her old friends. But although the nurses were happy to see the treats, Alice felt disappointed to discover that none of her old fellow nurses were on shift right now. "Please, tell them I said hello," she said, "and Merry Christmas."

"We'll try to save a few cookies for them," the LPN told Alice. But as Alice walked down to Lloyd's room, she doubted her friends would see a single cookie. She knew how fast sweets could disappear in this place. Oh well.

She found Lloyd with his cast-bound leg suspended and a disgruntled expression. "Dear Lloyd," she said cheerfully, "how on earth did you manage to do this?"

"The confounded ice," he grumbled. "What a way to spend Christmas, strung up like a kite."

"I'm so sorry." Alice patted his hand then pointed to the box on the table. "But at least Jane sent you molasses cookies."

"Jane's molasses cookies?" He brightened. "Ethel didn't tell me that."

Alice opened the box for him.

"All Ethel told me was that you've gotten some grumpy guest to play Santa tonight."

"Mr. Grover's not a grumpy guest." Alice held the box of cookies out for Lloyd. "It's just that he recently lost his wife, and he's still getting over it."

"And that's the best Santa replacement you could find for me?" He scowled at Aunt Ethel. "What about Barry Walters?"

"Barry and Betty are spending the holidays with their kids in New York. Remember?"

"Oh yeah, that's right." He scowled then took a bite of a cookie and, as he chewed, his countenance softened. "Well, I suppose you ladies know what you're doing. But I'll be doubly disappointed to find out that the pageant's grand finale was ruined by a reluctant Santa. It's bad enough to miss out on it, but if I hear that it's a failure, I'll be fit to be tied."

"Looks like you're already tied," Alice said lightly.

"And I'm overdue for pain medication," he grumbled. "Anything you can do about that, Alice? You used to work here. Maybe you can take over for those young'uns that don't seem to care about an old man's suffering."

"I'll go check on it right now." She headed for the door. "And I'll tell them that the cookies I gave them are a bribe to ensure better care for our illustrious mayor."

"You're a saint, Alice." His eyes twinkled. "Thank you, my dear."

Alice was soon chatting cheerfully with the receptionist, and when the LPN stopped by, she explained that Lloyd felt a bit neglected and seemed to be in need of pain meds. She was careful not to make them feel resentful and let them know that Lloyd was deeply disappointed that he was missing out on playing Santa at tonight's Christmas pageant.

"He's always done such a wonderful job, and the children just love him. So it's quite a blow to miss out on it this year. I'm sure that's part of the reason he's been a bit edgy. Well, that and being in pain."

"I'll get him those meds ASAP," the LPN promised as she checked the computer.

Alice thanked her and, feeling pleased for the relatively simple resolution, walked back to Lloyd's room. Now if only tonight's pageant could be as easily resolved. She prayed that all would go well...that Mr. Grover would want to cooperate...and that he would manage to smile.

Chapter Eight

A s Alice set the dinner table, she tried not to fret over Mr. Grover's absence. According to Dylan, the old man had left in a taxi a couple of hours ago. "And he took Suzie Q with him."

"Did he mention where he was going?"

"He didn't say anything," Dylan said with a dismal expression. "I just saw him as he got into the yellow taxi."

For Dylan's sake, Alice concealed her concern, but as the afternoon shadows lengthened, her worries increased. Finally, she confessed to Louise that she feared Mr. Grover could be on his way home.

"Did he check out with you?" Louise asked with a furrowed brow. "Because he said nothing about leaving to me."

"No, I was gone. And Jane already told me she hasn't seen him since before lunch."

"But you think he's gone for good?"

"I honestly don't know what to think." Alice explained about his reaction when she'd taken up the Santa suit.

"Well, we should probably check his room." Louise reached for the master key ring. "If he's gone, we'll need to find a replacement for tonight." Her sigh sounded exasperated. "I felt it was a mistake to talk him into this. He clearly didn't want to be involved. We shouldn't have pressured him like that."

"I know, I know...." Alice followed Louise up the stairs. "But I was thinking it would help draw him out a bit more. And Dylan was so hopeful."

Louise knocked on the door and waited. "Doesn't sound like anyone's here." She unlocked the door, cracked it open, and called out, "Mr. Grover, are you there?" Not hearing an answer she opened the door wider. The room looked nice and neat and, to Alice's relief, Mr. Grover's suitcase was still on the luggage rack.

"He hasn't gone."

"No." Louise closed and locked the door. "But he's not here."

"But at least he hasn't left town." Alice tried to think as they went back down. "I wonder where he could possibly be."

"Are you looking for Mr. Grover?" May Bernard asked.

"Yes, have you seen him?"

"Kay saw him in town," she said.

"Really? When was that? And where was he?" Alice asked eagerly.

"Kay spotted him outside the coffee shop as we were driving back here." May smiled. "I told her we should've stopped and offered him a ride."

"Yes, that would have been nice." Alice looked out the front window. "Especially since it looks like it's about to snow again."

"Well, then we'll just go back and get him," May told her. "I'll go fetch Kay." She giggled. "Oh my, this will be fun."

Alice hoped it would be fun for Mr. Grover too. Or at the very least, not too irritating. She knew that Mr. Grover wasn't overly fond of the chirpy Bernard twins. But if anyone could round him up and bring him back, she figured May and Kay were up to the task.

Other guests were already in the dining room. Jane had prepared an early buffet so dinner could be wrapped up in plenty of time for everyone to attend the Christmas pageant next door.

Beverly locked eyes with Alice. "Can I speak to you in private?" she whispered. Alice nodded and led Beverly through the living room and out to the foyer.

"What can I do for you?" Alice asked.

"It's Dylan. He really wants to play Mr. Grover's elf. But now he's worried that Mr. Grover isn't coming back. I don't know what to tell him."

"I'm sorry." Alice shook her head. "I suppose we shouldn't have talked Mr. Grover into doing this." She explained that the Bernard sisters had gone out looking for him. "But even if he comes back in time, I don't think he'll want to play Santa."

"Then who will? And what about Dylan? Will he still be expected to play an elf? Because I don't think he's willing— not without Mr. Grover. That was his motivation."

"We don't have a backup plan for Santa," Alice confessed, "but I'm willing to give it a try if no one else steps in to help."

Beverly's eyes grew wide. "Really? Don't you think the children will see through that?"

Noticing car lights outside, Alice paused to look. "That's the Bernard sisters now, and it looks like they have Mr. Grover with them."

"Well, I'm glad he's okay," Beverly said. "But I must admit, I'm irritated over how he got Dylan's hopes up that they'd do this together. And now it looks like he wants to pull the plug."

"Well, we don't know that for sure." Alice forced a smile. "Why don't you go get some dinner? I'll talk to Mr. Grover."

Alice waited in the foyer, praying silently for wisdom. As soon as the Bernard sisters came in, chattering away, Alice stepped over and took Mr. Grover by the arm. "I need to speak to you," she told him. "In the library." Before the sisters could object, she led him down the hallway. Then, trying not to treat him like an errant child, she asked him to sit down. Without protesting, he sat, holding Suzie Q in his lap and looking down at the rug with a guilty expression.

"I realize we may have talked you into something you'd rather not do," she began gently, hoping she could assert herself a bit more in order to get through to him. "But you did agree to play Santa. And I believe you're a man who keeps his word. And more importantly, Dylan believes the same thing. So I hope you won't let us down tonight."

He removed his hat. "Well, I had considered making my getaway this afternoon, but unfortunately, my car is still in pieces. The man at the garage said it won't be finished until after Christmas."

Alice sat down beside him. "I see. I can understand if you really don't want to be our Santa, but it seems that you could've told us."

"You're right. And I must admit, I felt a bit guilty about my escape plans. I suppose I deserve being stuck here in Acorn Hill."

"Which means you're stuck with us too." Alice attempted a smile.

"That's not so bad." The corners of his mouth curved up.

"So why not make the best of it, Mr. Grover? If nothing else, you could play Santa for Dylan's sake."

"Yes...and maybe it's more than just that."

"So you will?" she asked hopefully.

"I have always tried to be a man of my word."

"I'm glad to hear that." She studied him. "So will you keep your word by playing a *jolly* old Santa tonight? Or at least try to smile a bit more?"

"I will do my best." He pursed his lips. "But I should confess something to you."

"What's that?"

"The only time I was ever involved in anything theatrical, I failed miserably."

"When was that?"

"I was fourteen...in junior high. I tried out to play Romeo—of all things—can you imagine that?"

She smiled. "Yes, I can."

"It was only because I was head over heels for the girl playing Juliet. Colleen Stewart. I thought she was the best thing since sliced bread. I was a good student, good at memorization, and I got the part."

"And...?" She leaned forward with interest.

"As soon as I walked out on the stage and saw all those people, I completely forgot my lines. The drama teacher had to coach me through the whole first act."

"And after that?"

"I managed somehow. It's kind of a blank in my mind now. Except that it was so humiliating. And Colleen Stewart...well, she wouldn't even speak to me after that night."

"Well, that was a long time ago, Mr. Grover. And since then, you've been a teacher, standing up and talking to classes of kids, right?"

"That's right."

"So you obviously conquered your stage fright, right?"

He nodded with a look of realization. "That's right."

"And you don't even have lines to remember tonight. You only need to say 'Ho ho ho' and 'Merry Christmas.' Plus you'll be in costume and, really, no one in town even knows you. So, surely you can do that, can't you?"

"Yes, I think I can." He patted Suzie Q's head. "I feel a bit silly for trying to skip out on it now. Wasting the whole afternoon in town in a feeble attempt to hide out from all of you."

"I'm curious what you were doing all this time. I can't imagine there was much in town to interest you for so long."

He looked sheepish. "I, uh, well, I was looking for something in the stores…and then I went to the coffee shop to while away some more time."

"And then you planned to simply remain there all evening—until it was too late to come to the pageant?" she asked.

"Except they don't allow dogs in there." He shrugged. "And then the Bernard sisters showed up. Probably good thing too, since it was getting cold out there."

She shook her head, sad to think of the lonely man hiding out from them like that.

"I am sorry, Alice. I didn't want to disappoint you like that."

"Really?" She felt a tinge of hope. Mr. Grover hadn't made many apologies during his visit here.

"Yes. You've been kind to me. And I shouldn't repay you with my stubbornness."

"And Dylan too?"

"Yes. He deserves a bit more from me as well."

"Good. Now, I'm guessing you must be tired after spending the last few hours hiding out in town. And you're probably hungry." She checked her watch. "How about if I bring some dinner up to your room. You just relax and put your feet up. We want you in top form for tonight."

Mr. Grover agreed that was a good plan. But instead of taking his dinner up to him, Alice let Dylan do it, after explaining to him a bit about Mr. Grover's early bout with stage fright. "But that was a long time ago. I think he's over it now. Still, he might need some encouragement from you tonight. Maybe you two can practice together."

Dylan seemed relieved to hear this and eager to help. As he carried Mr. Grover's loaded dinner plate through the dining room, Alice could tell by the spring in his step that he was up for the task. Hopefully, Mr. Grover was too.

Chapter Nine

Because Alice had already promised to supervise her
ANGELs with their pageant responsibilities, she knew
she wouldn't be able to help Mr. Grover and Dylan get
ready for their roles. But Aunt Ethel had assured Alice she
could manage.

"I have no doubt you can manage helping with the costumes," Alice told her aunt as they discussed the pageant in
the kitchen. "But can you manage Mr. Grover?"

"What do you mean?" Aunt Ethel sounded defensive.
"You should know as well as anyone, but I'm quite capable
of managing most things."

"Yes, I realize that. But Mr. Grover is very nervous about
tonight. He'll need encouragement, but it needs to be gentle
encouragement."

"What Alice is saying is that he does not respond well to
being bossed around." Jane secured a large cookie plate with
plastic wrap.

"Yes, I suppose that's what I'm saying," Alice admitted.
"He needs to be handled with TLC." She quickly explained
about his stage fright. "I think if you remain uplifting and
positive, he'll be fine. Just don't prod or push him." Alice

exchanged glances with Jane. They both knew how bossy and pushy their aunt could be at times. And what worked with Lloyd Tynan would not work with Mr. Grover.

"Tell you what," Jane said to Alice. "You run these cookies over to the church, and I'll stick around to help Auntie with Santa and the elves."

"Thank you." Alice nodded with relief as she buttoned her coat. "See you both later." Then, with cookies in hand, Alice trudged through the snow to the church. As she went, she prayed another silent prayer for Mr. Grover. Oh, she knew it wouldn't be the end of the world if he messed up tonight. The pageant always had some little hiccups that everyone laughed about afterward. But for Mr. Grover's sake, she didn't want him to be a flop.

The ANGELs had been told to arrive early because they were supposed to usher and hand out programs before the pageant. After that, they would meet Alice in the basement to get into their angel wings. Then they would parade through the sanctuary—at just the right moment—singing "Angels We Have Heard on High." After that, the ANGELs and Alice would fade into the background while the younger children performed the Nativity play, followed by a caroling session with the older kids. And finally the ANGELs would close the children's part of the show with "Hark! The Herald Angels Sing."

After that, Santa would make his grand appearance, and all the children present, both performers and those in the audience, would be presented with little gifts that the church had been collecting throughout the year. If all went well.

When Alice met with her ANGELs, she reminded them that ushering was very important. "You're the first connection the audience has with the pageant. You want to make them feel welcome—and happy they came out on such a cold winter's night." She went over a few other things, and suddenly people were starting to arrive. "Do your best," she told them. "And I'll meet up with you again downstairs."

Down in the basement, Alice helped some of the other children with their costumes. A lamb needed help with lopsided ears. A shepherd couldn't find her hook. Alice had helped with dozens of Christmas pageants over the years, and yet she never tired of it. Seeing the enthusiasm of the children preparing for their performance was enough to put the spirit of Christmas into anyone's heart.

When her ANGELs came downstairs, everyone knew it was time for the younger children to go up and take their places. Alice could hear Louise's piano music filtering down the stairwell as she helped pin wings onto the oversized white T-shirts her ANGELs were wearing. They'd decorated their T-shirts with glitter glue, sequins, and rhinestones at their last meeting. Each one was unique, sparkly, and fun.

"That sounds like our cue," Alice told the girls when she heard the pastor finish his welcome. "Let's go up. Everyone break a leg." She chuckled. "Not literally, of course. Be careful on the stairs."

The ANGELs clustered in the church vestibule, waiting for Louise to begin playing their entry song. And then, singing brightly, they walked down the center aisle, splitting in the front, like they'd practiced, and going to opposite sides of the stage, standing and kneeling...waiting as the Nativity story continued to unfold.

But it was Jane, standing on the sidelines, who caught Alice's eye. Jane, standing by the door to the vestry, was motioning to Alice, mouthing, "Come here." So, trying not to draw any attention, Alice slipped up past the pulpit.

"We need you," Jane whispered as she tugged Alice into the vestry. "Santa meltdown." She quietly closed the door then turned on the light.

"He's balking," Aunt Ethel told Alice with a frown.

"Why don't you let Alice handle this now?" Jane tossed Alice a look as she reached for her aunt's arm. "You and I can go out and watch the pageant."

"Yes, I'll take it from here." Alice turned out the light as Jane and Aunt Ethel made their exit. Then she closed the door, turned the light back on, and turned to look at Mr. Grover. Smiling, she reached for his hand. "You make a fabulous Santa," she said to him.

"Mr. Grover didn't like it when your aunt put makeup on him," Dylan told Alice. "They kinda got into a fight."

"Not a real fight," Mr. Grover grumbled. "But nearly."

Alice looked at Dylan. "Oh my, you look fabulous too. Honestly, I don't think we've ever had a better-looking Santa and elf." She looked down at Suzie Q. "I should say elves." She chuckled. "You three are really going to be a big hit."

She pointed to a chair. "Santa, I think you should sit down. The program will take about a half hour. But if we turn off the light in here, I can open the door, and we can listen."

Mr. Grover sat in the only chair, and Dylan sat on the floor with Suzie Q in his lap. Alice turned off the light and quietly opened the door. They could easily hear in the small room, but because of the scenery, they couldn't see much. Still, the children's lines and sweet singing voices were charming and, Alice hoped, soothing to Mr. Grover.

Finally, it was time for her ANGELs to sing the last song. And then it was time for Pastor Thompson to wrap things up. As usual, he acted like he really thought the evening's entertainment was coming to an end, thanking everyone for coming and inviting them to share in treats afterward.

"Time for Santa and the elves," Alice said quietly. As Louise began to play "Here Comes Santa Claus," Alice nudged Mr. Grover to pick up the fully loaded Santa sack. Then she motioned for Dylan and Suzie Q to lead the way.

Alice whispered in Mr. Grover's ear as she gently guided him out the vestry door. "Your dear wife loved children, and I think she would be so happy that you're doing this for them tonight. She'd be cheering you on, Mr. Grover."

He looked at Alice with grateful eyes then followed Dylan out to the center of the stage to the accompaniment of uproarious applause. And then Mr. Grover, as if he'd done all this before, began to call out cheery greetings of "Merry Christmas!" and "Ho ho ho!" Standing tall, he waved to the audience in a very Santa-like way. "Thank you all for coming tonight! And thank you for inviting me to join you. Merry, Merry Christmas to everyone. And now I have some early Christmas gifts for the kiddies." He set the large brown sack on the floor, and children immediately began to cluster around him.

Alice could hardly believe her ears and eyes as Mr. Grover, aided by two adorable elves, took control of the stage. Not only did he continue to boom out glad tidings and jolly laughter, he began to ad-lib as well. Assisted by Dylan, "Santa" began to hand out gifts, greeting the children like they were old friends. He even made clever comments about the weather at the North Pole and shared greetings from Mrs. Claus, who was home with a cold. Then he made everyone laugh by sharing a funny joke about his reindeer demanding time off for a cocoa break. The man was a natural!

Dylan appeared to be having fun too, handing out gifts and helping the children pet the little canine elf. The Santa segment was truly a hit, and Alice couldn't have been happier. Or more relieved. After the gifts were all distributed,

Santa continued to visit with the children. He even made himself at home on a pulpit chair, allowing children to sit on his lap and express their Christmas wishes while their parents took photos. It was truly amazing.

"I can hardly believe it," Dylan's mother said quietly to Alice as they watched from the sidelines with Jane. "They're both doing really great."

"It's almost miraculous," Jane told Alice. "What did you do to calm him down?"

"I think his wife calmed him down," Alice said quietly. "I think he did it for Isobel."

Later that evening, after the festivities were over, the sets had been taken down, and everyone had gone home, Alice remained behind to straighten up the sanctuary for the next day's church service. This was a task she'd often performed for her father, back when he'd served as lead pastor of Grace Chapel Church. Alice had always enjoyed being in the sanctuary when all was quiet and calm like this.

As she lined pots of poinsettias beside the railing that surrounded the pulpit, Alice silently offered up a prayer of thanksgiving to her heavenly Father. She also felt grateful for her earthly father, wondering if he'd been watching tonight. And even more grateful to Isobel Grover...because it really did feel like she'd been involved somehow. Oh, Alice didn't understand the mysteries of heaven or the universe, but she knew that God's ways were higher than hers. And with God, anything was possible.

She finished up in the sanctuary then turned off the lights, put on her coat, and went outside. As she locked the door, she heard a familiar voice. She turned around and saw Mr. Grover, still wearing the Santa suit, talking to Dylan, still dressed as an elf. Mr. Grover was pointing out Canis Major. "There's the big dog," he told Dylan. "See, he's chasing the hare—that's Lepus."

"What about the little dog?" Dylan asked eagerly.

"Canis Minor is right there." Mr. Grover pointed upward again, explaining how to recognize the small cluster of stars.

"The little dog." Dylan held up Suzie Q. "Do you see that? That's your constellation, Suzie Q."

Not wanting to interrupt them, Alice went around the other side of the church, cut across the snowy backyard, and let herself into the back porch of the inn. As she hung her coat in the back closet, she could hear her sisters' voices in the kitchen.

"There you are," Louise said as Alice entered the bright warm space.

"We were about to send out a search party for you." Jane handed her a cup of hot tea. "You probably need this."

"Aunt Ethel just left." Louise set her empty teacup down. "But she wanted you to know that she appreciated your help with Mr. Grover."

"That's nice." Alice smiled.

"I promised the guests I'd play some Christmas carols," Louise told them. "Everyone is in a singing mood tonight."

"Will you let Beverly know that Dylan is with Mr. Grover?" Alice asked. "Stargazing."

After Louise left, Jane held a cookie plate up to Alice. "I bet you didn't get any treats tonight."

"Thanks." Alice took a sugar cookie. "I was too nervous to eat."

"Well, I don't think it could've gone better." Jane refilled her own teacup. "And I don't think we've ever had a better Santa." She held her teacup up. "Here's to Mr. Grover."

Alice clinked her teacup against Jane's. "Here's to him continuing to have a good Christmas here at the inn."

Jane nodded knowingly. "That's right. Christmas is not until Tuesday. But Mr. Grover seems to be full of surprises. Anything could happen."

Chapter Ten

Alice was pleased that Mr. Grover agreed to join everyone for the church service the next morning. As always
for the Sunday before Christmas, it was a joyful service.
Festive and colorful, the church was packed full and the
singing was exuberant.

As they walked back to the inn, everyone seemed in
good spirits. Well, nearly everyone. Alice wasn't so sure about
Mr. Grover. He was noticeably quiet again, perhaps simply
wrapped up in his own thoughts. But when they got to the
inn, without saying a word to anyone, he went straight up to
his room. Alice told herself it was to check on Suzie Q, but
when he didn't make an appearance for the midday meal, she
had her doubts.

Afterward, Alice made a plate of food for him, slipped
upstairs, and quietly tapped on his door. When he didn't
answer, she knocked a bit louder. When the door finally
opened, he looked sleepy and disheveled. "I didn't mean to
disturb you," she said gently. "But I thought you might be
hungry."

He checked his watch. "Is lunch over already?"

She nodded and handed him the plate.

"I didn't mean to miss it." He sighed. "I fell asleep. Thank you."

"Are you feeling okay?"

"Yes." He set the plate on the desk behind him. "I'm fine. Just tired, I suppose."

"You seemed a little blue after church."

"I was missing Isobel...and perhaps feeling a bit guilty."

"Guilty?"

"Last Christmas...I didn't want to go to church with her. And now, this Christmas...well, you probably can guess."

"But don't you think Isobel is happy that you went to church this year?" Alice asked him.

He shrugged, but his eyes looked misty.

"I don't know if you felt what I felt last night, Mr. Grover—I know you're a man of science—but I got the strongest sense that Isobel would have been glad you were there in church, that she would be pleased to see how happy you made the children."

"I know you said something to that effect last night. But did you really feel that at the time?"

"I genuinely felt something, Mr. Grover."

His expression looked slightly quizzical. "I think I did too."

"I'm not surprised. I also feel that somehow—in some unexplainable way—God orchestrated your whole visit here. It's as if He let Isobel know that she'd be gone this Christmas, and He knew she'd want to ensure you were not alone. Because she loved you so dearly."

His eyes were definitely glistening now. "She did love me...dearly."

"And I'm sure Isobel would hate to think you were feeling guilty, Mr. Grover. Over something that is over and done with."

He nodded. "I think you're right."

Alice smiled. "Young Dylan is hoping to play chess with you this afternoon. I told him I'd let you know."

Mr. Grover smiled. "Thank you."

"You're welcome." She started to step away, but he stopped her.

"Alice, may I ask you a favor?"

"Of course." She waited.

"I know you're busy with your inn responsibilities. But do you think you'd have time to take me shopping?"

"Shopping...?" She tried not to look overly surprised.

"Yes. I'd like to go to town, but I'd rather not take a taxi this time. I did that yesterday. I tried to do some shopping, but I don't really know your town. I walked and walked. Until my bad leg began to ache. And the sidewalks were icy and—"

"I'm happy to take you," she told him. "Does tomorrow morning work for you?"

"That'd be great. Thank you."

Alice was pleased to see that Mr. Grover and Dylan not only played chess together, they also found another one of her father's old astronomy books. As Alice set up the dining room for tea, she could overhear the pair discussing the book in the living room. Dylan was getting quite a cosmic education—and it sounded as if he was loving it.

But then she heard Myron's and Katie's raised voices drifting in from the foyer. Unfortunately, they were bickering over something that had happened in town. Katie had wanted to stop at the bakery for a snack, but Myron had insisted they return to the inn for tea. "After all, it's free," he said loudly. "And you're the one who's always harping about our finances."

"That's because you're always acting like such a cheap-skate," she retorted. And on they went—exchanging snipes back and forth until Mr. Grover interrupted them.

"Come in here right now," he called out in a stern teacher-like tone. "You two are acting like children. No, no, you are worse than children. Sit down on that sofa and listen up."

Alice paused from filling the sugar bowl to listen. What was Mr. Grover going to say to them? Should she intervene? And yet she felt the couple's arguments were impacting everyone within hearing distance.

"One might assume you two don't really like each other," Mr. Grover continued. "And maybe you don't. Tell me, do you even like each other?"

They both mumbled that yes, they did.

"And do you love one another?"

Again they both agreed they did.

"Then if you love each other, why are you arguing over something so trifling? How can you fight about going to a silly bakery?"

"Because I wanted to get a doughnut—and Myron said he wouldn't wait for me," Katie declared.

"Because I wanted to come back to the inn," Myron said defensively.

"That's only because you're such a skinflint," she shot back.

"Hold on," Mr. Grover said loudly. "Tell me, Myron, is it worth the price of a doughnut to put your wife through this kind of distress?"

"Well, no, I guess not."

"And you, Katie, is it worth a doughnut for you to call your husband all those names?"

"No, of course not."

"Someday, in all likelihood, one of you will be gone." His tone grew somber. "One spouse will outlive the other, and one of you, like me, will be left alone to pick up the pieces. And take it from me, sometimes you don't fully appreciate what you have. . .until it's too late."

"Yes, I'm sure that's true," Katie admitted. Myron quietly agreed.

"Because when you're left by yourself," Mr. Grover continued, sounding very much like a teacher now, "and you find yourself missing the one who was taken first, you start to remember things. So many things. Big things and little things. Good things and bad things. It all comes rushing upon you. Often when you least expect it. And it can be brutal at times. So think about this. Do you really want to look back on your first Christmas together only to recall how you argued and bickered over the silliest little things? That you fought over a doughnut?"

They both agreed they wouldn't like that.

"So for the sake of your marriage, and for the sake of those of us who don't enjoy overhearing your petty arguments, can you please try to keep your disagreements to a minimum or at least take them elsewhere?"

They both agreed to this and then they apologized—first to Mr. Grover and Dylan. And then to each other. After a bit more discussion, they even thanked him for his intervention.

"Maybe you should consider becoming a marriage counselor," Katie said.

He chuckled. "I don't think so."

"Well, I'm going to take my wife down to the bakery for a doughnut," Myron declared. "She can have a whole dozen if she likes."

"Oh, I don't want a dozen." Katie giggled. "But, yes, let's go. The Boston creams looked heavenly."

After they left, Alice joined Mr. Grover and Dylan in the living room. "You really handled that well, Mr. Grover. They needed an intervention like that."

"Thank you. Some lessons...well, you really do learn a bit late in life, but they're still worthwhile."

Alice smiled as she laid out the Christmas napkins. It seemed perhaps—at least with Mr. Grover—an old dog really was capable of learning some new tricks.

Chapter Eleven

Alice was curious about what Mr. Grover planned to shop for this morning, but thinking it could be something personal, she didn't want to ask. Dylan was "doggy sitting" Suzie Q, and Alice had promised to be back before eleven.

"Do you think stores will be open?" Mr. Grover asked as she slowly drove toward town. "I mean, since today is Christmas Eve."

"Oh, I think a lot of shops capitalize on last-minute Christmas shoppers."

"Like me."

"Are you doing Christmas shopping?" she asked.

"Yes. I want to pick up a few things."

"Where would you like to start?"

"Do you have a good bookstore?"

She snagged a parking spot near the Nine Lives Bookstore, and before long they were both perusing the bookshelves. Alice had already done her Christmas shopping, both for her sisters and for the rather generic gifts they would give to their guests at the inn. But, knowing her sisters' tastes in books, she decided to get them each a last-minute gift. It appeared that Mr. Grover had found several books as well as some Christmas wrapping paper.

"I suppose people might think it boring, but I like giving books for gifts," he said as they went outside. "But I'm still looking for a few more things." He pointed across the street. "Is that a gift shop?"

She confirmed that it was, and while he looked around the small shop, Alice visited with the owner. It didn't take long for Mr. Grover to make his selections. When the cashier offered gift wrapping, Mr. Grover gladly accepted.

"While those are being wrapped, I'd like to find a gift for Dylan," he told Alice. "But I'm looking for something very specific. Does your town have a toy and hobby shop?"

Alice thought. "Not exactly toy and hobby. We do have a nice toy store a couple of blocks that way. I'll drive down there so you don't have to walk on the icy sidewalk."

She pulled up in front of the toy store. "If you don't mind, I'll run down to the grocery store while you're looking in here. Jane asked me to pick up a few items for her."

"Yes, of course. And take your time. I'll be fine."

Of course, the grocery store was busy, and it took longer than she thought it would. When she got back to the toy shop, Mr. Grover was standing on the sidewalk with nothing in his hands and wearing a dismayed expression.

"They didn't have what you were looking for?" she asked as he got into the car.

"No. I really wanted to get Dylan a telescope. Not a toy one, mind you. But a real telescope."

"What a delightful idea."

"It seemed good to me, but the toy shop doesn't have anything like that. And the fellow in there didn't think any-one in this town has one either. He even made a couple of calls for me."

"That was nice of him."

"He suggested I get it online. But I'm not very good at that sort of thing."

"Jane is great at shopping online," Alice told him.

"Maybe so. But I doubt that anyone could get a telescope here by tomorrow."

"Yes, especially since it's Christmas Day."

"So now I have gifts for everyone—everyone except Dylan. And he is the one I most wanted to get something for. He's the reason I decided to get the others gifts."

"Is there something else we could look for? Perhaps an astronomy book?"

"Yes, I thought of that too. But I wasn't impressed with the books I saw at the bookstore earlier."

"We do have a sporting goods store on the other end of town. Is Dylan interested in any sports? Like baseball or football?"

"Not that I know of." He frowned. "And I'm not much of a sports person myself, so a gift like that feels insincere to me."

Alice parked near the gift shop. "How about if I go in and get your purchases for you?" she offered. "They should be wrapped by now."

"Thank you. I must admit, I'm feeling a bit worn out."

"I'll be right back."

As Alice waited for the clerk to bag up Mr. Grover's wrapped packages, she looked around the shop. Was there anything in here that an intelligent young boy would like? Most of the items seemed frivolous and more appropriate for women.

Alice carried the bags to the car and set them in the back seat, wishing she could think of some good solution for Mr. Grover's gift dilemma. But it was getting late, and she'd promised to be back in time to help Jane in the kitchen. As she started the car, Mr. Grover let out a happy whoop. "I've got it!" he exclaimed. "The perfect gift for young Dylan."

"What is it?"

"That space camp he wants to go to in Florida. I'll give him that for Christmas."

"Oh, he'll love that."

"You say your sister Jane is good on computers. Perhaps she can help me."

"I'm sure she'll be glad to help." Even if Alice had to take over the kitchen for a while, she was willing.

"Yes, this is perfect." He rubbed his hands together. "Of course, I'll check with Beverly first. I want to make sure I do this right. I can just imagine his face when he finds out."

Alice was surprised to hear Mr. Grover sounding so happy. Hopefully, it wouldn't be too difficult to figure out this space camp business. Not only because Mr. Grover was so excited but because she knew Dylan would be over the moon too.

As soon as they got to the inn, Mr. Grover practically sprang out of the car. Or as close to springing as an elderly lame man could. Alice helped him carry in his gifts and set the packages on the bench in the foyer.

"I'll talk to Jane," she told him as she unbuttoned her coat. "Hopefully, she'll be able to help you with the—" Alice stopped herself as Dylan, carrying the little dog, joined them. He told Mr. Grover that Suzie Q had been a "very good girl."

"How would you like to be my elf helper again?" Mr. Grover asked Dylan.

"Are we going to wear our costumes again?"

Mr. Grover grinned. "No costumes necessary. But could you put these packages under the Christmas tree for me?" As he handed the bags of wrapped gifts to Dylan, Alice hurried out to the kitchen and explained to Jane Mr. Grover's plans to give Dylan the space camp gift.

"Really?" Jane paused from frosting a cake. "That's so sweet and generous of him. But I'll bet a camp like that is expensive. Do you think he considered that?"

"I don't know." Alice grimaced. Hopefully, the cost wouldn't be overwhelming.

"And you know Mr. Grover seems, well, sort of frugal."

"You mean because of his appearance?" Alice had noticed from the start that Mr. Grover's attire suggested either an impoverished or penny-pinching nature.

"You mistook him for a homeless man when you met him."

"That's true. But I think that's partly due to his being widowed. His wife isn't around to help with his wardrobe choices. And even if he's frugal about clothing, that doesn't mean he's poor."

"Just the same, you might want to drop a hint as to the cost of a gift like that." Jane handed Alice the frosting spatula and pulled her cell phone from her apron pocket. "You finish this, and I'll do a quick search."

Alice continued frosting the cake while Jane clicked away on her smartphone. "While you're looking, can you find out if it's even possible to do this online?" Alice asked. "Or would it be better if Mr. Grover called someone himself?"

"Oh, anything can be done online." Jane held up her phone. "Here's a camp with the Kennedy Space Center."

"Yes, that's what Beverly said," Alice said eagerly. "I'll bet that's the one."

Jane read a figure. "Wow, Alice, do you really think Mr. Grover will want to cover that?"

"I, uh, I don't know." Alice bit her lower lip.

"Well, before he gets in too deep, you'd better let him know the cost." Jane took the spatula back. Alice thanked her then went to look for Mr. Grover.

"He's in the library with Louise," Beverly told Alice. "He's helping her wrap some Christmas presents."

"Is Dylan around?" Alice asked quietly.

"He just took Suzie Q outside."

"I don't know if I should say anything...." Alice considered. "But it might help to get your input."

"My input?" Beverly put down the book she was reading, and Alice explained Mr. Grover's idea for Dylan.

"But I'm not sure he can afford it—and he doesn't know how much it costs yet," Alice finally said.

"Oh, it's terribly expensive." Beverly shook her head. "But how sweet of him to want to do that for Dylan."

"My question is, if he really does decide to do it, are you okay with it? Is there anything he should know? And is there more than one camp? It would be sad if he went to all that trouble and booked the wrong camp."

"Yes—and there are a number of options. My mother sent me the brochure for the camp that's nearest her. She offered to provide transportation and pay for the airfare to get him down there. That will be a stretch for her, but she's willing." Beverly reached for her purse. "I have the information right here." She dug out a rumpled brochure and pointed to where she'd marked one of the camps in pen. "This is the one that works for us."

"Do you mind if I share this with Mr. Grover?"

"Not at all. I just hope he doesn't keel over from the shock of how much it costs. And I wouldn't want him to feel any pressure to do this. I'm sure he doesn't realize how expensive it is."

"Well, for what it's worth—" Alice heard the front door open and saw Dylan and Suzie Q bound into the inn. She slipped the brochure into the pocket of her cardigan and smiled at Beverly. "We won't be holding our breath over this, will we?"

"I sure won't." Beverly picked up her book. "But it was nice of him to think of it."

Alice found Mr. Grover and Louise up to their elbows in gift wrap in the library. "Santa's workshop?" Alice asked as she closed the door behind her.

"Santa is all thumbs," Mr. Grover told her. "But your sister needed an elf, and I was all she could find."

"Louise happens to be one of the best gift wrappers around," Alice assured him.

"Well, unless you want creative wrapping." Louise tied a bow. "You'd need Jane for that."

"Speaking of Jane..." Mr. Grover set the scissors down, looking at Alice.

"I have the information right here." She handed him the brochure. "I took the liberty of having a quick conversation with Beverly. I hope you don't mind. I was worried there might be more than one option. It turns out there are many. This is the one that works for them. It's marked."

"What are you talking about? It sounds so mysterious." Louise reached for the tape dispenser.

"You'd have to ask Mr. Grover." Alice watched as Mr. Grover read over the brochure. "I did tell Beverly that nothing is written in stone. And she understood."

"Can Jane help me with this?" he asked.

"Yes, of course. She's more than happy to help." Alice wanted to ask if he'd seen the price of the camp but didn't want to insult him.

"Is it all right if I go speak to her about it now?" he asked.

"Sure. She's in the kitchen." Alice smiled. "She might make you help frost a cake or something."

"That's fine with me—as long as she lets me lick the bowl." He chuckled as he left.

"What is going on?" Louise demanded as she set down the neatly wrapped gift.

"I'm not sure I get to say. It might be something he wants to keep under wraps. Kind of like a good deed. Or you could ask Mr. Grover."

"Well, I don't want to be nosy." Louise measured off some ribbon. "And I must say that Mr. Grover has thoroughly won me over. Sometimes first impressions are misleading. Because I don't think I could've been more wrong about the man."

"He really is a sweetheart." Alice handed her the scissors.

"You know what we were just talking about?"

"I haven't a clue."

Louise wrapped the ribbon around the package. "He confided to me about how he'd gotten so blue at church yesterday...because he missed Isobel."

Alice nodded.

"The ironic thing was that I had just been feeling a bit down myself."

"Oh Louise, I didn't know that. What's wrong?"

"Well, you know I was disappointed that Cynthia isn't coming for Christmas."

Alice wasn't surprised that Louise was missing her daughter. "I'm sorry about that. But at least she'll be here for Easter."

"That's true. But it wasn't just Cynthia. I was missing Eliot too. And it's not like I'm freshly widowed. Not like Mr. Grover. But the holidays sometimes remind me of times gone by. And I suppose I was feeling a bit sorry for myself."

Alice put an arm around Louise's shoulders. "I'm sorry. It's been so busy around here, I didn't notice."

"That's all right. But it was what Mr. Grover said to me...it was a comfort." She sighed. "It really helped. And I appreciated it."

"I'm so glad he came here for Christmas. I think we needed him as much as he needed us." As Alice pressed her finger into the ribbon so Louise could tie the bow, the door to the library opened.

"Well, it's all settled," Mr. Grover announced. "Jane is a whiz at that sort of thing. She had them email the confirmation to the inn. She said Louise might be willing to print it out for me in the office."

"So I get to be in on the secret?" Louise's brows arched.

"As long as you keep it a secret." Mr. Grover grinned. "But I think I can trust you ladies."

Alice was still curious about Mr. Grover's reaction to the expense, but she decided it wasn't any of her business and left them to finish up the gift wrapping. It was sweet to hear Louise, a woman who wasn't inclined to flattering praises, express her genuine admiration of Mr. Grover. Not only had Mr. Grover not ruined Christmas, like some had predicted, he had greatly enriched it!

After a festive breakfast the next morning, everyone, including Aunt Ethel, gathered around the Christmas tree. First to sing carols then to exchange gifts. Dylan, wearing his elf hat, did the work of retrieving and distributing the gifts from under the tree.

Everyone was in good spirits. Alice was relieved that the gifts she'd picked out for the guests were appreciated. And her sisters seemed to like theirs as well. It was fun to see Suzie Q model the little sweaters—one in pink and one in purple—that the Bernard sisters had made for her.

Mr. Grover's gifts to everyone were surprisingly thoughtful and appropriate. Alice loved the snow globe he gave her. It had a lovely angel inside, but it was his note that made it truly special—thanking her for being the "angel who'd rescued him from the snow."

"Are we done?" Louise asked. "We can sing more carols."

"Wait." Alice pointed to the top of the tree like Mr. Grover had asked her to. "Is there something up there?" Everyone looked up to see that a white envelope was tucked just beneath the star on top. Alice had used a stepladder to get it up there. "It's so high up, I don't think anyone can reach it," she said.

"Myron can reach it," Katie said. "Can't you, honey?"

"Maybe with the help of this step stool." He scooted it over then got on it and carefully removed the envelope. "It says it's for someone named Dylan. Anyone know who that is?"

"That's me!" Dylan sprang to his feet.

"Here you go." Myron handed it over.

"What's in it?" Jane asked as he opened it.

"No way!" Dylan started to jump up and down. "No way!"

"What is it?" Beverly asked eagerly. "Tell everyone."

"Space camp!" he shouted. "I get to go to space camp this summer! I can't believe it—I'm going to space camp!" He danced around the room, waving the paper in the air.

"Who's it from?" Louise asked him.

"Santa." Dylan paused, looking around the room at everyone.

"Well, of course it is," Jane said.

Dylan went over to where Mr. Grover was sitting quietly watching. "But we all know that Santa's not real."

"Well, the spirit of Santa is real," Jane told him.

Dylan nodded. "But this is from Santa himself." Then Dylan threw himself at Mr. Grover and wrapped his arms around his neck. "Thank you, Santa!"

Mr. Grover waved his hand dismissively. He pretended to know nothing about the whole space camp thing, but Alice could tell that Dylan wasn't fooled by his act. She felt pretty certain this was a friendship that would last for more than just one Christmas. In fact, it would be that way for all of them. No one would ever forget Mr. Grover.

Louise Remembers...
By Beth Adams

Prologue

"M y favorite unexpected Christmas guests were those newlyweds we had a few years back." Louise took a misshapen bell and studied it. "Lauren and Jordan."

"That's right," Jane said. "I almost forgot about them. He was Viola's nephew?"

"It was their first Christmas after the wedding," Alice added, nodding. "You did take a liking to them, didn't you, Louise?"

"There was something about them that reminded me of me and Eliot," Louise said. "Those early years can be hard."

"But that Christmas was pretty special," Alice said.

Louise nodded. "It sure was."

Chapter One

Louise Howard-Smith pushed aside the curtain and looked out the window of the parlor, searching for headlights. The clouds hung thick and heavy in the dim evening light, but there was no sign of the predicted snow yet. And no sign of her daughter, Cynthia, either. Louise turned back with a sigh. The curtain fell gently back into place.

"She'll be here soon," Alice said. She was curled up under a wool blanket with a book and a cup of tea, and she had been urging Louise to sit down and relax too.

"I know. I just can't help but worry," Louise said. She glanced at the spot on the couch next to Alice. It did look inviting, with the white lights from the Christmas tree casting the room in a soft, warm glow. The tree was trimmed with beautiful hand-painted glass ornaments and topped with an antique star that had graced the Howard family tree since Louise was a girl. There was another tree, with the Howard sisters' own personal ornaments, in the living room, and electric candles graced each window, an old-fashioned symbol meant to signal that travelers were welcome here.

Maybe she *could* sit down and relax for a moment. But as soon as she thought it, she realized she would never be able to unwind while she was on edge about Cynthia, who was driving down from Boston tonight. Maybe she could use this time to practice the pieces she would be playing at the Christmas Eve service on Thursday. Pastor Kenneth Thompson had changed up the program this year, and she would need to learn some new music before the service in two nights. Playing the baby grand in this room always helped her relax. But the music would no doubt disturb Alice. Then again, it probably wouldn't be worse than the pacing Louise was doing already.

"What's Jane up to?" Alice asked.

"Last I checked she was baking gingerbread cookies," Louise said. Maybe she could go and help Jane with that. Louise usually left the baking to the youngest Howard sister, but she could play sous-chef, or at least start on washing the dishes. But just then, a sweep of headlights indicated that a car had pulled up next to the inn. Louise dashed back to the window but let out a sigh when she saw it wasn't Cynthia's car.

"Not her?" Alice asked.

"Those must be our new guests," Louise said. They had been expecting one last set of guests, a couple from New York, to check in this evening. They already had two older couples—friends who always spent Christmas together in a new place, they'd told Louise—upstairs. The couples had gone out for an early dinner and were now settled in for the night. The New York plates on the CR-V in the driveway confirmed these were their new guests. "I'll go check them in."

"Thank you," Alice said, giving her sister a grateful smile before turning back to her book.

Louise headed out to the reception desk, which was draped in evergreen boughs and lit with a trio of white pillar candles on a gold charger. Louise worried about using real candles in this more than hundred-year-old house, but her sisters had overruled her, and she had to admit the light and scent the candles gave off were beautiful.

The front door opened, and Louise smiled as a young man wiped his feet on the mat before he stepped in, carrying a suitcase in one hand and lugging another behind him. He was so bundled up that she could barely see his face.

"Hello. Welcome to Grace Chapel Inn," Louise said. "Let me help you."

"I'm all right," he said, holding the door open with his foot. A woman stepped in behind him. She shut the door as he set the suitcases down, and then she looked around and sucked in her breath.

"Oh goodness. This place is beautiful! It's even better than the pictures." She pulled back the hood of her puffy coat and took in the gold-and-cream wallpaper and the beech coatrack.

"Let me take your coats." Louise walked forward as they peeled off their jackets, and she hung them neatly in the coat closet. "You must be the Nelsons."

"That's right. I'm Jordan." The man was tall, with sandy blond hair and a wide smile. "And this is my beautiful bride, Lauren."

Lauren beamed. Her brown hair was pulled back in a ponytail, but curly wisps escaped. A large diamond glinted on her left hand.

Louise's heart warmed at the obvious love this young man had for his wife. "Newlyweds?"

Jordan laughed. "How could you tell?"

"It's nice to see such a happy couple." She led them to the reception desk. Lauren seemed delighted by the old-fashioned porter's bell and the collection of antique fountain pens.

"It's a pleasure to meet you," Louise continued. "I'm Louise, and I run this inn with my sisters, Alice and Jane. We welcome you to Grace Chapel Inn."

"Thank you. We're happy to be here," Jordan said.

Louise checked the reservation book. "It looks like you're going to be staying with us until the day after Christmas?"

"That's right. We're actually visiting my aunt here in town."

Louise smiled. "Viola mentioned you were coming. She said she's sorry she doesn't have enough space for you to stay with her."

"Oh wow. You know Aunt Viola?" Jordan asked.

"It's a small town," Louise said. "You'll quickly discover that pretty much everyone here knows each other."

"Just like where we come from," Lauren said.

Louise stared at her. Hadn't she read that they were from New York City? Weren't there more than eight million people there? What was she—

"That was a joke," Lauren said with a smile.

"Got it." Louise laughed. "That makes so much more sense."

Louise handed them the key to the Sunrise Room and gave them a quick tour of the first floor, showing them the parlor, the library, the living room, and the dining room, where breakfast would be served. Lauren exclaimed over the Queen Anne dining room table and the Eastlake chairs in the parlor, and she clapped when she saw the beautifully decorated trees in both the parlor and the living room.

"Two Christmas trees! This place is amazing."

Louise introduced them to Alice, who looked up from her book and welcomed them, and Jane, who was busy in the kitchen making tray after tray of gingerbread cookies. She would decorate them in the morning when they had cooled,

Louise knew. Then Louise led the young couple up the stairs to their room, which was painted a light blue and had a blue, yellow, and white quilt on the bed.

"It's so beautiful." Lauren dropped her purse on the dresser and took in the high ceilings and the large windows. "That bed is an antique, isn't it?"

"That's right."

"I love antiques," Lauren said, sighing. "I love to imagine the people who used them all those years ago."

Louise always liked to see a young person who appreciated history. So many were only impressed by the latest gadgets.

She pointed to the bathroom. "My daughter will be staying in the Symphony Room, so you'll share this with her. I hope that's all right."

"That's just fine," Jordan said. "We look forward to meeting her." They both thanked her, and she left them to settle in. Just as she reached the bottom of the staircase, the front door opened, and Cynthia stepped in.

"Hi, Mom," she said, dragging her suitcase in behind her and shutting the door. "Oh my goodness. It smells so wonderful in here. What is Aunt Jane making?"

Louise wrapped her daughter in a tight hug and pulled her close. "Gingerbread cookies. I'm sure she'll let you have a taste. I'm so glad you made it." She pulled back and looked at Cynthia. Her daughter's dark hair was gathered into a ponytail, but she had dark smudges under her eyes, and her cheeks looked thinner than usual. "You look tired."

"It's been crazy at work. I'll be fine after a few days here."

Cynthia was an editor for a children's book publisher in Boston, and she loved her work. Louise was glad for that but sometimes worried that she worked too hard. Well, she was here now. Though she had warned Louise that she would be working all day tomorrow. She had apparently run out of vacation days and convinced her boss to let her work from here. It wasn't ideal, but Louise was happy she was here, no matter what. "I'm so glad you made it."

"I'm glad to be here." Cynthia hung up her coat and then picked up her suitcase. "I'm in the Symphony Room?"

"That's right. Let me help you carry that."

"I'm fine, Mom." Cynthia waved her hand to indicate that she could handle it. "I'll take this up and get settled in, and then I'll come back down, and maybe we can have a cup of tea and catch up?"

"That sounds wonderful," Louise said. "Have you eaten?" Sometimes Cynthia got so busy with work that she would forget to eat.

"I grabbed something on the way. Thank you, though."

While Cynthia carried her suitcase to her room, thunking it against the stairs with each step, Louise went into the kitchen and filled the teakettle.

"She made it?" Jane was just taking a tray of cookies out of the oven. Sweet-smelling air wafted out along with them.

"She did." Louise set the teakettle on the stove and turned on the burner. "Safe and sound."

"Now you can relax." Jane set the tray on the counter and used a spatula to pry a corner of one cookie from the pan. "Here. I need a taste tester."

"Your cookies are always delicious."

"Because I taste test." Jane scooped the cookie onto a plate and then pried up another and set it on a second plate. "One for Cynthia too. They'll taste better with frosting, but I can't decorate them until they're cool."

Louise set sachets of mint tea into mugs decorated with hand-painted Christmas trees, and when the kettle whistled, she poured the hot water over them. Warm wisps of steam rose up from the surface.

There were footsteps on the stairs, and Lauren and Jordan walked past the kitchen.

"We're going out for dinner," Jordan announced. "We won't be back too late."

"Where are you headed?" Jane asked.

"Do you have any suggestions?" Lauren asked. "We were just thinking we'd wander and see what we found."

"Your best bet would be Zachary's," Louise said. "It's a nice place, with very good food. They're only open for dinner, and it shouldn't be too crowded."

"That sounds great," Jordan said.

Jane told them where to find the restaurant, and they headed out. A few minutes later, Cynthia came downstairs, and Louise and her sisters all gathered around the table to talk to her. Cynthia told them about some of the books she was editing for work and about a new friend who had joined her Bible study. She mentioned a bestselling mystery book series she was loving and a play she had seen the past weekend. Jane caught her up on all the news in Acorn Hill—a painting class she and Clarissa Cotrell had attended through the fall and the holiday concert Vera Humbert's fifth-grade class had put on and a fire at the library that had closed the children's section for a few weeks earlier in the month. Alice told her about a toy drive she was heading up for a shelter in Potterston and about an activity she had recently done with her ANGELs—the group of local girls she led on service projects. Wendell, their beloved tabby cat, purred in Cynthia's lap.

After they'd all consumed several mugs of tea and eaten many of the cookies Jane had intended to decorate in the morning, Louise finally yawned and stretched her arms up.

"It's probably time for bed," she said, noticing that Cynthia's eyes were drooping as well, and Alice was stifling a yawn. The newlyweds had come back from dinner a while ago, and the upstairs was still.

They all headed up, trying to keep quiet on the stairs, and Louise got ready for bed in her third-floor bedroom. She peeked out the window and saw that there was no snow yet, and the night was dark and calm. Before she settled in for the night, though, she pulled a soft robe on and went back down to the second floor. She knocked gently on the door to the Symphony Room.

"Come in," Cynthia called, and Louise pushed open the door. She loved this room, with its climbing rose wallpaper and its tall windows. Cynthia was tucked up under the covers, reading a paperback novel by the warm light of a bedside lamp.

"I just wanted to make sure you have everything you need," Louise said, though they both knew it wasn't true. She just wanted to see her daughter again and give her one more hug. She didn't get to see Cynthia enough and missed the chance to talk to her more regularly. Seeing her now, Louise was struck all over again by how wonderful Cynthia was and how lucky she was to be her mother.

"I'm good, Mom." Cynthia used her finger to mark her place in the book. "I'm just going to read for a while and then go to sleep."

"All right. Don't stay up too late."

Louise knew Cynthia was a grown woman now and knew how to take care of her herself, but Louise couldn't stop herself. She would always be a mom.

"I won't." Cynthia gave her a knowing smile.

"You're almost done," Louise said, gesturing toward the book she was holding. "Is that the mystery series you were telling us about?"

"That's right. I'm about to find out who did it."

Louise took the hint. "All right then. Have a good night."

"Good night, Mom."

Louise turned and began to walk out of the room but then she stopped, listening.

Was that... It almost sounded like someone was crying in the bathroom. Louise hesitated, not sure what to do.

It sounded like a woman, which meant it had to be Lauren. She looked at Cynthia, but her daughter had already buried herself in her book and apparently heard nothing. Should she knock on the door and make sure the young woman was all right?

But if she was in the bathroom, she most likely didn't want anyone to know she was upset, Louise reasoned. She waited a moment and then slowly turned away. Best to let her have some peace, she decided. Hopefully, she would feel better in the morning.

With one last indulgent look at Cynthia, Louise made her way to her own room and to bed.

Chapter Two

It had snowed overnight, though it had been just a fine dusting and not the two inches that had been predicted. Still, it was just enough to cover the yard and the street in a soft white coat, and it sparkled in the rays of sunlight that peeked through the trees. It was gorgeous. Louise sighed deeply as she got dressed for the day. The Lord was a master artist, and she was continually surprised by His masterpieces.

The scent of cinnamon and something warm and yeasty filled the air as Louise went downstairs. Jane was serving apple-cinnamon pancakes drenched in butter and maple syrup when Louise came into the kitchen. Alice was nowhere in sight, and Louise figured she must be out walking with Vera Humbert, a ritual they did most mornings.

The two older couples were eating in the dining room, and Jane was chatting with them about their travels. Louise piled several pancakes on a plate and sat down.

"Hi there, Louise. Melinda was just telling me about the trip these guys all took to Arizona last Christmas," Jane said, indicating a woman with graying blond hair. She was married to Matthew, to her left, who had glasses and a mustache. Louise was pretty sure their last name was Wallace.

"It was beautiful," Melinda said. "The colors of the mountains out there are unreal. The most gorgeous reds and purples. And the plants that grew there—I'd never seen anything like the cactus out west."

"It was hot," Matthew said, shaking his head. "There was no snow."

"It didn't exactly feel like Christmas," the other woman— Priya, Louise was pretty sure—said. Priya Walton and her husband, Rupert, were British, but had been living in Ohio near the Wallaces for several decades.

"You can stick a wreath on a cactus, but it still doesn't make it a Christmas tree," Rupert said over the rim of his coffee cup.

Louise laughed. "No, I suppose it doesn't."

"We decided we wanted to come somewhere that looked like a Christmas card this year," Melinda said. "And I'd say we did exactly that."

Louise asked how they'd gotten into traveling together for Christmas, and Priya explained that the first year the Wallace's daughter, Carrie, had spent with her in-laws, they'd planned a trip together so they wouldn't be sitting home alone stewing in memories and feeling lonely. "And we all loved it, so we've just kept it up." She used the edge of her fork to cut off a piece of pancake. "Rupert and I never had children, so we've got nothing tying us down at the holidays, and it's so expensive to travel overseas to visit our families at that time of year, so it's worked out quite well."

"Do you ever disagree about where you want to go next?" Jane asked. "It sounds like it could be challenging to get four people to agree."

"Not really." Matthew shook his head. "There are so many beautiful places in the country, and if we don't get to one we'd like to see this year, maybe we'll get to it next year."

"We all get along really well," Rupert added.

"The only thing we ever really disagree on is politics." Melinda gave a knowing smile. "And we've agreed to just not talk about it."

Jane laughed. "That seems like a smart strategy. Politics can be so divisive."

"Sometimes you just have to agree to disagree," Louise said.

"But as long as we stay away from that subject we get along great," Matthew said. They moved the conversation to the list of places they were considering for next year's trip. Utah, Maine, and California were all in the running, apparently.

Louise finished up her breakfast and loaded her plate into the dishwasher. Alice had come back from her walk and was changing upstairs, but she would be back down shortly. Since Cynthia was working remotely today and Louise knew that she was planning to spend much of the day in her room in front of her computer, she decided to use this time to practice the pieces she would play at the Christmas Eve service at Grace Chapel Church tomorrow night.

Louise left the parlor door open in case anyone needed her, and she had barely settled down on the upholstered piano bench when the doorbell rang. Louise popped up, since she was the closest to the door. She pulled open the door and was thrilled to see Craig Tracy standing on the porch, holding a box wrapped in shiny red paper. Craig owned Wild Things, a charming florist shop in town that the sisters frequented. The potted poinsettias that graced the porch had come from his shop.

"Hello, Craig." Louise held the door open for him. Craig had helped Jane bring the gardens that surrounded the inn back to life after the sisters moved back home, and even now, when the trees were bare and the grass brown, witch hazel and holly brightened up the yard, thanks to his good landscaping advice. "Please come in. That must be for Alice's toy drive."

"That's right." Craig wiped his feet on the mat and stepped inside. "I was supposed to buy for a four-year-old girl, so I bought a baby doll. I hope that's all right."

"My daughter loved baby dolls at that age," Louise said. "I'm sure she'll love it."

"Craig!" Alice appeared in the hallway and clapped her hands. "Thank you for bringing this over."

"I'm happy to do it."

Alice took the gift from him and placed it under the tree in the living room, where she was storing the shelter gifts, and Craig went with her, discussing the pros and cons of various baby dolls he'd had to decide between. Louise went back into the parlor to practice. Pastor Thompson had decided that instead of ending the Christmas Eve service with everyone holding a candle and singing "Silent Night," which was the traditional ending to the service, this year they would sing a new arrangement of the beloved song earlier in the service and end with the less familiar "I Heard the Bells on Christmas Day."

Louise wasn't sure how she felt about the change—she would wait to reserve judgment until she saw how it played out in the service. But she knew it had evoked some strong feelings among members of the congregation. Word of the decision had already caused plenty of longtime members of the church to get up in arms about the change and argue for the importance of adhering to tradition.

Louise sat down at the piano and began working through the new arrangement of "Silent Night" when she heard Craig go out and footsteps on the stairs. She looked up to see Lauren standing in the hall, head cocked, listening.

"Was that you playing 'Silent Night'?" Lauren asked.

"It was. I hope I didn't wake you," Louise said. "The room is soundproof, but I didn't close the door in case my sisters needed me. But maybe I should have—"

"You didn't wake me," Lauren said. "I've been up for a while. I just asked because, well, it was beautiful."

"Oh." Louise couldn't help smiling. She loved how music could bring so much joy into the world. "Thank you. It's such a simple song, but it's always been one of my favorites."

Louise could see that the skin around Lauren's eyes was puffy. Remnants of last night's tears, no doubt. Louise pressed her lips together. Should she say something? Was it better to pretend she hadn't noticed? She was never sure what to do in situations like this. Maybe it would be better to keep things normal.

"Have you had breakfast?" she asked, her voice sounding just a bit too bright.

"Oh yes, we ate more pancakes than we should have," Lauren said. "They were delicious. The reviews online were right about the amazing food here."

"Jane is a really good cook. We're very blessed." Louise hesitated again. Was Lauren just waiting for Jordan? Or did she need something else?

"What are you up to today?" she asked, her voice once more sounding just a bit too chipper. "Anything fun?"

"We're going over to Jordan's aunt's house now to see his mom," Lauren said. She smiled, but there was something in her eyes that didn't seem to match up.

Once again Louise hesitated. She didn't want to be the nosy innkeeper butting into their guests' business. At the same time, if there was something she could do to help...

"Are you all right?" she asked.

"Oh." Lauren let out a forced laugh. "Oh yes, I'm fine. I know I look terrible, right? I had a hard time falling asleep last night, and it always shows on my face. I just drank a lot of water. Hopefully, that will help me look more normal again soon."

"I'm sorry to hear that." Louise didn't believe that everything was all rosy, despite Lauren's cheerful tone, but she didn't say that. "Do you need anything? Another pillow or an extra blanket?"

"Oh no. The bed is so comfortable, and the room is great. I just sometimes have a hard time sleeping in a new place."

"Well, please let us know if you need anything," Louise said. She wasn't sure what else to say.

"I will." Lauren turned as her husband walked up beside her.

"Ready to go?"

"Ready."

He leaned in and planted a kiss on Lauren's lips. Lauren's face brightened, and she took his hand and looped her pinkie around his. Then Jordan turned and smiled at Louise. "Good morning."

"Good morning." Louise gave a little wave. She couldn't figure it out. These two were clearly in love. But something was bothering Lauren, that was clear. Ah, well. It was none of her business. "Have a great day," she called, and they thanked her and moved toward the front door. Louise said a silent prayer as the door closed behind them, though she wasn't really even sure what she was praying for.

∽

Louise continued to work through the new arrangement of "Silent Night" and practiced "Hark! The Herald Angels Sing." Nancy Colwin, who owned Zachary's Supper Club with her husband, Zack, and Patsy Ley, who was married to Henry Ley, the associate pastor of Grace Chapel Church, dropped off presents for the toy drive that morning. Both of them dropped into the parlor to chat, and Nancy expressed concern about the changed order of the songs.

"I just don't see why we can't do what we've always done," Nancy said. "It's tradition. It's beautiful. Why go stirring things up when it's perfectly fine the way it is?"

Patsy had a different take on the change. "Every year, I hold my breath when those candles are lit," she said. "With all of that old dry wood and not enough fire exits and all those kids waving lit candles around, I just keep waiting for a tragedy to happen. I'm quite happy to nix the candlelight portion of the service and sing a different hymn instead."

Louise had never seen it quite that way, but she could see Patsy's point. Mostly, though, she thought how interesting it was how everybody seemed to have an opinion on the song that had ended the service for so many years. She hadn't realized how attached people had grown to the ritual of ending the service that way.

After they left, Louise ran through the two pieces one more time, and she felt fairly confident about them by the time Cynthia came down for lunch. She would need to spend some time practicing "I Heard the Bells on Christmas Day," which she hadn't played in years, as well as "Joy to the World," which would be played during the offering.

Louise joined her sisters and Cynthia as they enjoyed cheddar broccoli soup and sandwiches on freshly baked bread, and then, when Cynthia vanished back upstairs, Alice announced that she needed to finish up some last-minute Christmas shopping. "Does anyone want to come into town with me?" she asked.

"I thought you were done with your shopping," Louise said, carrying her plate to the sink.

"I thought I was too," Alice said. "But when I was walking with Vera this morning, I realized I hadn't gotten anything for her. Then it occurred to me that I should get something for the ANGELs. And, well, I'm not sure about the sweater I bought for Aunt Ethel."

"But it's a lovely sweater." Louise had been with Alice when she'd found the chunky hand-knit piece at a craft fair a few weeks ago. It was a dusty rose color, and it looked as warm as it was soft.

"I know. That's the problem," Alice said, a guilty look on her face. "I think I may want to keep it for myself."

Louise and Jane both laughed.

"I'm going to stay here and whip up some more cookies, since so many of the ones I baked vanished before I could frost them," Jane said. "That way if anyone else comes by with gifts for the toy drive, I can be here to receive them."

"Thank you, Jane. That would be very helpful," Alice said.

Louise had bought and wrapped all her gifts weeks ago, so she was about to decline to join Alice when she remembered something. This morning she'd had an idea for something small she could get for Cynthia.

"Actually, maybe I will come with you," she said. She could practice the piano pieces later. She might as well take advantage of Cynthia's being distracted with work for now.

"That would be great. I'd be happy for the company." Alice finished loading her plate into the dishwasher and rinsed her hands. "I'll be ready to go in about ten minutes. Would that work for you?"

"Perfect," Louise said. She headed upstairs and pulled on a wool sweater and heavy socks, and then she knocked gently on the door of the Symphony Room.

"Come in!" Cynthia called. Louise opened the door and found Cynthia looking up at her over the screen of her laptop.

"I'm going to run into town with Alice," Louise said. "Do you need anything?" She cast a stealthy glance at the book on Cynthia's bedside, making sure she would recognize the cover.

"I'm good," Cynthia said. "I'm hoping to just knock this out and finish up with work a bit early. I should be done by the time you get back."

"That sounds great." Louise closed the door behind her and headed downstairs. She and Alice pulled on their heavy winter coats and stepped out onto the porch.

"It's so beautiful," Alice said as they shuffled through the soft snow. "It really looks like Christmas, doesn't it?"

"It does," Louise agreed. "And the weather report said it's supposed to snow tomorrow night too."

"Oh, that would be lovely," Alice said. "A white Christmas."

"Let's hope so." Louise hitched up her purse as they made their way down the steps and onto the sidewalk. They passed Grace Chapel Church, the little church their father had pastored for decades, and the carriage house, where Aunt Ethel lived. The lights were on inside, and it looked cozy, with smoke trailing out of the chimney. Louise hummed "O Holy Night," which the church choir would perform during the Christmas Eve service. They'd had their final practice earlier this week. "So where are we headed?"

"I was thinking I might stop in at Nellie's to see if I could find something for Aunt Ethel," Alice said. "I saw some pretty silk scarves in the window there over the weekend."

Louise nodded. Nellie's was a clothing boutique in town that sold colorful clothing and accessories. Aunt Ethel loved that place.

"And I thought I might stop in at Time for Tea and get Vera some of Wilhelm's Winter Blend," Alice continued. "She mentioned how much she likes it this morning on our walk. How about you? I thought you were done with Christmas shopping?"

"I was." Louise grimaced. "But I thought I might get Cynthia the next book in the mystery series she mentioned last night. She was about to finish the one she was reading."

"That's a good idea, assuming Viola carries it," Alice said. "It might be too popular for her tastes."

Viola, the owner of Nine Lives Bookstore, was not shy about her preference for great literature and often looked down her nose at many of the bestsellers and more commercial fiction so many of her customers seemed to prefer.

"Let's hope she has it," Louise said. They turned onto Acorn Avenue, and Louise smiled when she saw the Christmas lights strung up along the lampposts and the wreaths hung on them. Acorn Hill was always a beautiful little town, but at Christmastime, it really looked like something out of a Norman Rockwell painting. They walked past the Good Apple Bakery, where the sign on the door announced IF YOU LOVED IT, WE BAKED IT AT THE GOOD APPLE. Beyond that, they passed Parker Drugs, with its old-fashioned soda fountain, and Fred's Hardware, run by Vera Humbert's husband.

"What bout Mark? Did you send him something?"

Alice's cheeks flushed. She had recently reconnected with Mark Graves, the head zookeeper at the Philadelphia

Zoo, with whom she'd been romantically involved many years ago. Alice wouldn't admit to them being anything more than friends now, but sometimes Louise suspected that her sister might someday sell up her portion of the inn and move to Philadelphia to marry Mark. But Alice denied it, so they would just have to wait and see.

"Yes. I sent him a necktie with little tigers on it," Alice said. "It should have arrived yesterday."

A necktie? It seemed a bit impersonal to Louise, but then, what did she know? She hadn't dated in decades.

"I'm sure he'll love that," Louise said. "And that means we don't need to find something for him."

Alice asked what Louise had gotten for Jane, and as Louise explained that she'd picked out half a dozen tubes of Jane's favorite colors of oil paint, they made their way into Time for Tea.

A bell tinkled over the door, and Wilhelm Wood stepped out from the back room. "Hello," he called. He smiled when he saw it was Louise and Alice. "Welcome. How are you both doing today?"

"We're doing well," Alice said. Louise took in a deep breath. She loved how it smelled in here—earthy and sweet, with just the slightest hint of mint. Wilhelm had a Mozart piano concerto playing over the loudspeakers. Jars of dried teas lined one wall, and beautifully packaged boxes of tea bags and teapots and strainers filled the rest of the shop. There was a special display of Jane's Madeline and Daughters chocolates on a table near the front of the store. "Oh, it all looks so tempting," Alice said. "I just want to try it all."

"That's the idea," Wilhelm said with a smile. "Tea makes a great Christmas gift, you know."

"I do know," Alice said. "I'm actually hoping to get some of your Winter Blend for Vera Humbert, please."

"Coming right up," Wilhelm said. "Vera loves that tea. She'll be thrilled."

"Are you traveling anytime soon?" Louise asked as he used a metal scoop to tip some of the dried leaves into a brown bag. Wilhelm was a bachelor who lived with his mother here in town, but he loved to travel and had seen more countries than Louise could count.

"I'm hoping to take a trip to New Zealand in February." Wilhelm tipped another scoop into the bag and set it on the scale.

"New Zealand?" Louise didn't know a lot about the country, but it sounded exotic.

"It is supposed to have dramatic landscape, plus it'll be summer there," Wilhelm said. "Which sounds pretty nice right about now."

"That sounds lovely," Alice said. She paid for the tea and thanked him. They went to Nellie's next, where Nellie Carter helped Alice pick out a beautifully embroidered silk scarf in a deep eggplant color.

"This will look wonderful on your aunt," Nellie said as she wrapped it in tissue paper. "I saw her admiring the display just the other day."

"I hope she'll like it," Alice said. Louise smiled, knowing that Alice could now keep the sweater.

"She'll love it," Louise insisted.

They stepped back out onto Acorn Avenue and headed east. The sidewalks and streets were crowded with shoppers, and Louise waved at Clara Horn, who was pushing her pot-bellied pig, Daisy, in a stroller as she walked down the street. Today Daisy was dressed in a red and green Christmas sweater and tucked under a tartan blanket. Louise had never quite understood why Clara pushed Daisy around like a baby, but she was a beloved part of the community.

"Hello, Clara," Alice called.

Clara waved and pushed the stroller closer to them.

"Hi there." Clara was in her seventies, and good friends with Aunt Ethel and Florence Simpson.

"Is Audrey coming for Christmas?" Louise asked. Audrey was Clara's daughter and the same age as Jane.

"Yes, she'll be coming in tomorrow. Daisy and I can't wait. Isn't that right, Daisy?" She stroked the little pig with her finger, and Daisy grunted.

"I hope you have a wonderful visit," Louise said, and then she and Alice moved along down the sidewalk. Just up ahead was Nine Lives Bookstore. BOOKS MAKE GREAT GIFTS declared a sign in the window. It hung above a display of hardcover books piled one on top of the other to make the shape of a Christmas tree. Louise recognized great holiday classics like Charles Dickens's *A Christmas Carol* and O. Henry's *The Gift of the Magi* as well as beautifully illustrated copies of *The Little Match Girl*, *The Polar Express*, *The Night Before Christmas*, and *The Nutcracker* piled beneath the book tree.

Louise stepped into the store and inhaled the lovely scent of paper and ink, and sighed. There were several people browsing in the aisles, and Alice went off to peruse the tables at the front of the store. Louise waited while Viola finished helping a customer pick out a colorful edition of *The Secret Garden*. Some young girl was going to get a lovely gift under the tree. Cynthia had loved that book when she was young. Once Viola had rung up the purchase, she turned and smiled at Louise.

"Whew. Sorry about the wait. I hired a college girl to help me during the Christmas rush, but she's got that nasty flu that's going around, so I'm shorthanded."

"That's quite all right. I'm in no rush."

"Well, that would make you the only one." Viola laughed. "So. What can I do for you? Have you come to check out the dead Russians like I've been urging?"

Today Viola had a purple scarf draped around her neck, and she gazed at Louise over her bifocals.

"*Anna Karenina* looks serious, but it's a page-turner, trust me," she continued. "Perfect for cold winter nights."

"No, I'm afraid not," Louise said. She hadn't read the book, but she knew how it ended, and it did not sound very Christmassy. "I do intend to read it at some point, but today I'm here looking for a gift."

"You are?" Viola cocked her head. "You don't strike me as a last-minute shopper."

Louise laughed. "I'm not, usually. But Cynthia just got into town—"

"Now there's a girl who knows good literature." Viola's eyes lit up. "Has *she* read *Anna Karenina*?"

"I don't know." Louise was used to Viola's ways by now. She knew Viola's goal was to get everyone to read the classics. She carried popular books in her store to meet the demand of her customers, but she was always trying to sell more serious books. "I'm here to get her the next book in a mystery series she loves. She just mentioned it to me yesterday."

"I see." Viola arched an eyebrow.

Louise told her the name of the series, and Viola heaved a heavy sigh. "Come with me."

She led Louise to the mystery section, helped her find the next book, and then led her back to the counter.

"I hear you have visitors," Louise said as Viola scanned the barcode on the back of the book.

"That's right. My sister Irene came to visit me this year. And her son and new daughter-in-law are staying with you."

"They're a lovely couple," Louise said. "And how nice that you get to have visitors this year."

"It is nice. I'm glad they came. Irene…" Viola broke off, and Louise handed over her credit card. "Well, it's been a tough year. Her divorce was finalized this spring, and the family wanted to do something different for Christmas this year. A way to leave all the things associated with Brian behind and make new memories."

"I'm sorry to hear that," Louise said. "That must have been hard for them."

"It was good, in the end." Viola slipped the book into a paper bag imprinted with the store's logo. "Irene had put up with a lot, for a long time, and it finally just got to be too much. I let out a cheer when I heard she was finally leaving him. We'd all been trying to get her to leave for years."

"That had to have been hard." Louise wasn't sure what else to say.

"Well, it made Lauren and Jordan's wedding interesting." Viola smirked. "Everyone was on their best behavior, even though Brian showed up with his new girlfriend. She's closer to Jordan's age than Brian's."

"Oh goodness."

"Jordan was more gracious than I would have been able to be." Viola slipped the receipt into the bag and handed it to Louise.

"Was that the wedding you went to in June?" Louise knew Viola had closed the shop for a few days in early summer to travel to a wedding, but she hadn't gotten many of the details.

"That's right," Viola said. "It was this lavish affair at a country club in New Jersey."

"That sounds lovely." Louise imagined Lauren must have made a beautiful bride.

"It was too much. Too many bridesmaids, too many pictures, too much money."

Louise wanted to laugh. Only Viola could complain about a beautiful wedding at a country club. "So you didn't enjoy it?"

"I was glad to be there to support my sister and her family," Viola said with a sniff.

"And I'm sure they were glad to have you."

"It was kind of them to invite me. Though given how many people were there, I'm not sure they would have noticed if I hadn't come."

"It was a big wedding, then?"

"Lauren's family alone must have been several dozen people. They are a big, tight-knit family, that was clear right away. But they were nice enough."

"Well, I'm glad that she was willing to come here and spend her first married Christmas with you. And with us," Louise added.

"It was very kind of her. I know she wishes she could be with her family this year, but Jordan really wanted to support his mom, and you can't exactly argue with that." She shrugged. "Well, I know Irene is grateful to have them both here at any rate."

"And I'm thrilled to be hosting them."

Louise took the bag and found Alice looking through a display of novels set in the English countryside, but she wasn't planning to buy anything here, so she and Louise stepped back out into the cold winter air.

"Where to next?" Louise asked.

"Well…" Alice pressed her lips together. "I was thinking I might go to Sylvia's to pick up some little things for the ANGELs, but right about now, I could sure use a doughnut."

The Good Apple Bakery was just up ahead, and suddenly a doughnut sounded like a fantastic idea. "I could use a break," Louise said. "Shopping is hard work."

"It sure is."

When Louise and Alice returned to the inn later that afternoon, they found Aunt Ethel seated at the kitchen table sampling some of Jane's fresh-baked cookies.

"Hello, Auntie." Louise stopped in the doorway while Alice headed upstairs to keep Aunt Ethel from spotting her gift.

"Hi, Louise. I brought over the gift I signed up to buy for that little boy in the shelter." Aunt Ethel smiled, pleased with herself. "And wouldn't you know it, Jane had just finished decorating these beauties."

Louise held back a smile. Aunt Ethel, their father's younger sister, had a habit of turning up just when food was ready.

"Aunt Ethel was just telling me her thoughts on Pastor Thompson changing the Christmas Eve service," Jane said, giving Louise a knowing look.

"Why would you go and mess with something like that? Ending the service with candles during 'Silent Night' was the way my brother did it for years. There's no good reason to change it. He just wants to try something newfangled, probably to appeal to the younger generation." The sniff she gave made it clear exactly how she felt about that.

"I don't know," Jane said. "Maybe he just wants to try something different for a change." Of all the Howards, Jane was the most excited by trying new things.

"If it was good enough for Daniel, it should be good enough for him."

Part of Louise agreed with her, but she was going to wait and see how it went. She was open to the idea that this could be an improvement. She decided to change the subject. "It was nice of you to contribute to the shelter toy drive."

Louise knew Alice had worked hard to organize this toy drive, and it warmed her heart to see so many people from town contributing.

"Well, I couldn't let those poor kids go without presents, now could I?" Aunt Ethel took a bite of the cookie. "Of course, back in my day, we didn't have as many toys and never would have expected the electric doodads kids want these days. We were happy with a handful of penny candy and an orange. But I suppose times change. I hope the kids at the shelter will appreciate it."

Louise wasn't quite sure how to respond to that, especially as she'd seen Aunt Ethel's daughter Francine unwrap her fair share of elaborate gifts over the years. But she knew better than to mention that. "Your hair looks nice," she said instead. "Did you have it touched up?"

"Yes. Thank you." Aunt Ethel set the cookie down and patted her bottle-red hair. "I went down to the Clip 'n' Curl yesterday. I wanted it to look nice for the service tomorrow night. Lloyd is supposed to read scripture, you know, and so all eyes will be on us."

Louise held back a smile. Her aunt was "special friends" with Lloyd Tynan, the mayor of Acorn Hill, and while he was a lovely man, Louise couldn't see why his reading scripture would necessitate a new hairdo for Aunt Ethel. But if it made her feel good to have her hair done, Louise was in full support.

"You know, it wouldn't hurt you to get yourself down to the Clip 'n' Curl to get your hair shaped. You're past due," Aunt Ethel said. "I bet Betty Dunkel still has some appointments before tomorrow night."

"Thank you, Aunt Ethel." Louise kept a smile on her face and decided to change the subject again. "Wow, Jane, these cookies turned out beautifully."

Jane had applied thin layers of icing in delicate pastel colors to create delicate flowing dresses and lederhosen on the cookies.

"Thank you." Jane was leaning back against the counter, drinking tea from a cheerful red mug. "I have to admit, I'm happy with how they turned out."

"They're delicious too," Aunt Ethel said, helping herself to another one.

Louise chatted with the two of them for a few minutes, and then she took her bags upstairs and checked on Cynthia. Cynthia said she only had a little more work to get done and would be down shortly, so Louise headed back downstairs. As she passed by the library, she found Lauren inside, holding her cell phone up to the window.

"Oh. Hello." Louise stopped short in the doorway. "You're back."

"Hi there. I hope it's okay that I came in here," Lauren said.

"Of course. You're welcome in here." Louise had always loved this room, with its mossy-green tweed wallpaper and its mahogany bookshelves. It had been her father's study for so many years, and it still reminded her of him whenever she came in. "Let me guess. You're hunting for a signal?"

"Correct," Lauren said. "I have two bars right here, which is more than I've gotten anywhere else."

"The reception's not great here," Louise said, though Lauren clearly already knew that. "But you're welcome to use our landline."

"Thank you," Lauren said. "I appreciate it. I probably should have stayed at Viola's, but, well, if I'm honest, I just needed a break."

"I completely understand." As much as Louise had loved Eliot and his family, who were lovely people, it had always been draining to visit her in-laws.

"And then I realized that today was the day my family was going out to chop down the tree, and I thought I'd try to call and see if I could join in the fun virtually." She shrugged. "It's the first time I've ever missed it."

Louise took a step into the office. "Is it a family tradition, then?"

"Yes." Lauren sighed. "Every year we drive out to this family-run Christmas tree farm out in South Jersey and chop it down together. It's a whole big thing. We stop at the same diner for lunch on the way there, and then after we get the tree and bring it home we have hot chocolate and these Italian cookies my mom always bakes, and we play carols while we decorate the tree. My parents have these boxes of ornaments for each of us kids, and they're the same ones we've been hanging on the tree for years. It's... Well, it's totally dorky, but we loved it when we were kids, and we've been doing it the same way ever since."

"It sounds lovely." Louise and her sisters had enjoyed a similar tradition when they were younger. "Did you always wait until right before Christmas to get the tree?"

"No." Lauren's curls bounced as she shook her head. "When we were all younger, we did it on Saint Nicholas Day,

which is December sixth. But now with so many of us out of
the house or away at college, we do it the first day that everyone's home for Christmas."

"That is such a sweet tradition," Louise said. "I hope you
get ahold of your family. It would be lovely for you to be there
with them, even if it's just virtually. And let us know if you
need anything."

Louise hesitated a moment, and then she started down
the hallway, intending to give Lauren privacy to make the
phone call, but after she'd only gone a few steps, she started
to wonder if privacy was really what the young woman
needed.

Louise went into the kitchen and talked with Jane and
Aunt Ethel for a few minutes while she made a cup of herbal
tea. She carried the mug back to the library and found Lauren
seated in one of the russet-colored chairs staring down at her
phone.

"Were you able to connect with your family?"

"No." Lauren sighed. "I think they must be out of cell
range. They like to go pretty deep into the property looking
for just the right tree. I texted my sisters to ask them to send
me photos when they can, but nothing has come through yet.
Maybe when they get back into cell range."

Louise stepped into the room and held out the mug. "I
brought you some tea."

"Oh my goodness." Lauren pressed her lips together, and
Louise realized she was tearing up. "Thank you. Everyone is
so nice here."

"We try to make our guests feel at home." Louise set the
mug on the little side table between the two armchairs. "Do
you mind if I join you for a minute?"

"Not at all." Lauren gestured to the other chair.

"Is this the first time you've missed Christmas with your family?" Louise asked.

Lauren nodded. "A part of me really wanted to spend the holiday with my family. I have five brothers and sisters, and it would be the first time we've all been together since the wedding. We always have so much fun together. But, well, with Jordan's mom…"

"I hear it's been a tough year for her?" Louise asked gently.

"That's one way to say it. His dad is… Well, Jordan is trying hard to maintain a relationship with him, but he feels pretty strongly that his mom was wronged, and he was worried about her being alone for Christmas. His sister is in Texas with her husband's family, and we were close by, so it just seemed like we kind of had to be here. Irene wanted to get away and get a change of scenery and start some new Christmas traditions for their family, and of course I couldn't say no," Lauren said. "Not that I would have," she added quickly. "I'm glad we're here. It's lovely."

"I'm glad you're enjoying it here." Louise adjusted the pillow behind her and leaned back. "But it's natural, you know, to miss your family and your holiday traditions. Especially if this is your first year missing out on them."

"Thanks." She gave Louise a shy smile. "I appreciate it. I guess I'm just feeling a bit homesick."

"That's totally normal. I remember my first Christmas away from my family. I loved my husband and his parents, but they ate different food and had a fake tree instead of a real one, and they didn't sing the same songs…" She shook her head. "I missed my sisters like crazy. My parents too."

"What did you do?"

"The same thing you're doing." Louise smiled. "I tried to make the best of it and called home several times. And did my best to remember that I loved Eliot and had chosen to spend my life with him and wanted him to be happy. All of that was true and good. But still, it's hard to adjust to another family's way of doing things."

Lauren nodded. "It doesn't help that this is all new for them too. I know they used to have their own family traditions, but that's all changed now. They wanted to do something different this year. I think the idea of facing the things they used to do, but without Jordan's dad, was too much. So they're kind of lost, and Irene doesn't seem to have too much interest in baking or decorating or anything. And with his aunt at work so much, Jordan and his mom are just sitting around watching TV, and it just feels... Well, I don't know."

"Viola is so busy at the shop this time of year," Louise said.

"I know. And she's not used to hosting for the holidays, so it's not really her fault. But there aren't any decorations up, and there are no Christmas cookies or treats, and no music, and... I don't know. It just doesn't really feel like Christmas, I guess."

Louise wasn't sure what to say. She knew how paralyzing grief could be. How the aftermath of a divorce was devastating, no matter how long it was in coming. How scary it could be to face the holidays alone for the first time.

That first year after Eliot died, Louise hadn't wanted to celebrate at all. She couldn't bring herself to get out the decorations they had collected over the years. Thank goodness for Alice, who had picked her up and taken her to buy gifts and driven her and Cynthia home to spend the holiday here with Father. She doubted she'd have even bothered to go shopping or make any sort of effort otherwise. She could only imagine the loneliness and pain Irene must be dealing with.

"I'm sure they both appreciate your being here."

Lauren lifted up her mug and blew on it. "I'm sure they do. And they're my family now too." She took a sip of the tea.

"Have you told Jordan how you're feeling?"

"No. Of course not." Her denial was so quick and vehement it surprised Louise. "He's already dealing with so much. I can't complain about missing my family when his family has totally fallen apart."

Louise could see where she was coming from, but she wasn't sure she agreed.

"Plus, I'm sure we'll spend the holiday with my family next year," Lauren continued. "It's not like this is a forever situation. It's just..."

She let her voice trail off.

"Jordan clearly loves you. I'm sure he would want to know how you're really feeling."

"Maybe." She took another sip of tea and set the mug down.

Louise was thinking about how to respond when they heard footsteps. They both turned and saw Jordan in the doorway.

"There you are." He smiled when he saw his wife. "I came back to see how you're doing." He stepped into the room and looked around. "This room is so cozy."

"I'm doing all right." Lauren gestured toward the mug. "Louise brought me some tea."

"That's really nice." He smiled at her. "Mom was going to take a nap, so I thought now might be a good time for us to go up and wrap the presents we brought."

"That's probably a good idea." Lauren sighed and pushed herself up. "Thank you, Louise. I really appreciate this."

"Of course." Louise watched Lauren follow her husband out of the room, still carrying her tea, and heard them go up the stairs. She sat still for a few moments, thinking about what she had shared, and then she closed her eyes and said a prayer for Lauren, asking God to help her find unexpected joy and a deepened connection with her new husband and his family this Christmas. And she asked that the Lord would show her how she could help in her own way too.

Chapter Three

Cynthia finally came downstairs, declaring herself officially on vacation until the New Year. Jane had a pot roast and potatoes cooking in the oven, and they filled the house with a delicious rich aroma. Louise made Cynthia a cup of hot cocoa to celebrate and then put on Christmas carols in the living room and handed Cynthia the box of her ornaments. The living room tree—the family tree, as she thought of it—was quite a contrast to the tree in the parlor, which was hung with tasteful glass ornaments and white lights. The tree in the living room was hung with the sisters' own ornaments they had collected over the years and lit with colored lights, which Jane had declared more "fun."

"The family Christmas tree isn't done until you add yours," Alice said.

"Just don't put them all on the bottom half of the tree like you did that one time." Jane laughed and leaned back against the couch.

"I was a kid! Those were the only branches I could reach!" Cynthia laughed. She opened the box and pulled out a chipped ceramic angel painted in garish shades of pink and purple. "I thought this was the most beautiful ornament in the world when I was little."

Louise remembered that. Cynthia had had a long phase where she only wanted things to be pink and purple, and seeing her hold the ornament now, she pictured her as a little girl with pigtails again. She had been such a sweet little girl.

"What's that one?" Alice asked as Cynthia lifted out the next ornament in the box.

"I got this when I was studying abroad in London in college." Cynthia held up a silver-colored cast of Big Ben.

Louise remembered that year. She had spent the whole semester worrying about Cynthia being an ocean away. Meanwhile, Cynthia was having the time of her life learning about Shakespeare and Jane Austen and exploring the English countryside on the weekends. She hadn't wanted to come home that Christmas, and when she did, she'd seemed to have grown older in those few short months.

The doorbell rang, and Alice got up to answer it. A moment later, Carlene Moss, who ran the *Acorn Nutshell,* came in with a gift wrapped in gold paper. She greeted each of them and put the gift with the pile under the living room tree. Several people had stopped by to drop off gifts for the shelter while Louise and Alice had been out, and there was now an impressive number.

"You've got quite a pile there," Jane said. "There are going to be some happy kids Christmas morning."

"As there should be," Alice said. "Those kids should have a happy Christmas, and being in a shelter doesn't change that."

"You might need to make more than one trip to Potterston tomorrow," Louise said to Alice. "I don't think this will all fit in your car."

"I'll make as many trips as it takes if it brightens Christmas for those kids," Alice said.

"It's really nice of you to organize this," Louise said.

Alice shrugged. "We have so much here. I wish I could do more than drive over a few presents. I wish there was a way we could make lasting change in the lives of those kids."

"Maybe we could," Jane said. "What if we put a tag on each of them that says something like 'Jesus is the gift that keeps on giving?'"

"Hmm." Louise liked the sentiment, but she wasn't sure about the wording. "It kind of makes it seem like He's a camera or something."

"Okay, that's probably not right," Jane said.

"'Jesus is the reason for the season,'" Alice suggested.

"How about nothing that you'd find on a bumper sticker?" Cynthia said, pulling a pink satin ballet slipper ornament out of the box.

"What if we just had the tags say something simple, like 'Merry Christmas from Your Friends at Grace Chapel Church'? Then they'd know the gifts are from a church," Alice said.

"I think that's a nice idea," Jane said. She tapped her chin with her finger. "I think I have something we can use to make tags. Hang on."

Jane returned a few minutes later with some plain white 3×5 cards, a few rubber stamps with Christmas designs, red and green stamp pads, and calligraphy pens.

"I was thinking I could cut these into the shape of a holly leaf," Jane said, holding up the index cards. "And then we could decorate them with the stamps and add the message."

"That's a lovely idea," Alice said. "If you could make the template for the leaf, we can use that to trace the designs onto the other cards."

"Sure thing."

Jane knelt down at the coffee table and sketched out the shape of a leaf and then cut it out. Louise put on a Bing Crosby album, and they all worked together in companionable silence. It felt nice to spend time working on a project like this with her family. Soon they had all the gifts tagged, and when Cynthia's ornaments were on the tree, Jane pulled the pot roast out of the oven and they all settled down at the dining table for dinner. Their guests were all out, so they didn't need to worry about keeping the noise down, and they laughed and joked and had a great time catching up with Cynthia. She told them a funny story about trying to retrieve a package that had been misdelivered to an apartment on the far side of town, and about the scheming and conniving that had happened during the white elephant gift exchange they'd done at her office Christmas party. Louise wished, once again, Eliot was here to see her. He would be so proud of how she'd turned out.

After dinner, Louise and Alice helped clean up the kitchen, and then Cynthia settled in at one end of the parlor couch with a book, Alice at the other, both tucked in under a wool blanket. Wendell hopped up in between them, while Jane sat in an overstuffed chair nearby, knitting what looked like a warm chunky scarf. A fire in the hearth cast the whole room in a warm glow. Louise decided to use the quiet hours before bed to run through the music for "I Heard the Bells on Christmas Day." She settled at the piano in the parlor and spread out the sheet music. She placed her hands on the keys and started the song, but her fingers stumbled on the second measure, and she reset her fingers and started again.

"That's a pretty song," Cynthia said, looking up from her book.

"It is, isn't it?" Louise turned around on the bench and looked at her daughter. "I recently learned it was originally a poem written by Henry Wadsworth Longfellow." Louise had done some research about Longfellow, and she'd learned that he was the author of "Paul Revere's Ride" and "The Song of Hiawatha," among other poems she recognized.

"Really?" Jane looked up from her knitting. "I didn't know that."

"It actually has quite an interesting history," Louise continued. "The poem was written in 1863, during the height of the Civil War, and in some ways it's about the tragedy of slavery and the grief of a nation that's divided."

"Wait. What?" Cynthia cocked her head. "I don't know the song all that well, but I assumed it was just about bells and peace on earth and all that jazz."

"Listen to the words," Louise said. She began to sing:

I heard the bells on Christmas Day
Their old, familiar carols play,
and wild and sweet
The words repeat
Of peace on earth, good-will to men!

And thought how, as the day had come,
The belfries of all Christendom
Had rolled along
The unbroken song
Of peace on earth, good-will to men!

"Okay, I got that," Cynthia said. "People don't use the word *Christendom* enough these days, but otherwise, yep, pretty standard."

"Just wait. The later verses are far less well-known. They're usually left out when the song is sung these days, because, well, you'll see." Louise sang the next three verses:

Till ringing, singing on its way,
The world revolved from night to day,
A voice, a chime,
A chant sublime
Of peace on earth, good-will to men!

Then from each black, accursed mouth
The cannon thundered in the South,
And with the sound
The carols drowned
Of peace on earth, good-will to men!

It was as if an earthquake rent
The hearth-stones of a continent,
And made forlorn
The households born
Of peace on earth, good-will to men!

"Whoa." Alice leaned back.

"I had no idea *that* was part of the Christmas song," Jane said, shaking her head.

"It's about how the sin of slavery made the wish for peace on earth and goodwill toward men hollow," Cynthia said, eyes wide. "I had no idea."

"And about the grief of a nation, torn apart," Jane added.

"Yes, it's about all that, and more," Louise said. "Now, just listen to the next verse. This is where it really hits home for me."

And in despair I bowed my head;
"There is no peace on earth," I said;
"For hate is strong,
And mocks the song
Of peace on earth, good-will to men!"

"It's such a depressing song," Jane said. "I never realized."

"Well, it was written soon after Longfellow's wife died in a tragic fire," Louise said.

"And, you know, during the Civil War, when it was legal to *own another human being*," Cynthia said. "So yeah, it's not really very uplifting, but I think there's good reason."

They were all quiet for a moment, thinking about the lyrics to the song.

"Pastor Thompson really wants to end the Christmas Eve service with this depressing song?" Alice tilted her head. "Why?"

"Just wait," Louise said. "It doesn't end on despair. It actually ends on a hopeful note. Listen."

Then pealed the bells more loud and deep:
"God is not dead, nor doth He sleep;
The Wrong shall fail,
The Right prevail,
With peace on earth, good-will to men."

"It's saying that even in the midst of all that's going wrong in the world, God is in control," Alice said.

"And good will triumph over evil in the end," Jane said. "I love that."

"And in Longfellow's time, it did," Cynthia said. "Slavery was abolished, and the nation joined together again."

"And God is still in control today too." Jane nodded.

"Yes," Louise said. "I think that's the message Pastor Thompson wants to send this year. I think that's why he chose to end the service with this. It's a reminder to not lose hope and that God is still in control, because of what Christmas means."

"That's lovely," Alice said quietly. "I had no idea that was what that song was about." She seemed to be mulling the words over in her head.

Louise turned back to the first page of her music and started playing the song again. This time she played it without stumbling as her fingers started to feel the right rhythm. Alice hummed along.

"That was beautiful."

Goodness. Those newlyweds had a habit of appearing in doorways when she didn't expect them. Lauren had spoken, but she was standing next to Jordan, who had his arm around her. They were both smiling.

"Thank you. It's a new one for me. I'm still working on it," Louise said.

"It reminds me of the songs I used to hear on the piano at church when I was a kid," Lauren said.

"Well, I'm going to be playing it on the organ at church tomorrow night," Louise said. "For the Christmas Eve service. You both should come. It's always a beautiful service."

"That sounds nice," Lauren said and looked over at Jordan, who nodded. "We're not especially religious, but it seems like a nice thing to do on Christmas Eve."

"We'll have to see what my mom and aunt have planned." Jordan shifted his weight from one foot to the other. "For now, let's head upstairs. I'm exhausted."

"Sitting around all day *is* exhausting." Lauren was teasing him, and Jordan didn't seem to mind, but Louise knew too much to not hear the edge in her voice.

After they had vanished up the stairs, Louise sat back on the piano bench. It wasn't her business. She didn't need to interfere. But…their marriage was so new. If they didn't address this now, it would only fester and get worse. Louise couldn't exactly go up there and act like a marriage counselor, but she could show them some extra kindness on this cold winter night.

"I'll be right back," she said, and pushed herself up from the piano bench. She went into the kitchen, poured milk into a pot, and set it on the stove. While that warmed, she set a few of Jane's freshly baked gingerbread cookies on a plate. When the milk was hot, Louise stirred in cocoa powder, sugar, and a hint of nutmeg, and then she poured the hot cocoa into mugs. She set it all on a tray and carried it upstairs and knocked gently on the door to the Sunrise Room.

"Oh wow. Are you for real?" Jordan blinked when he saw Louise standing there. "This is amazing. Lolo, look what Louise brought us."

Lauren came out of the bathroom, toothbrush in her hand, and laughed. "I guess I'll be brushing my teeth again."

"Thank you," Jordan said. Louise set the tray on the dresser and walked out, closing the door gently behind her. She went to the kitchen, rinsed out the pot, and then headed back to the parlor.

When she entered the parlor, Jane looked up from her knitting. "That was really nice."

"They're sweet kids."

"Mom. They're not kids," Cynthia said. "They're in their twenties."

"My point exactly. They're just babies."

Cynthia shook her head.

"You've taken a special liking to them," Alice observed.

Had she? Louise liked most of their guests and tried to get to know each of them to some degree. But she didn't always bring them tea or hot cocoa and cookies.

"I guess I have," Louise said. What was it about them that had elicited the mother hen response? "The first year of marriage is always challenging, and then with Jordan's parents splitting up... It's a hard way to start off a marriage."

And maybe, she thought, it also might have had something to do with the fact that she too had struggled with spending holidays away from her family early in her marriage. Jane hadn't seemed to have similar qualms—she'd moved to San Francisco and loved it there and hadn't always made it home for the holidays. For some Christmases, they'd gone to visit Justin's family, and sometimes they'd stayed at home in their apartment overlooking the San Francisco Bay. It had never seemed to bother Jane to be so far away.

Then again, Jane had always been more free-spirited and independent than Louise, who'd spent her first Christmas with Eliot's family missing her parents and sisters desperately. Even though Eliot's parents were lovely people who tried to make her feel welcome, everything had felt wrong. They'd gone to a church that wasn't Grace Chapel, and they'd sung different songs, and his mom had made meat loaf instead of ham. Eliot's mother had given her a plain set of hand towels, and when she unwrapped them, she had to force herself to show gratitude. She was thankful—they would be very useful. It was just that compared to the thoughtful, personal gifts she was used to unwrapping from her father and sisters, it had seemed kind of sad. Louise had spent the whole holiday longing for home.

Had Eliot felt the same way when he'd come to visit her family here in Acorn Hill? She'd never really thought about it, if she was honest, but she felt sure he must have. Once Cynthia came along, they'd made the decision to stay in their own home in Philadelphia for Christmas and start new traditions for their own family, and she hadn't had to really think about it. It would've been tricky, no matter how they'd handled it.

Well, maybe she had taken a liking to Lauren and Jordan. She empathized with them and wanted them to have a nice Christmas. There was nothing wrong with that.

Louise sat back down at the piano and played the piece through several more times until she felt confident she could play it well tomorrow night.

When she looked up, Alice was gathering her things, and Cynthia was yawning. Louise suddenly realized how tired she was too. When she was concentrating on music, she often didn't notice things like hunger or exhaustion.

"I think it's time to turn in," she said, and Cynthia nodded. Alice was already heading for the door.

"I just need to finish this row," Jane said, holding up the scarf she was working on. "And then I'll head up too."

Louise closed the cover on the piano keys and nudged the fireplace doors closed, but she left the Christmas tree lights on. Jane would turn them off when she left. Then she steered toward the kitchen.

"Buttermilk?" Cynthia said with a laugh.

"Just a small glass." Louise didn't understand why everyone thought her love of buttermilk was so funny. It was delicious, and it was good for her. It wouldn't hurt them to drink some too, but she knew she was alone in this.

"I'll see you in the morning," Cynthia said and followed Alice up the stairs.

Louise flipped on the kitchen light and moved toward the fridge. She poured herself a glass—all right, maybe it wasn't as small as she'd intended—and was turning to put the buttermilk back in the fridge when someone walked into the kitchen behind her.

"Oh." Louise had expected one of her sisters but was pleased to see that it was Lauren, carrying the tray of empty mugs and the plate.

"I wanted to bring this down," Lauren explained. "Hot cocoa can be a bear to scrub off the next day."

"Thank you." Louise took the tray and set it on the counter. "That was really thoughtful."

"It was so nice of you to bring it up." Lauren turned to go but then paused. "And thank you for playing those Christmas carols today. I really enjoyed hearing them. They remind me of the church I went to growing up. I was in the Christmas pageant every year, and hearing those songs again brings back so many memories."

Louise didn't want to pry, but she sensed Lauren wanted to talk about it, so she asked, "Will your family be at the Christmas Eve service at your home church tomorrow night?"

Lauren nodded. "Of course. My mom always makes lasagna and meatballs, and there's cannoli for dessert. It's a late dinner, and it's always a long lazy meal because we go to the midnight mass, so there's always time to kill. And then we go off to the mass, and it's the same priest who was there when I was a kid. He's ancient now, but he's a great guy. When we were kids we always thought the service was so long and boring, but now I think it's really beautiful."

"I love the idea of a midnight mass, but I would struggle to stay up late."

"There's an earlier one for people who don't want to stay up, but we've always gone to the late one. There's something really beautiful about celebrating the birth of Jesus in the middle of the night, when He might really have been born."

Louise smiled. "It sounds special."

Lauren nodded. "Then we all go home and get to bed, because my younger siblings still get up at the crack of dawn for presents in the morning."

Louise laughed. "I remember those days. We had to make a rule that Cynthia wasn't allowed out of bed before seven, otherwise she'd have gotten us up in the middle of the night."

"My parents wouldn't let anyone touch the gifts until we'd all had breakfast, which made me crazy when I was a kid, but I appreciate it now," Lauren said. "And we had to take turns, opening gifts one at a time, and I have a big family, so it took *forever*. I hated that when I was a kid. But now I get it. It's nice to have everyone appreciate each gift."

"It sounds lovely."

Lauren didn't say anything. She seemed to be lost in her memories.

"I know it will be different this year," Louise said. "Does Jordan's family have any traditions like that?"

"They used to go visit his dad's extended family on Christmas Eve." She sighed. "Obviously, they aren't doing that now. Everything is so different this year. They all seem kind of lost and not really sure what to do. I almost wish…"

She let her voice trail off. Louise waited, but when she didn't go on, Louise suggested gently, "Is it that you wish you were with your family?"

Lauren nodded. "It's horrible, I know."

"It's natural," Louise said. "And it's not midnight mass, but you really would be welcome at the service tomorrow night. It starts at seven."

"I'd love to come," Lauren said. But something in her voice made Louise understand there was something she wasn't saying.

"But?" She'd sensed Jordan's hesitation when she brought it up earlier.

"I asked Jordan about it after you mentioned it earlier," Lauren said. "And he isn't sure he wants to go. He's not much into church, and so I haven't really been either. He's—

well, he's spiritual, but he's pretty skeptical about organized religion. But I don't know. I think there's something special about gathering together with people who believe the same thing."

"I do too," Louise said. "Maybe he would make an exception for Christmas Eve?"

"Does Viola usually come?" Lauren asked. "That might make it easier."

Louise laughed. "No, I'm afraid Viola rarely comes to church. She's firmly in the 'spiritual but not religious' category as well." Viola actually had many things to say about religion, none of them good, and she and Louise had shared many frank discussions about their differing opinions.

Lauren shrugged. "That might make it harder, then."

"We would love to have you if you decide to come."

"I'll ask Jordan again." She sounded dubious. "I would like to go. It's hard for me to imagine Christmas Eve without church. But we'll see. It'll probably depend on what his mom wants to do."

"That's fair." Louise put the mugs and the plate into the dishwasher and rinsed off the tray. "Well, you're all invited, and we would love to see you there."

"Who's coming where?"

They both turned as Jane walked into the kitchen.

"I was encouraging Lauren and Jordan to come to church tomorrow night," Louise said.

"Oh yes. You should definitely come. It's a lovely service," Jane said.

"I don't know what Jordan and his mom will want to do. I was telling Louise that their family's Christmas Eve traditions all involved his dad, so they're kind of at a loss."

"Ah." Jane nodded. "I get that. The Christmas after my husband and I separated, I was a total mess and had no idea how to celebrate."

"You're separated?" Lauren cocked her head.

"Divorced, unfortunately." Jane sighed. "It was quite a while ago, and things are better now. I get to live here with my sisters and run this inn, and I'm very happy with how things have turned out. But it took a while. That first year—" She shook her head. "It was tough."

"I can imagine."

"Justin and I both worked in restaurants, so we didn't have a lot of time off over the holidays, but we always slept in late Christmas morning and then made a big gourmet breakfast and ate together. We wouldn't get around to opening the gifts until the afternoon, and then we'd go for a walk down by the Bay."

Louise looked at Jane. She hadn't known that. She hadn't known any of that.

"It took a while for me to stop expecting to smell that briny sea air on Christmas," Jane said, shaking her head. "In some ways, holidays were the hardest part of the divorce. I couldn't stop remembering what it had been like before. And suddenly, all the things I'd thought would be the same for the rest of my life... They just weren't."

"I get the sense that's kind of what Jordan's mom is feeling," Lauren said.

"I'm sure that's part of it," Jane said. "It sounds like she might be feeling lost and not really sure what to do. That's where I was the first year."

"So how did you move past that?" Lauren asked.

"I don't know that you ever really move past it," Jane said. "But I moved back here. I moved home and started a new life with my sisters. And we made new memories and new traditions."

Lauren nodded. "I think that's what we were hoping for coming to Acorn Hill this year. But so far, my mother-in-law has spent most of her time just watching HGTV."

"Maybe you need to be intentional about it," Louise said. "For her, but also for you and Jordan. You won't always be with your family at the holidays. And you won't always be with his, I'm sure. So what about the two of you? Are there traditions that you two, as a couple, want to start? Are there ways you can bring his mom into those ideas?" Louise shrugged. "Maybe that's a place to start, anyway."

"That's an interesting idea," Lauren said. "I like the idea of starting traditions for our own little family."

"Talk to Jordan about it." Louise closed the dishwasher and started it. A low hum filled the kitchen.

Lauren hesitated, and then she nodded. "I will."

Chapter Four

auren and Jordan ate breakfast early and were gone when Louise came downstairs on the morning of Christmas Eve. The sky was heavy and gray, with a chance of snow in the forecast, but for now the clouds simply hung low and thick.

Louise wore her favorite cherry-red sweater and black slacks, and she chatted with the Waltons and the Wallaces over eggs and French toast. When the two couples left to go to an Amish Christmas market in nearby Lancaster County, Jane went upstairs to dust and wipe down the guest rooms and refresh the linens, and Louise helped Alice load the gifts for the shelter into her car.

"You won't be able to see out the back window," Louise said, gesturing at the stack of presents they'd carefully fit like Tetris pieces on the back seat. The trunk was so full they'd barely been able to get it to close.

"I can catch a few glimpses," Alice said from the front seat.

"Are you sure you wouldn't rather take my car?" Louise's car was bigger, with more leg room and trunk space.

"I'd rather drive my own," Alice said. "But thank you."

"Would you like me to take them for you?"

"Louise." Alice smiled. "I'll be fine."

"All right." Louise watched Alice back up and turn her car around. She did seem to be able to see somehow, so Louise tried not to worry. After Alice pulled out of the driveway and turned on to the street, Louise went back inside the house and found Cynthia drinking a cup of coffee.

"Good morning," she said, noting that Cynthia looked better rested than she had since she'd arrived. "Did you sleep well?"

"Like a rock."

"I'm so glad." Louise looked around. Jane had put away the French toast, but there was oatmeal and cereal and plenty of eggs. "What would you like for breakfast?"

"Oh, I don't need breakfast."

"What are you talking about? Of course you do."

"I'll just grab a banana or something. There's no time for a full breakfast anyway. We need to get going."

"Going where?"

"Christmas shopping." Cynthia drained the last of her coffee and set the mug down on the counter. "I haven't bought a thing."

Louise stared at her. "Nothing?"

"Not one thing. I've been so busy with work, I haven't had a chance. Will you come with me?"

Louise laughed. Cynthia took after her in so many ways, but there was no doubt she was her father's daughter. Eliot had always left his shopping to the last minute too. She'd received more than one sweater from her favorite boutique in Philadelphia over the years because he had waited until the last minute and hadn't known what else to get. It hadn't mattered. She'd loved them just the same.

"Do you want to go to Potterston?" The mall would be a nightmare today. Avoiding that parking lot on Christmas Eve was reason enough to getting her shopping done early.

Cynthia gave her a guilty smile.

"All right." Louise sighed. "Let me get my purse."

"Thanks, Mom."

"You're lucky you're my favorite child."

Cynthia loaded the mug into the dishwasher. "I'm going to brush my teeth. I'll be back down in a minute."

The roads to Potterston were busy, and they had to circle the mall twice before they found parking, but once inside, Cynthia did her shopping quickly. Louise helped her pick out a flowy blouse for Jane and new slippers for Alice, as well as a neat patent leather purse for Aunt Ethel. As they walked back to the mall entrance, Louise noticed that the line to see Santa Claus stretched out of Santa's Village and halfway to the department store. The tinny mall music and the crowds were enough to make her long for the peace and quiet of Acorn Hill. They climbed back into the car gratefully and drove back. Louise felt the tension leave her body as they got farther from the crowded city and back into the charming small streets of town. Cynthia said she wanted to make one more stop before they headed back to the inn, but wouldn't tell Louise where she wanted to go.

"So what am I supposed to do? Just hang out in the car?" Louise asked as she parked in a spot along Acorn Avenue.

"Of course not. Just don't go into the shop I'm going to."

"Which shop is that?"

"I can't tell you that. That would give away what I'm getting you."

Louise shook her head. "So how do I know where I'm allowed to go?"

Cynthia looked around, scanning the shops along the block. "Why don't you go into the bookstore? That's safe."

"So you're not getting me a book?" Louise arched her eyebrow.

"Mom. I work in publishing. I don't have to buy books. I just ask my friends for whatever books my company doesn't publish."

"Well." Louise sniffed. "I would think you'd want to support local bookstores."

"I do. Just, you know, not today."

"I just went there yesterday." As soon as the words left her mouth, Louise wanted to pull them back. What if Cynthia asked why she had been to Nine Lives the day before? Luckily, Cynthia didn't seem to notice.

"You love bookstores. And Viola is your dear friend. Go visit her." She shooed Louise off. "Now scoot."

Louise climbed out of the car and walked toward the bookstore, trying to figure out when she'd started to allow herself to be ordered around by her daughter.

The bell over the bookstore door dinged, and Louise let the door fall closed behind her. The store was even more crowded today than it had been yesterday. Several people were browsing the aisles. Rose Bellwood was looking through a table of stocking stuffers, and Rhea Eagan, who taught at the elementary school with Vera Humbert, was flipping through a lush full-color cookbook.

"Back again. You just can't stay away."

Louise turned and smiled at Viola, who was wearing a red-and-green checked scarf.

"Cynthia wanted a few minutes to shop in peace, so here I am."

"There's no better place to kill time than in a bookstore," Viola said. "And who knows, you may accidentally find something to improve your mind."

Louise laughed at Viola's dry humor.

"It's packed in here today," Louise said.

"It usually is on the day before Christmas." Viola shrugged. "My seasonal help is still sick. Luckily, I have some new helpers today."

She gestured toward the back of the store, and Louise did a double take when she saw Lauren kneeling down on the floor of the children's section showing a woman about Louise's age a collection of colorful picture books.

"Lauren is here?"

"Jordan too." Viola smiled. She pointed toward the history section, where he was unloading and shelving a pile of thick books. "They showed up at the house first thing this morning and said they wanted to help out. Maybe they were just bored. I don't know. I didn't ask too many questions, honestly. I knew I'd need the help today, so I said, sure, come on over."

Louise watched as Lauren talked with the woman about the different picture books. Louise couldn't hear what they were saying, but it looked like Lauren was talking about something she truly loved.

Louise felt a wave of longing rush through her. Would she ever have grandchildren to select picture books for? Cynthia was bright and beautiful and successful, and she would make such a caring, wonderful mom. But she wasn't dating anyone that Louise knew about, and though she'd had a few boyfriends over the years, none had been serious enough that she had considered introducing them to her mother. Louise couldn't understand what was wrong with young men these days. Why weren't they falling over themselves to ask Cynthia out?

Louise reminded herself that Cynthia was only thirty-four and there was still plenty of time. In any case, God knew who the right man for Cynthia was, and He would bring them together at the right time. Louise just hoped it would happen while she was young enough to crouch down on the floor of the bookstore and flip through picture books.

Finally, the woman selected a book. Lauren put the other books back onto the shelf, and then she helped the woman up. Louise could see from here that she had chosen *Knuffle Bunny: A Cautionary Tale*. Such a great book.

"I see you put them straight to work."

"I'm not dumb."

"No, you're not. No one has ever accused you of that." Louise laughed. "They seem to be doing just fine."

"They're loving it." Viola smiled. "And I have to admit, I don't mind the company."

That might be as close to acknowledging she liked some-one as Viola got. "How is it going with your sister? Is she doing all right?"

Viola sighed. "Honestly? I don't know. She came here for a change of scenery and a chance to do something different for Christmas. To make new memories, ones that don't involve that lying, cheating scumbag of a husband."

"Tell me how you really feel."

"Sorry. But he really did treat her terribly. After twenty-five years of marriage, after she gave up her career to stay home and raise the kids and followed him around the country so his career could advance, he up and leaves her for a girl not much older than his son?" Viola shook her head. "It's hard not to get the tiniest bit bitter."

"I can understand why," Louise said. She knew marriages were often more complicated than they looked from the outside, but it did sound like Irene had been treated badly. "But it sounds like the visit is not going quite as well as you'd hoped?"

"She just doesn't seem to want to do anything but sit inside and watch television. I know it doesn't help that I have to be here during the day. I'd love to be able to close the store and stay with her, maybe take her out and see some sights, but this is the busiest time of year in the bookstore. The week before Christmas is when I make a good chunk of the money that will carry me through until tourist season begins in the spring."

"Of course. I understand that." Things at the inn quieted down after Christmas too, and they had only a few dozen visitors planned for most of January and February. They wouldn't be fully booked again until May, when the tourists started coming back to Acorn Hill more regularly. "But surely there are things she and the kids could do to get her out of the house? We have some guests who went to Lancaster to visit a Christmas market," Louise suggested.

Viola shrugged. "They tried. I have to give it to Lauren and Jordan, they really have done their best to get Irene out of the house and to take her to see things. But so far she's refused. She just wants to stay in. And what can you do? She's a grown woman. You can't exactly force her to go out and do things."

"No, I suppose you can't." It sounded like she was battling depression. Certainly, she had reason. And Louise knew that grief could never be rushed. Irene would have to walk through it at her own pace, in her own way. Louise had gone through a similar time after Eliot's death, where she hadn't wanted to leave the house or sometimes even get out of bed. Visits from Cynthia had been a comfort, but even her presence couldn't lift Louise out of her mourning. "I'll be praying for her."

"Thank you," Viola said. "Lauren is trying to convince her to go to the church service at Grace Chapel tonight."

"She should come. You should too."

Viola's response was a snort.

"I hope to see you all there," Louise said. Viola nodded and then excused herself to head to the counter and ring up the purchase of *Knuffle Bunny*.

Louise looked around the shop. There was no sign of Cynthia yet, so she wandered over to the display of stocking stuffers and started to browse. There were beautifully decorated bookmarks and hand-tooled leather journals and pocket calendars and foldable reading lights. Louise picked up a journal bound in smooth brown leather and opened its thick, creamy pages. Jane would love this, she thought. But she already had a gift for Jane, so she set it down. She then picked up a turquoise planner etched with the words FOR I KNOW THE PLANS I HAVE FOR YOU. That was from Jeremiah 29, Louise knew. It was a lovely verse and a beautiful planner, with thick, smooth pages and wide spaces to write. Louise hadn't bought a planner for the next year yet, actually. She knew Cynthia thought she was a dinosaur for continuing to use a paper calendar when everything was online these days, but there was something so satisfying about recording one's plans in ink, on actual paper. Louise flipped through the pages and then closed the book softly. It would be her Christmas present to herself, she decided. She started to carry it to the counter.

"Louise! Hi!"

Louise turned and saw Lauren making her way around the display tables toward her.

"Hello there." Louise smiled. "I see you got yourself a job."

"It's not the first time I've worked retail." Lauren smiled back. "Yesterday at dinner, Viola was talking about how busy the shop had been and how it was sure to be even busier today, so I asked Jordan what he thought about volunteering to help out."

"Viola seems quite pleased to have you."

"We're having fun. And guess what? You and Jane are the reason we're doing this."

"We are?"

"Yep. Last night after we talked in the kitchen, I went up and told Jordan I wanted to start some of our own traditions, just our family. Him and me. Not my parents and brothers and sisters, and not his family either. Some traditions for our new little family. He loved the idea, so we talked about the kinds of traditions that are important to us. One of the things we came up with was that we want to do something to help people in need as part of our holiday traditions. In the future, we want to try to help out at a soup kitchen or organize a toy drive like Alice did or something of that sort. But at the last minute, we weren't sure how to do that, and, well, we realized that Viola needed help."

"She certainly does." Louise chuckled. "Viola thought you were just bored."

Lauren laughed. "Okay, there may be a bit of that too, if we're being totally honest. But mostly it's an attempt at our first annual tradition of helping someone who needs it during the holidays."

"Well I think that's wonderful. And I know Viola appreciates it."

A beep sounded from Lauren's pocket, and she pulled out her phone. She smiled when she looked at the screen. "Aw. My sister just sent me a picture of the Christmas tree, all decorated." She held up the phone so Louise could see.

"That's lovely," Louise said. It looked pretty much like most family Christmas trees, but it was special to this family, and that made it beautiful.

"They've been sending me updates all day. Look. Here's my niece, Sadie. Isn't she adorable?" She held up the phone to show a photo of a toddler in a beautiful green-and-red plaid dress.

"She's precious." She really was a very cute baby, Louise had to admit, with big brown eyes and strawberry-blond hair and a little dimple in her right cheek. Louise hesitated. "But getting all these photos… Does it make it harder to not be there?"

"Not really." Lauren slipped the phone back in her pocket. "Yesterday when we were just sitting around the house, yeah, it definitely did. But since we decided to get out and do something today, it's not so bad. It's kind of nice to see what's going on, you know? And it's nice to know they're thinking of me."

"I'm so glad." Louise held out the planner. "Is there any chance you can ring this up for me?"

"I'm afraid I don't know how to use the register, so I'll have to let Viola take care of that. But if you need any recommendations for great Victorian literature, let me know. I was an English major and am itching to use my degree."

"I'll be sure to let you know." Louise laughed and made her way to the register, where Viola rang her purchase up.

"Leave it to you to pick out the only book in the shop that doesn't have words in it," Viola said with a wry smile.

Louise tucked her purchase into her purse just as the door opened and Cynthia stepped inside. She didn't seem to be carrying anything. If she'd bought anything, it was either small enough to fit in her jacket pocket or else she'd dropped it off at the car.

"Ooh. Did you buy anything fun?" she asked, letting the door close behind her.

"I did. I got a Christmas present for myself."

Cynthia tilted her head and narrowed her eyes. "Okay…" Then she turned to Viola. "Did you explain to her that that is not how this holiday works?"

"Don't look at me. I just work here." Viola held up her hands in self-defense.

"Well, I guess I'm glad you found a way to keep yourself occupied. Even if it means buying Christmas presents for yourself."

Louise and Cynthia went toward the door, and they waved goodbye to Lauren and Jordan and Viola before they stepped out into the cold winter air.

By this time, Louise's stomach was rumbling, and she realized that Cynthia, who'd had nothing but a banana, must be starving. They had sandwich fixings at home, but Jane would be in the kitchen, getting started on the ham for their supper tonight.

"How about a stop at the Coffee Shop before we head home?" Louise suggested. Cynthia agreed that sounded great, and soon they were tucked into a booth, chatting with Hope Collins, who waitressed at the homespun diner.

"Whew. It's been crazy today," Hope said, setting two glasses of icy water down on the laminate table. Her hair, which was naturally dark but today was dyed a bold shade of red, was pulled up into a bun on top of her head. "How are you doing today? It's great to see you, Cynthia. How long are you in town?"

"Just a few days," Cynthia said.

"She works too hard," Louise explained.

"Well, we're glad to have you here for a few days if that's all we can get. Have you all had a chance to check out the menu today?"

June Carter changed the menu daily, and she always posted the day's offerings on the windows at the front.

"We sure did." Louise ordered the turkey and cheese, while Cynthia opted for the vegetable soup and a Cobb salad. They talked about Cynthia's work for a while and some of Louise's piano students, and then they fell silent for a moment. Louise wasn't sure if it was because of the conversations she'd recently been having with Lauren, or if it was the sentimental time of year in general, but Louise couldn't help thinking about Christmases when Cynthia was little.

She remembered the way Cynthia's face would light up when she saw the presents under the tree on Christmas morning, or her excitement as she added a number to the Advent calendar each day, counting down the days until Christmas. She remembered how Cynthia would snuggle into Eliot's arms as he read the story of Jesus's birth to her from their illustrated children's Bible, and how little Cynthia was full of questions about the story. How could the wise men follow a star that far? Why did Herod want to kill the baby Jesus? What's frankincense? Why didn't they bring Jesus something better, like a bike or a pony? She would sometimes fall asleep listening to the story, wrapped safely in her father's arms. Louise would sit quietly nearby, sure she would never get tired of the sight.

"What are you thinking about?" Cynthia asked.

Louise wasn't sure how to explain all of the emotions that were rushing through her. "I was just thinking of how much fun Christmas was when you were little," she said. "And how I miss your father."

"I miss him too." Cynthia took Louise's hand and held it as tears welled up.

"He would be so proud of you."

Neither of them said anything for a moment, and Louise jolted with surprise when Hope came back and set plates down in front of them.

"Sorry about that. Didn't mean to scare you. Here you go," Hope said, pushing Louise's sandwich toward her. The bread, baked fresh at the Good Apple, was thick and hearty, and the turkey and cheese looked delicious. She set the soup and salad near Cynthia, and then with a cheerful wave, she said, "You two have a Merry Christmas."

The food was wonderful, as always, and as they drove back to the inn, Louise was full and happy. She smiled as she saw the house, decked out in wreathes and lights. It looked like an oasis on this gloomy day. The skies still threatened snow, although nothing but a few flakes had fallen yet. When they stepped inside, the house smelled like cinnamon and baking apples and the ham Jane was baking for dinner.

"It smells amazing in here," Cynthia said, clutching her shopping bags. "When do we eat dinner?"

"We just ate lunch!" Louise laughed.

"I can't help it. Aunt Jane's cooking is too tempting."

"We'll eat at five," Louise said. "So that there's time to have a nice meal before the service tonight."

Cynthia vanished upstairs to wrap the presents she'd bought, and after Louise took her new planner to her room, she went over to the church to practice the pieces for tonight's service on the old pipe organ. It was similar to the piano but different enough that she wanted to practice on the actual instrument.

Louise entered the quiet sanctuary and walked down the center aisle. The sky was dark, but she could still see the stained glass windows with the sanctuary lights. She looked at the window that showed Christ holding a lamb and the one that showed the Ascension, but she focused her gaze on the window that showed the baby Jesus in a manger. Sometimes it was hard to believe that God really came to earth as a baby. It didn't make sense. He could have come in any form. Why would he show up as a helpless baby? But that was what made it so special, she knew.

Louise reversed her direction, went to the back of the church, and sat down at the familiar organ. She ran her fingers along the keys. The church community had gathered together to raise the money to repair the old organ and its pipes a few years ago, and the instrument played better than ever. She pressed down on the keys, and the notes sounded out over the quiet pews. Louise loved it when this space was filled with people worshipping God together, but she especially loved it when it was quiet like this and it was just her and God and the music. It was holy in a way she couldn't put into words.

Louise ran through the pieces until she felt comfortable, and when she returned, Alice was back from the shelter and was resting in her room, and Jane told her that the Waltons and Wallaces were back from the Amish market. She also said that Lauren was upstairs but Jordan was still out. Louise raised her eyebrows, but Jane said she didn't know what the story was. Louise tried not to worry. It didn't mean that there was a problem, she reminded herself. Newlyweds didn't have to spend every moment together. But something about it still concerned her.

Louise went into the kitchen to feed Wendell and to snag a taste of the ham that was resting on the stove. Jane shooed her out just as Jordan came back into the inn. He had black plastic bags in each hand. He smiled and said hello, and Louise stepped aside to let him go upstairs. A few minutes later, both he and Lauren came back downstairs, and Lauren had a big smile on her face.

"Guess what?" Lauren poked her head into the parlor, where Louise had settled onto the settee.

"What?"

"Jordan went out and got Christmas decorations!" Lauren's eyes were shining. "He saw how upset I was that there were no decorations at his Aunt Viola's house, so he went to Potterston and bought lights and wreaths and ornaments, and we're going to go over and make Viola's house look cheerful and festive."

"That's wonderful." Louise was so pleased to hear it. It would be good for all of them, and it was especially touching that Jordan had noticed Lauren's sadness and had done something about it. Louise had never doubted that Jordan loved his wife, but it was touching to see how he cared for her. "I'm so glad."

"Yeah. It won't be the same as the decorations at my family's place, but at least it will make the house feel a bit more cheerful."

"Have fun."

The two hurried out of the house, and before long, Jane was calling her sisters and Cynthia to the dining room. Aunt Ethel was already in the dining room, waiting for them to arrive.

Louise had heard Jane's plan to go with a neutral palate for the tablescape this year, and she had worried that it would look awfully plain without the cheery red napkins and special Christmas china Louise had bought years ago. Louise had seen the new table linens Jane had made from lace and off-white linen she found at Sylvia's Buttons, and she had also seen the pinecones and juniper branches Jane had gathered for the table. She'd even seen the white candles that had been warming up the entryway and washroom for the last several weeks. But she hadn't imagined how they would all come together to make the table look simple and clean and naturally beautiful.

"It's stunning," Alice said. She seemed to be as surprised as Louise was by the sight.

"Thank you." Jane was beaming as she set the platter of carved ham down on the tablecloth. "Please, sit."

They all sat down around the table and, after saying grace, started passing dishes of baked sweet potatoes and rolls and creamed spinach.

"Jane. It's only Christmas Eve. You can't possibly be planning to do this all over again tomorrow?" Alice asked, as she scooped spinach onto her plate.

"Of course not." Jane shook her head. "Tomorrow we're having turkey and mashed potatoes, and I'll do crescents instead of rolls, and we'll have braised kale instead of spinach."

"You're too much." Alice gave her an indulgent smile.

"I enjoy it." Jane shrugged. "I truly enjoy cooking. Just let me spoil the people I love."

"I am happy to oblige," Alice said.

"This looks amazing," Louise said, seeing how beautifully the colors on her plate played off one another. Jane had just used their plain white everyday dishes, but she had set a silver charger underneath each plate, and along with Mother's good silver, which had been polished to a high sheen, the result was stunning.

"And it tastes pretty good too." Aunt Ethel had just swallowed a bite and was moving in for another one. The sisters all laughed.

"So how was your trip to the shelter?" Cynthia asked Alice.

"It was really special," Alice said. "I got to meet the kids who live there, and it was nice to be able to put faces to the names. I knew I was shopping for a seven-year-old boy, but today I got to meet Marcus, and it made me even more excited to think about him opening that basketball tomorrow morning."

"I bet they were excited to see all those presents," Jane said.

"Oh yes," Alice said, nodding. "After the shelter director helped me carry them in and put them under the tree, the kids all crowded around looking for their packages. There was a good deal of shaking of presents going on before the director shooed them out and told them they had to wait until the morning to see what was inside."

"I hope they'll be pleased," Louise said.

"I think they will be," Alice said.

"Imagining it kind of reminds me of a picture book my company published this year," Cynthia said. "It was about a family that saved up all year to afford gifts they gave away to total strangers."

"That sounds lovely," Louise said. Cynthia explained that it was based on a true story and that they had hired an award-winning illustrator to bring the story to life. The conversation drifted, and Aunt Ethel told them about a trip her good friend Florence was planning to take to visit her grandchildren after the holidays. Jane talked about a series of handmade greeting cards she was hoping to create in the New Year. The candlelight cast a soft, warm glow over the room, and as Louise looked around the table, she realized just how lucky she was that she got to spend this evening—this life, really—with these wonderful people.

But soon it was nearly time to go over to the church, and as much as Louise hated to leave this table, she knew she needed to help clean up and get ready. They all carried plates and empty serving dishes to the kitchen and loaded them into the dishwasher, and then Louise headed upstairs while Aunt Ethel called her goodbyes. She would head back to the carriage house to change, and they would see her at the church.

Louise changed into the cranberry-colored dress and black pumps she had picked out, and after running a brush through her hair, she headed back down the stairs to gather her sheet music.

She heard voices in the Waltons' and Wallaces' rooms and knew that Lauren and Jordan were in their room. Each of the guests had been invited to the service tonight, and Louise hoped they would all come.

Louise and her sisters and Cynthia all bundled up in coats and hats and scarves and walked out into the winter air to troop across the yard to Grace Chapel. The light pouring through the stained glass windows of the white clapboard building was bright against the dark night. They made their way carefully up the steps and inside the old church, and Louise felt her shoulders relax. The smell of the old building, a mixture of wax and wood and must, was one from her childhood, and walking in the doors made it feel like she had come home.

How many Sundays had she walked in that door to find Father at the pulpit, praying over the church and the congregation before a church service? Mother had usually been scurrying around downstairs, chatting with some of the ladies as they set out food or prepared to teach Sunday school or worked on some other task that few would ever notice they'd done. She and her sisters had sat wedged into that first pew every Sunday she could remember until she'd gone off to college.

Pastor Kenneth Thompson greeted the sisters as they walked into the church, and he asked Cynthia about her life in Boston. He wasn't Father, but he was a good pastor and a good man, and Louise knew they were blessed to have him. They walked into the sanctuary, their footsteps silenced by the thick red runner that went up the aisle. The creamy white walls were hung with simple evergreen wreaths, and the upright piano at the front of the church was hung with evergreen boughs. But Louise didn't head to the piano. While Jane and Alice and Cynthia went to find seats, she carried her music to the pipe organ at the back of the church and sat down on the bench.

She arranged her music on the stand and ran through it briefly in her mind, and then, before she knew it, it was time to begin the prelude. She'd picked Bach's Aria from the Goldberg variations to start the service, and she loved how it sounded as the notes rose out of the old pipes and echoed through the church.

After the last notes of the prelude, Pastor Thompson walked onto the stage. As Louise looked across the church, she saw many familiar faces. There was June Carter and Clara Horn, and Polly Humbert and her husband, Alex, sitting between her parents, and Nia Komonos. And there was…Viola Reed?

Louise had to do a double take to make sure she was seeing things correctly, but yes, there she was, with a gauzy silver scarf wrapped around her neck.

It was a Christmas miracle.

Next to Viola was a woman who had to be her sister, seated next to Lauren and Jordan. They had come after all. She loved to see that so many members of their beloved community were here to celebrate the birth of their Savior.

She played the organ as the congregation sang "Hark! The Herald Angels Sing" and then donned her choir robe and joined the choir on stage for their rendition of "O Holy Night." Then she returned to the organ.

Lloyd Tynan rose and walked to the stage, wearing a suit and bowtie, and rested his Bible on the pulpit. He opened it, his face serious, and then he adjusted his glasses and looked down to read from the book of Luke. "In those days Caesar Augustus issued a decree that a census should be taken of the entire Roman world. (This was the first census that took place while Quirinius was governor of Syria.) And everyone went to their own town to register," he began, his voice rich and deep. "So Joseph also went up from the town of Nazareth in Galilee to Judea, to Bethlehem the town of David, because he belonged to the house and line of David. He went there to register with Mary, who was pledged to be married to him and was expecting a child. While they were there, the time came for the baby to be born, and she gave birth to her first-born, a son. She wrapped him in cloths and placed him in a manger, because there was no guest room available for them."

Louise noticed that Aunt Ethel sat up a little straighter as he read, and she kept glancing around.

After the mayor had finished the passage and returned to his seat, Pastor Thompson preached about the miracle of Christ's birth, and then it was time for "Silent Night." Louise couldn't help but notice several people whispering, presumably about the lack of candles, but it sounded nice nonetheless.

After Pastor Thompson said a few more words, Louise played the first notes of "I Heard the Bells on Christmas Day," and everyone in the congregation rose to their feet.

I heard the bells on Christmas Day
Their old, familiar carols play,
and wild and sweet
The words repeat
Of peace on earth, good-will to men!

The voices of her friends and neighbors joined together in beautiful harmony, and Louise blinked back the tears that stung her eyes.

She'd probably heard the lyrics dozens of times in her life, but now that she knew the story of the song and why it was written, she saw the words in a new light. The original poem had been written in grief and centered on the pain of a nation divided against itself.

> *It was as if an earthquake rent*
> *The hearth-stones of a continent,*
> *And made forlorn*
> *The households born*
> *Of peace on earth, good-will to men!*

As she played, she couldn't help but think about Jordan and Lauren and Irene. A family had been torn apart this year, divided by strife and difficulty and broken promises.

> *And in despair I bowed my head;*
> *"There is no peace on earth," I said;*
> *"For hate is strong,*
> *And mocks the song*
> *Of peace on earth, good-will to men!"*

But even as Louise heard the words, she knew that though they were true, they were not the end. There was more to this story. Irene and Jordan and Lauren might be in grief today, but a family torn apart—tragic as it was—was not how this all ended.

Because even in the midst of that grief, a new family had been born. Even knowing that his parents' marriage had been broken beyond repair, Jordan had been brave enough to pledge his life to another. Lauren had promised to spend her life with him, no matter what. Knowing the challenge ahead of them, they had still promised to love and be faithful to one another, just as Christ loved and was faithful to His people. Their story did not end with despair but with hope in the midst of despair.

> *Then pealed the bells more loud and deep:*
> *"God is not dead, nor doth He sleep;*
> *The Wrong shall fail,*
> *The Right prevail,*
> *With peace on earth, good-will to men."*

Louise felt a sense of expectation well up within her. God would bring peace on earth, even when it seemed impossible. He would bring unity to the divided, and His truth would prevail. That was the message of Christmas—that the little baby born in that manger would bring peace and redemption to the people separated from God.

As the last notes of the tune faded from the pipes, she felt the truth of those words as never before. For a moment, no one moved, and no one said anything. They all seemed to be absorbing the peace that had settled over the sanctuary.

Then, solemnly, Pastor Thompson ended the service by thanking them all for coming and wishing them a wonderful Christmas, and slowly the congregation started to make their way to the door. Louise sat a few minutes and let the memories of the music settle over her.

Slowly, she gathered up her sheet music and packed it into her bag, and then, with one last look around the sanctuary, she walked out into the foyer. The space was crowded with people clutching cups of tea and eating sugar cookies.

"You did such a great job," Sylvia Songer said, pulling Louise in for a hug. "That last song… Well, I guess I didn't realize how beautiful it was."

"It was a lovely service," Louise said. She felt peaceful and serene in a way she couldn't explain. The best she could do was to say that the Lord had been present in the service tonight.

"I still like 'Silent Night,'" Aunt Ethel was saying as she walked on past them. Her friend Florence Simpson walked next to her.

"I don't know," Florence said. "It was different, but that's not a bad thing. It's fun to shake things up sometimes."

"Oh please, Florence. When have you ever been all right with shaking things up?" Aunt Ethel asked.

Louise couldn't hear Florence's response as the women vanished out of earshot, but she smiled nonetheless.

"Well, I should get going," Sylvia said, giving Louise a wave. "It looks like you have someone who wants to speak with you anyway. Have a very Merry Christmas, Louise."

"Thank you, Sylvia." Louise waved and then turned to see who wanted to speak with her. She smiled when she saw that it was Lauren. She looked beautiful in a black dress with gauzy sleeves, her curls tumbling down around her shoulders.

"Hi there." Lauren gave her a shy smile.

"Hello. I'm so glad you made it. And you somehow got Viola here too. I'm impressed."

"She wanted to come."

Louise cocked her head. Viola never wanted to come to church.

"Okay, maybe it was more that she didn't want to be left home alone. And she knew that if she stayed at home she would have to clean up the dishes. In any case, she came without kicking and screaming."

"I'm so glad."

"I am too. It was a lovely service." She leaned in a bit closer. "I also wanted to thank you."

"For what?"

"For being so kind and encouraging." Lauren shook her head. "I mean... I'm not going to lie. I didn't really want to be here when we first arrived."

"You hid it well."

"It wasn't anything to do with the inn. The inn is lovely. It's just that, well, you know that I was missing my family and our traditions."

"Of course. It's only natural."

"But then, when I was talking to you and Jane last night, you helped me think about it differently. Don't get me wrong, I still wish I were home with my family." She gave a guilty laugh. "But just like you suggested, Jordan and I spent a lot of time talking today about what we want our traditions to look like for our family."

"You mentioned making it a point to help someone else every year," Louise said.

"That's right. I'm already thinking of ways we can help people next year."

"I'd say you really helped someone today. More than one person, in fact. Viola would have been overwhelmed without you there. And what about the customers you helped? When I saw you in there, it sure looked like you were helping a woman find the right gift for her granddaughter."

"Yeah, but that was fun. Next year we'll do something that's more of a sacrifice."

"All right," Louise said. She wasn't going to try to talk Lauren out of it, but she didn't necessarily believe that every act of service had to be unpleasant.

"And then, after we put up the decorations, I offered to make dinner. Viola was exhausted from working in the store, so she was thrilled to let me. I made lasagna, just like they were having at home. My mom sent me the recipe. I made meatballs too and picked up cannoli at the Good Apple."

"I'm so glad. What a wonderful way to keep that tradition alive."

"Yeah. And it was good. Not as good as my mom makes it, obviously, but good enough."

"I'm sure it was delicious."

"It was, if I do say so myself." She smiled. "Anyway, tonight we decided on another tradition. Jordan really liked the service tonight, and he agreed that we should try to find a church in our neighborhood that we can go to."

At first, Louise wasn't sure she'd heard right. "You're going to find a church?"

Lauren nodded.

"That's wonderful news. I'm sure there are many churches in New York that have beautiful Christmas Eve services."

"Yes, I'm sure you're right, but I don't just mean for Christmas Eve. I don't think we'll go every Sunday, but he was interested in finding one where we could get to know people and attend more often."

Louise tried not to let the surprise she felt show on her face. Hadn't Lauren just said the day before that she didn't think Jordan would be interested in attending church? How had that change happened in just the last day?

"That's great to hear." And it was. Louise may not understand what had happened, but it truly was great. The Lord worked in mysterious ways.

"Anyway, I wanted to thank you. None of this would have happened without you and your sisters. This may not have been the kind of Christmas I'm used to, but it hasn't been bad. And it's... Well, I guess it's the start of new traditions for Jordan and me. For our little family."

"I'm so glad to hear it." Before she could think about what she was doing, Louise leaned in and gave her a hug. Lauren returned the hug with a tight squeeze, and when she pulled back there were tears in her eyes.

"Thank you for everything," Lauren said. Then she turned to catch up with Viola, who was making a beeline for the door.

Louise watched her go, and she couldn't help the smile that spread across her face. Louise and her sisters never knew who was going to come in through the doors of Grace Chapel Inn, but God did. He brought the right people at the right time, and Louise was constantly amazed at how He always knew.

"Are you about ready to go, Mom?"

Louise turned and saw that Cynthia had come up beside her.

"I suppose." Louise would have been happy to linger, but she could see that Cynthia was ready to head out. She had her coat on and was wrapping her scarf around her neck. "You look ready."

"Florence Simpson just asked me when I'm going to get serious about finding a man so I can settle down and have babies, so yeah, I'm ready to be away from here."

"Oh dear." Louise laughed. "I'm sorry."

While Louise couldn't deny she sometimes wondered the same thing, she knew better than to say it to Cynthia. She knew Cynthia wanted those things for herself someday too.

"It's all right. But let's get out of here." Cynthia threaded her arm through Louise's, and together they started to make their way toward the double doors. The crowd in the foyer was thinning out, and Louise saw that Jane and Alice were already walking across the yard ahead of them together. Well, Alice was walking. Jane was…was holding her arms up and jumping up and down. What in the world…?

"Look, Mom. It's snowing," Cynthia said as they stepped outside the doors of the church.

Ah. That explained Jane's reaction, then. It would be a white Christmas after all. She held on to Cynthia as they walked carefully down the church steps, crunching on the rock salt someone had thoughtfully spread, and then they stepped out into the yard, which was already gathering a fine layer of white powder. Fluffy white flakes of snow were falling all around them. Across the yard, Grace Chapel Inn was lit up against the dark night, the candles in each of the windows a beacon of welcome and rest.

"Look up."

Louise lifted her gaze, and she saw millions of tiny white flakes falling from the pitch-dark sky, spiraling toward the ground.

"It's so beautiful, isn't it?" Cynthia said.

"It really is."

Around her, she heard others exiting the church exclaiming over the snow, but the noise was muffled, and for a moment it seemed like she and Cynthia were alone in the quiet churchyard. Then, as if by some magic—though Louise knew it had been scheduled well in advance—the bell at the top of the steeple began to peal, announcing and celebrating the coming of the Savior.

And as she walked through the delicate snowflakes, Louise couldn't help the song that echoed in her mind, the strains of the last hymn they had sung in the church.

I heard the bells on Christmas Day
Their old, familiar carols play,
and wild and sweet
The words repeat
Of peace on earth, good-will to men!

That was what she felt more than anything right now, she realized. The hope that this Christmas there might be peace on earth and good news for everyone. God had come to earth and had given all of them the gift of His taking on flesh. It was good news, great news, to be shared just as the sound waves of the bell spread far and wide.

"Merry Christmas, Mom," Cynthia said.

"Merry Christmas." Louise looked at her daughter, all grown up and walking beside her, and then at the inn that she ran with her sisters, warm and welcoming. She couldn't think of a better place to be for Christmas than Grace Chapel Inn.

Jane Remembers...
By Anne Marie Rodgers

*For Regina and Leo, whose vision brought
Grace Chapel Inn to life.
I hope our latest offerings honor you.*

Prologue

"There's a memory that sticks in my mind," Jane said, after reminiscing with her sisters, "but it's different from either of those. Do you remember the year the Ericksons were supposed to come in a few days before Christmas, but they canceled? I thought we were going to have empty rooms, but then that mother-daughter duo walked in without reservations. What was their name again? Oh, the Rosdahls. Chris and Calla."

"Calla," Alice said. "How could we ever forget her? A more miserable child I've never seen, especially at Christmas."

"She had good reason," Jane said. "Her whole world had changed...."

Chapter One

A week before Christmas, Grace Chapel Inn was ready for the holiday. The sisters' stockings were hung from the mantel in the parlor, and swags of greenery tied with red ribbon festooned the reception desk in the foyer and the banister of the staircase. Christmas trees had been wrestled into tree stands and decorated in both the parlor and the living room. A large pine wreath with frosted pinecones, sprigs of holly with clusters of red berries, and a large red bow hung from a hanger centered right in the middle of the glass panel in the front door, casting its shadow onto the gold-and-cream rug that complemented the lovely wallpaper in the hall.

On the Monday before Christmas, Jane Howard hung up the telephone on the reception desk of Grace Chapel Inn. The festive Christmas decorations she'd so carefully placed sparkled a bit less than usual.

"What's wrong?" asked her eldest sister, Louise, seeing the downcast expression Jane couldn't hide. Louise had just placed several new Christmas cards they'd received from friends and former guests in the large basket on the hall table.

Jane grimaced. "That was Sandy Erickson. Dylan has been diagnosed with mono, and they've had to cancel their reservations."

"Oh what a shame!" Louise exclaimed. "I was looking forward to sharing Christmas with them and seeing how those dear children have grown."

The whole Erickson family from San Diego—Paul, Sandy, and their children, Dylan and Claire—had discovered the inn on a visit "back East" a few years ago. This year, they had planned a return trip. Jane's cooking, they freely admitted, was part of the draw.

"Poor Dylan," Jane said. "Mono is not fun, especially when you're young and accustomed to having loads of energy."

"Poor us too," added their other sister, Alice, who had entered the hallway just in time to catch the conversation. "That's half our week's income right there." She sighed. "And I doubt we'll have any more guests booking for Christmas at this late date." They had reservations for each of the two upstairs front bedrooms with private baths, one a couple and another a single gentleman. Both had family in the area and did not plan to spend a lot of time at the inn, although Jane had told them they were welcome for breakfast each day.

"Oh well, I guess it will be a quiet Christmas. That's too bad," Jane said. "I much prefer it when it's lively around here."

Just then, the sound of footsteps pounding across the porch made all three sisters startle and turn toward the door. It burst open to reveal a young girl of perhaps ten wearing a purple coat that clashed horribly with her shoulder-length, coppery-red corkscrew curls. "Do you have room for us to stay?" she demanded.

"Be careful what you wish for," Alice murmured beneath her breath, making Jane grin.

"Calla!" A dark-haired woman ascended the porch steps behind her, hurried in, and closed the door that was admitting frigid air into the house. "Were you born in a barn?" she asked in a tone of fond exasperation. She rolled sky-blue eyes the same shade as the child's and looked at Jane, who had stepped forward. "Hello. I'm sorry for my daughter's lack of manners. We're seeking a room, preferably with two beds, for a week or two." The bright smile she'd pasted on wavered. "We may stay through New Year's Day if the rooms are available. We're not exactly sure of our plans yet."

"Welcome to Grace Chapel Inn," Jane said. "I'm Jane Howard, and these are my sisters Alice Howard and Louise Smith. As it happens, we just had a cancellation. We don't have a room with two beds, but we do have two rooms with a connecting bath."

"That might work," the mother said.

Louise went to the desk, scribbled a note on a piece of paper, and handed it to Alice, who nodded and passed it to Jane.

"I don't want to stay here," the girl said. "Let's just go home, Mom."

The mother's smile looked forced, and Jane suspected she was gritting her teeth behind it. "We're having a holiday adventure, remember? Your home is beautiful," she said, looking around and smiling.

Jane glanced at the note as the woman returned her attention to her. *Offer reduced rate,* along with a suggested discount. She cleared her throat. "Since we have these rooms because of a last-minute cancellation, we could offer you a reduced rate for the double bed-single bath combo."

"That's very kind of you." The mother didn't even ask about the total. "I'm Chris Rosdahl. This is my daughter, Calla, and we'll take both rooms." She glanced at the child, who was wandering toward the tree visible in the parlor. "Don't touch anything," she said in the tone of voice that suggested this was an oft-used phrase. Lowering her voice, she confided in a whisper, "Sleeping with her is no fun. She kicks like a mule."

Jane chuckled. "I'm glad we have the double-room setup available." She waved them forward. "If you'd like to step over here, I'll get you checked in, and then I'll help you bring in your things."

Chris was soon checked in, and Jane handed her two large, old-fashioned keys. She ushered her guest back toward the front door. "I'll follow you—" she began, but her sentence was interrupted by the sound of something hitting the floor and shattering in the parlor. Everyone's startled gaze was drawn toward the sound.

Calla stood over the remains of a glass ornament, looking stricken.

"Calla!" Her mother's voice was sharp. "I *told* you not to touch anything."

Instantly the child's expression fell into sullen, distant lines. "It was an accident."

"Sure it was," said her mother. "Like the one with your baby picture was an accident? Come over here and—do—not—touch another thing."

But it truly had been an accident, Jane felt sure. She'd been able to see through the doorway, and Calla had barely brushed the ornament.

"Oh, it's not a big deal." Alice hurried to intervene. "It's not old or valuable. It'll only take me a moment to clean it up while Jane shows you to your rooms."

By the time Alice finished speaking, the child had already yanked open the front door and headed outside. Her mother's troubled eyes followed her, and she sighed. "Thank you," she said. "You're sure it wasn't anything expensive or sentimental…?"

"Absolutely not." Jane touched her elbow. "Are your bags still in your car?"

Chris nodded, and together they followed Calla outside.

There was a chilly wind blowing, but the sun still shone brightly on the early afternoon landscape. They hadn't had snow yet this year. The sisters had decorated the inn for the holidays right after Thanksgiving. Bright red ribbons were affixed to the light pole, the evergreen roping that hung in scallops along the porch railing, and to the wreath on the door. A basket of pinecones rested to one side of the door, also sporting a red bow, and in every window an electric candle glowed in welcome.

Only snow could make it better, Jane thought as she helped the mother and daughter carry in suitcases, an extra pillow, a laptop case and an iPad, toiletry bags, and another shoulder bag stuffed with what felt like rocks but appeared to be books, games, and snacks.

Jane led the way back inside and up the stairs to the two rooms at the rear of the inn. She stood aside to allow Chris to unlock the door of one room.

"Oh! This is lovely," Chris said as she stepped inside. She parked the large suitcase she'd brought up and dumped the other things on the bed. "Just set them anywhere," she said to Jane. "We'll sort it out and unpack them. Did you and your sisters decorate the rooms yourselves?"

Jane nodded. "This is the Sunrise Room." She and her sisters had found the pretty patchwork quilt in pale blue, white, and yellow, and they'd painted the walls a matching shade of pale sky, adding other accents over the years. "The Symphony Room is right through the connecting bath this way." She opened the door between the rooms and passed through the nicely appointed bath into the room done in shades of cream, green, and soft pink to match the wallpaper pattern of climbing roses.

Chris drew in a breath. "This one's equally pretty." She turned to her daughter. "Which one do you want, Calla?"

"I don't care." The girl flopped down on her stomach across the bed and pillowed her head on her arms, face turned into the crook of one elbow.

"Fine. You can stay here, and I'll take the other one." Chris turned to Jane. "Thank you so much. I'll be down in a bit to ask about restaurants and places for meals and things to do."

"If you like," Jane said, thinking of the length of the stay Chris was planning, "I'd be happy to take you to a Christmas tree farm tomorrow. We could get a little tree to set up over here." She indicated a corner of the spacious guest room. "There's plenty of space in this corner, and we have loads of extra lights and decorations you could use to trim it."

"Really? That would be awesome!" Chris's eyes were shining. "What do you think, Calla? Wouldn't that be fun?"

"This is stupid." The child's voice was muffled. "I don't care what you do."

The sparkle winked out of Chris's eyes, and Jane saw the effort it cost her to shrug off her daughter's attitude. "Well, I think it's a lovely idea," she told Jane. "And it's very kind of you. I'll look forward to it."

"Great!" Jane said brightly. "We'll go after breakfast then. I'll leave you to get settled in now."

Slipping out the door, Jane was troubled. Calla seemed a bit young to be in the throes of adolescent defiance, and Jane sensed a weary sadness resting on Chris's shoulders. Plus, there'd been no mention of a father joining them. She suspected the current tension between the two was not the normal state of affairs. What could be wrong with the Rosdahls?

Chapter Two

On Tuesday morning, Jane baked one of her personal favorites for breakfast, a French toast casserole made with a large loaf of French bread slices and a tasty mixture that included eggs, milk, sugar, cinnamon, and nutmeg. She served it with heated Vermont maple syrup, crispy strips of bacon, cranberry juice, and a large bowl filled with tasty green Granny Smith apples, ripe yellow bananas, and petite clementines.

After surveying their guests' wishes, Jane had decided to serve the casserole hot at nine. The single guest who preferred to rise late had assured her he'd be happy with something heated up or even a bagel. Laughing, she had assured him the inn could certainly manage that.

The couple who'd booked the Sunset Room would not arrive until midweek, so it would just be Chris and Calla for breakfast. Jane set two places at one end of the mahogany dining room table with a pretty set of pale green crackle-glazed pottery that she'd found at a yard sale a year or so ago. It had been priced so low she couldn't resist it, especially since it perfectly matched the greens of their dining room.

As she carried in the steaming casserole dish and placed it on hot pads on the sideboard, Chris entered the room. She sniffed the air. "Wow, that smells amazing. What is it?"

"French toast casserole." Jane turned from the buffet. "I hope your room is comfortable. Do you have everything you need?"

"It's perfect," Chris said. "I slept like a log."

"And how did Calla find her room?"

Chris's smile faded a bit as she approached the food. "Fine. She said she's not hungry, so I came on down." But then she grinned. "She eats like a horse though, so I bet it won't be long until the smell of this gets to her."

Right on cue, a figure hesitated in the dining room doorway. "I figured I'd better eat if you're going to drag me out to some field this morning," Calla said gracelessly.

"Good morning, Miss Howard," her mother prompted.

"Good morning, Miss Howard," Calla recited.

"Good morning, Calla," Jane replied. "Please call me Jane. I have coffee, tea, and hot chocolate available if either of you would care for a hot drink."

"Oh, coffee please," Chris said gratefully.

"What kind of hot chocolate?" Calla asked. "The kind out of a package is no good."

"Calla!" her mother said.

"I agree," Jane told the child. "Mine is homemade from my secret recipe. My sister Alice often drinks it to help her fall asleep at night. Want to try it?"

"I guess." Calla wandered over to the buffet and began to fill a plate as her mother set down her own loaded plate at the table.

Jane returned to the kitchen and began making the drinks. As she got out a serving tray to carry them into the dining room, Alice entered the kitchen in the uniform she wore for her nursing shifts at Potterston Hospital. "Good morning."

"Good morning," Jane replied. "Want some breakfast? There's plenty of French toast casserole in the dining room."

"Yum," Alice said. "What's on your agenda for today?"

"I'm taking our guests over to Bellwood Farm to get a small tree for the daughter's room," Jane said. "And then I thought I'd spend some time balancing the books after I finish icing the sugar cookies and working on some gifts I've made."

"What a nice idea," Alice said. "There's at least one extra Christmas tree stand in the attic, along with several boxes of lights and ornaments we haven't used in a while." The attic of the inn was a jumble of discarded treasures from decades past.

Jane nodded in response to Alice's comment. "I thought Calla might enjoy decorating her own tree."

Alice looked doubtful but said, "I hope so."

As Jane set the steaming drinks on the tray and picked it up, Alice smiled and said, "Good luck today."

Their eyes met across the room, and Jane chuckled, understanding perfectly that her sister meant, *Good luck with that difficult child.* Alice, who worked with a group of slightly older preteens and teens called the ANGELs at church, recognized an unhappy child when she saw one. "Thanks," Jane said.

After breakfast was finished and Jane had cleaned up the dishes, she went to the attic. She knew where the extra decorations were, but she had to move several items aside to get to them—an old coffee table, a Bentwood rocking chair, and a stack of elaborately carved wooden picture frames. Jane found one of the extra Christmas tree stands and carried it down to the second floor, where she knocked on the door of the Sunrise Room. When Chris opened the door, Jane handed her the tree stand. "Here you go. You can decide where you want it before we go get the tree."

"Thanks. We'll meet you downstairs in a few minutes."

"Great." Jane descended to the first floor and donned her outdoor clothing. As promised, she soon met the Rosdahls in the foyer for the short drive over to Bellwood Farm.

"How are we going to bring back a tree?" Calla asked, when she caught sight of Jane's compact car.

Jane held up a coil of rope and several Bungee cords. "We're going to tie it on the roof," she said.

Calla rolled her eyes, but she climbed into the back seat, while Chris sat in front with Jane.

Jane had decided to go to Bellwood Farm just outside town rather than driving ten miles to the North Pole Christmas Tree Farm in Merriville. She and her sisters had gotten their own trees in Merriville, but this drive took only minutes. As they approached the farm, Chris leaned forward in her seat. "Oh how charming! Look, Calla, it's like a postcard."

That was an accurate description, Jane decided. The old farmhouse was Victorian in style, long and white, two stories, with an attic that boasted peaks, gables, and large windows. It sat in the middle of a wide swath of pasture, with large shade trees and pines dotting the yard. At the far edges of the fields were thick stands of forested acreage. Several fields off in the distance displayed orderly rows of evergreens on Samuel Bellwood's Christmas tree farm. Above the front door was a welcome plaque, a traditional round Pennsylvania Dutch hex design with the world WILKUM painted on it.

Near the barn was a small area of wooden racks against which leaned a variety of Christmas trees already cut. Jane parked, and she and her guests got out and walked over to inspect the trees.

"Hello, Jane." Samuel Bellwood, the patriarch of the Bellwood clan and owner of the spread, ambled out of the barn. Samuel was a bear of a man, tall and broad, but as gentle as a lamb. His dark eyes twinkled as he surveyed her guests. "Welcome to Bellwood Farm."

"Thanks. You have a lovely home," Chris said. She introduced herself and her daughter. "We're guests at Grace Chapel Inn. Jane thought we might find a small tree here to put up in our room."

"That's our Jane, always dreaming up fun things to do," Samuel said, smiling. He gestured to the stand of trees. "You're welcome to look there, but I think many of the smaller ones have been sold. We might have to go out to the field and cut one down."

Calla clutched her mother's arm, all pretense of bored preteen falling away. "Mom, can we do that?"

"We've never cut down a tree of our own," Chris said to Jane and Samuel. "That would be wonderful."

"Okay, then." Samuel beckoned for them to follow him over to a tractor with a hay wagon attached. "Climb in, ladies, and we'll take a little trip out to the Christmas tree fields."

Jane, Chris, and Calla scrambled up a staircase of wooden fruit boxes nailed together and into the back of the wagon. They took seats on the hay bales at one end. It was chilly but not frigid outside, and the day was sunny, for which Jane was grateful. Samuel climbed into the driver's seat of the tractor, and it rumbled to life.

The trip out to the tree field was cold and bouncy and jouncy, throwing them off-balance and making them cling to the sides of the wagon as the vehicle toiled over a rough, rutted track. Still, Jane thought the delight on Calla's face was worth the uncomfortable trip.

At the edge of the tree field, Samuel cut off the tractor engine and helped them clamber out of the wagon. "Off you go," he said to Calla. "When you find your tree, I'll cut it down for you."

Jane smiled at her friend as Calla darted off along an avenue of evergreens. "Thanks," she said to him.

"She looked like she needed to cut down a tree," he said, smiling gently.

Jane chuckled, nodding her agreement and silently thanking him again for his perceptiveness, before joining Chris as she strolled among the trees at the edge of the field.

"Don't go too far, Calla," Chris called.

"Mo-om." Jane couldn't see Calla, but she'd bet there was some eye rolling going on. "There's no one out here but us. I couldn't get lost if I tried."

"I found a pretty little tree over here," Chris said. "Want to look at it?"

Calla appeared a moment later. She surveyed the tree her mother indicated. "Nope. I don't like that one."

"Okay. Let's look a little farther."

"I like this one." Calla stood by a fat blue spruce that was nearly tall enough to brush the twelve-foot ceilings in the main floor rooms of the inn.

"That one won't fit," Chris told her. "It can't be any taller than I am."

Calla made a sound of disgust. "That's tiny. Five ornaments will cover the whole thing."

That was patently untrue. Calla disappeared again along the next row of trees as Chris slowly inhaled and exhaled. Jane could almost see her counting to ten.

"Oh, the joys of childrearing," Chris muttered under her breath. She turned to Jane, looking apologetic. "I'm sorry

Calla's being such a killjoy. Her life has changed dramatically recently, and she's not handling it very well."

"Change can be hard for all of us," Jane said diplomatically.

"It's always been tough for her," her mother said. "I've tried really hard to make her life as predictable and orderly as possible, but it's not always easy, and her father doesn't help much. He lives well over an hour away, and when she was younger, he used to just pop up and take her to dinner or something, never mind our planned activities or homework or anything else. She'd go, but then I'd have to deal with the temper tantrums afterward." There was bitterness in her tone. "That finally got better about two years ago."

"How long have you two been...apart?" Jane asked.

"We divorced when she was less than a year old," Chris said. "We were really young and not ready for parenting when I got pregnant. Erik played in a band and spent his nights either practicing or playing gigs in local bars. I did most of the baby care on my own. Of course, I grew up in a hurry, but he sure didn't."

"Mm-hmm."

It appeared that Chris needed a listening ear, and Jane's implied understanding appeared to be all she needed to add more. "He met someone and remarried two years ago, and since then, he's been much better about taking Calla every other weekend, but she never sees him midweek anymore. She doesn't get it, of course, since even though he wasn't super-reliable when she was younger, he at least came around fairly frequently."

"That must be hard for Calla."

"So hard." Chris dodged to the next row for a second to ensure she could keep her daughter in sight. "Although it could be worse. His new wife seems to like her, and she even worked with me to set up a more regular visitation schedule. Calla was adjusting and doing pretty well, I thought, until Erik and Claudia told her this spring that they were going to have a baby. She came home acting almost manically excited about getting a new baby brother or sister, but I felt like it was forced, you know?"

"She's been an only for a long time," Jane said. "It must be hard, thinking about how you're going to have to share a parent. Even though he may not be perfect in your eyes, he's all she's ever known."

"Exactly," Chris said flatly. "And then things got even crazier. The baby was due in January, but she was born super early, in November."

"Oh no!" Jane thought of a couple in her church who'd had a preemie not long ago. "Did she survive?"

"Yes. I think she's doing okay." Chris shrugged, looking vaguely uncomfortable. "Her father sends Calla an email every few days through my account, but she doesn't want to read them or see the pictures he's sent. I usually skim a sentence or two to make sure everything's going okay, but they're not addressed to me, so I haven't read every one in detail. And I haven't looked at the pictures."

Jane heard a hint of defensiveness in Chris's voice, and her heart ached for the younger woman. She knew how difficult it was to navigate the end of a marriage, but it must be so much worse when one was forced to stay in touch for the sake of a child. It would be hard to ever really move on completely. "Do you know how much the baby weighed?" she asked.

"Just over three pounds."

Jane cringed involuntarily, mentally thinking of a five-pound bag of flour she'd just opened. Three pounds was so tiny! "That's really little."

Chris nodded, looking troubled. "I think she's doing okay so far. Eric hasn't mentioned any big setbacks or major medical problems."

"I understand why Calla's struggling," Jane said. "That's frightening, even for a child who may not understand all the ramifications associated with babies born prematurely."

"Well," Chris said wryly, "it's a little more personal for her. She hasn't gotten to see the baby, because flu season started early, and the NICU banned all visitors except parents. I can't blame them, but Calla was desperate to visit, and she was horribly disappointed."

"Oh, I bet," Jane said.

"And she hasn't seen her father since the baby was born. First he was spending every minute at the hospital. Then Calla was supposed to spend the first half of her Thanksgiving break with Erik and Claudia, and of course they had to cancel that. I get that they had to be at the hospital and couldn't have her at the house, but Calla sure doesn't." Although Chris sounded resentful enough that Jane wondered if she really did understand.

"I'm sure." Jane's heart ached for the child.

"I'm afraid she thinks they've replaced her with a new baby and they don't want her anymore." Chris's voice trembled.

"And who could blame her?" Jane asked. "This is a difficult situation for an adult, much less a child."

"And then," Chris went on, "last week her dad told her they aren't sure what their Christmas plans are."

"What did he say to you about it?" Jane knew sometimes children got things wrong or misunderstood.

"He and I don't talk," Chris said. "Now that Calla's old enough to communicate reliably, she just passes things on to me."

Oh dear. That didn't sound like a very healthy way to deal with a child's needs. And what was it teaching Calla? Not to mention the fact that Calla wasn't reading her father's emails at present anyway. But Chris was still talking.

"Since she's been out of diapers, she's spent Christmas Day with me and then gone to his house afterward for a couple of days. But I guess there's some talk about the baby being able to be released and come home during that time frame, so Erik and Claudia don't feel like they can commit to a specific schedule." Chris sounded glum.

Bringing home a healthy, normal baby would be stressful enough, but bringing home a preemie who might still be on monitors and was still itsy-bitsy would be downright terrifying. A young mother in the Grace Chapel congregation had given birth prematurely a few months ago, so Jane was slightly familiar with the challenges preemies experienced. She was a little surprised Chris didn't sound like she understood that—but the other woman's main concern appeared to be focused on how all this was affecting *her* child. It certainly didn't seem fair to the other couple, but then again, divorce often left people unable to see anything clearly that had to do with their former spouse.

"So Calla may not understand why everything is up in the air," Jane clarified.

"Probably not." Chris shuddered out a breath, and bitterness was unmistakable. "I just knew once this baby came her father would put her second. She was always a happy little girl, and it's so upsetting to see her acting so—well, you've seen her. She's awful."

But couldn't Chris see that a newborn with serious medical issues was going to change even the best-laid plans? "She's unhappy," Jane said carefully. "Unhappiness makes many people behave in ways they'd never dream of under normal circumstances."

"Hold that thought." Chris stepped through a pair of trees in the row they were walking along. "Calla?" Then her voice grew more urgent. "Calla! Answer me!" She turned back to Jane. "I don't see her."

Chapter Three

"It's a big field, but there's very little out here that could be dangerous to Calla," Jane soothed.

"I think I'm more concerned that she's hiding from me deliberately," her mother said.

"I imagine that between that coat and her hair, we'll soon spot her," Jane said. "Why don't we cut across the rows until we find her?"

"Good idea. So you noticed that awful coat." Chris rolled her eyes as she and Jane began to cross through row after row, pausing at each to take a good look down the length of the field. "A couple of weeks ago, when I thought this was just a passing nose-out-of-joint kind of thing, I told her I'd buy her a new coat if she talked to her dad on the phone. So she did. Granted, she mostly listened and hung up as quick as she could, but she did it. And then she chose that hideous purple coat. I tried and tried to talk her into another color. With her hair, there are certain shades that just don't work, you know?"

Jane had to laugh. "I do. Where'd that red come from?"

"Erik's mother apparently had bright red curls as a younger woman." Chris shook her head. "But neither he nor his brother does. We were all a little shocked when Calla was born with wisps of unmistakable flaming red quirking straight up atop her head like tiny springs."

Jane laughed.

"Oh, hey. There she is." Chris waved. "Calla!"

Jane could see her too, deep in the field, waving vigorously.

"Mom! I found our tree."

"Of course you did," Chris muttered, as she and Jane began to trudge along the row. "As far away from the wagon as possible. I hope it's not too heavy."

The two women made their way through the trees. As they got near enough to see the tree at which Calla was pointing, Jane began to giggle. "I don't think we're going to have any trouble carrying it back to the tractor."

Chris, after one incredulous glance, rolled her eyes and began to laugh. "Why am I not surprised?"

The tree was the spindliest, saddest-looking little Fraser fir Jane had ever seen. It stood crookedly between two bigger trees that had crowded it out and kept it from getting much sun. The branches were sparse, and one side bore two gaping holes. Halfway up, the trunk split in two, creating a double crown, one that shot straight up while the other angled out oddly. Perhaps the best thing Jane could say about it was that it was almost exactly as tall as Chris, just the size she had indicated.

"This is the tree I want." Calla sounded truculent, as if she'd already imagined arguing with her mother.

"Okay," Chris said. "Let's call Mr. Bellwood and have him cut it down."

Calla squinted at the tree and looked at her mother suspiciously. "I can choose this one?"

"Sure," Chris said cheerfully. "It's the right size, and that was the only thing I said."

Jane couldn't help grinning. "It'll look great with decorations on it." She turned to signal for Samuel, who had waited by the tractor near the bottom of the rise.

When he came striding along the row with the big saw in his hand, Samuel stopped dead at the sight of the tree Calla had chosen. "Oh," he said. "We weren't going to sell that. It's so misshapen we were planning to cull it in the spring so it won't inhibit the growth of the ones on either side."

"But this is the tree I want," Calla said plaintively, looking up at the huge farmer.

Jane smiled at Samuel and shrugged. "It'll save you cutting it down later."

"That it will." Samuel shook his head in resignation, grinning. "All right, but I'm not charging you, since you're doing me a favor taking it away."

Back at the inn, Jane and Chris unstrapped the tree from the roof of Jane's car and carried it inside, with Calla rushing ahead of them, opening doors. She appeared to have temporarily forgotten her woes.

First, they took the tree up to the Symphony Room where Chris had set the tree stand. It didn't take much work to maneuver the pitiful little evergreen into position, and while Chris held it upright, Jane and Calla crawled beneath it and tightened the screws that would hold it in place.

Next, Calla carried several pitcherfuls of water from the connecting bathroom to fill the tree stand.

"You'll have to check it a couple of times today," Jane warned. "Fresh-cut trees really suck up the water for the first twenty-four hours or so."

"I will," Calla promised. She set the pitcher Jane had loaned her on the corner of a dresser nearby.

She trailed Jane up the attic steps to bring down the boxes Jane had found, and together they carried the boxes to the Symphony Room. "Why do you have all these extra ornaments?" Calla wanted to know.

Jane shrugged. "I believe some are from when my sisters and I were young. Some of the others are extras Louise and I brought along when we moved back here to open the inn with Alice. We haven't all lived here together our whole lives."

"I guess I didn't realize that," Chris said. "Where did you live before?"

"San Francisco."

"I've always wanted to visit there," Chris said. "It looks like such a pretty city."

"I enjoyed it," Jane said. "But I'm happy to be living here again with Alice and Louise." She didn't really want to get into a discussion of her own past at the moment, so she shifted the subject back to the ornaments. "The trees downstairs have some of our really old family heirloom ornaments as well as sentimental ones, like a handprint salt clay mold from my first-grade Sunday school class. But there's a pretty good selection here of different things you might enjoy using on this tree."

Chris knelt, carefully pulling open the flaps of one box and extracting a smaller box with a cellophane front. "Oh cool," she said. "Icicles! I haven't seen these in years! My gram used to put them on her tree. We can't use these. A whole unused box of them is probably valuable these days."

Jane laughed. "That I doubt. Those things were the bane of our existence. You couldn't go near the tree," she told Calla, "because they held so much static they'd stick to your hair and your clothes."

"And look at these. My grandparents had some similar to these too." Chris held up another package with a windowed front that displayed its contents: glass ornaments in various shapes, among them a cluster of grapes, a Santa head, a glittering pinecone, and a streetlamp with a flickering candle painted on its sides. "I wonder where they got to. It would be fun to decorate with them."

"Here are some strings of lights." Calla had tugged open another box. "But look—the bulbs are huge."

"That's the way they used to be made," Jane informed her. "And the only other color besides those red, blue, green, orange, and white was yellow, but I don't think our tree had any yellow."

Chris plugged one of the two-pronged plugs into an outlet, and the soft glow of the large bulbs lit up the room. "I believe we'll only turn this on when we are in the room," she said. "I don't know if these things are up to current fire code standards."

Jane nodded. "Wise decision. These bulbs can get pretty warm if they're left on for hours and hours, and we wouldn't want them on a dried-out tree, but I think for this one week, they'll be fine." She gestured toward the bathroom. "And should you ever need it, there is a fire extinguisher beneath your bathroom sink."

"And look at these glass Santa heads." Chris's face looked troubled. "Are you sure you don't mind if we use these?"

"Not a bit." Jane held out a package of ornament hooks she'd stashed in one pocket. "Here you go. Have fun!"

Jane exited the Rosdahls' suite. Louise had dusted and prepped the two front rooms for the guests who were due in within the next couple of days, and she paused, dustcloth in hand, to look inquiringly at Jane as she stopped at the top of the stairs.

"Mission accomplished?" she asked. "I'm off to practice at the church for a bit now." She meant, Jane knew, that she would be practicing music for Christmas Eve on the pipe organ in the sanctuary.

Jane nodded. "We got the tree, and I helped them set it up." She grinned. "It's the saddest little Charlie Brown tree you've ever seen, but Calla chose it and seems pleased with it. Then we brought down some decorations, and I left them to it. I'm headed downstairs to make up a gazillion sugar cookies for the cookie exchange."

"Twelve dozen is not a gazillion," Louise said tartly. Then she smiled. "But I'm glad you're the one doing it. I'd hate to have to decorate a hundred and forty-four sugar cookies."

"And I'd hate to have to practice the 'Hallelujah' chorus over and over and over," Jane said with a grin, "so we're each well-suited to our tasks."

Putting a hand on the banister, she headed down the stairs and back to the kitchen. The recipe she planned to make was as easy as it could be. She didn't even have to chill the dough before rolling it out. The icing was equally easy— she used a recipe that dried hard, so the cookies could be stacked for easy storage. There was little worse, in Jane's opinion, than soft, sloppy cookie icing that got all over everything.

Assembling the ingredients and her baking tools on the butcher block counter, she mixed and rolled the dough before using Christmas cookie cutters to make trees, bells, stockings, stars, and snowflakes. She placed the first batch in the industrial-sized gas oven to bake and set a timer. Then she gathered her used baking utensils and bowls and took a few minutes to wash everything up.

The timer was about to go off, so she moved to the counter nearest the oven to grab a set of oven mitts.

Just then, Calla slid through the door from the hallway. The effect was that of a very small storm cloud suddenly scudding across the sky.

"Hey," Jane casually said by way of greeting.

"Hey." Calla didn't say anything more, so Jane decided she would wait a bit.

Calla wore a familiar, mulish look on her face, so Jane refrained from asking why she wasn't decorating her tree. Picking up the oven mitts, she lowered the big oven door, pulled out her trays of cookies, and set them on trivets to one side of the counter to cool.

Jane quickly rolled out more dough and cut out more shapes before using an offset baking spatula to transfer them from the floured counter to her baking sheets. She bit her tongue several times just as she was about to speak. She figured that waiting for Calla to make the first conversational overture was her best move.

"You need one more star," Calla observed. Jane had tried to cut approximately the same number of each shape.

Jane laughed. "You're right." She cut one more star and rearranged to make room for it on the second baking sheet. Then she popped both trays in the oven and set her timer again. "That will make six dozen when those come out," she said. "Two more batches that size, and I'll have them all baked."

"That's a lot of cookies," Calla said. "Why so many?"

"We have a cookie exchange at church," Jane said. "Twelve people each bake twelve dozen of one kind of cookie, and then we swap so everyone gets a dozen of everyone else's plus a dozen of their own. It's a great way to have a nice variety of Christmas cookies without losing your mind baking."

"Who's going to eat all those?"

Jane winked at her. "I suspect I'll have plenty of people around here interested in helping to eat them, don't you?"

Calla grinned and ducked her head. "Yep." Her mood appeared to be lightening.

"And we have more guests arriving this week, so we'll need plenty. Would you like to help me decorate them?"

"Sure." Calla straightened in anticipation. "With what?"

"I'm going to make some special icing," Jane said. "You can help."

Together, they mixed confectioner's sugar, milk, almond extract, and corn syrup into a smooth, glossy icing. "Now we divide it into smaller bowls and add food coloring to get the shades we want," Jane told her, suiting words to action. "Once we mix all the colors we want, we can start decorating." She pointed to a pile of paintbrushes in various sizes she'd laid on the counter along with several plastic bags for piping thin lines of icing. "I use those for cookie decorating."

"We're *painting* them?" Calla sounded surprised.

Chapter Four

Jane laughed at the look on Calla's face as she handed her a paintbrush. "Yes, we're painting the cookies. It's easy. Here, I'll show you."

As they began to ice the first batch of cooled cookies, Jane said, "Are you out of school this whole week?"

Calla shook her head. "No, but I'm a good student, so Mom asked if she could take my assignments for this week and we'd do them together while we're on our trip. Break starts Friday, and I already have everything done except my journal for language arts."

"Do you like to read?" Jane asked. "When I was around your age, I used to hide so I could read without doing my chores."

"I bet your mother always found you," Calla said. "Mine does."

"My mother died right after my birth," Jane said, "so I was raised by my father. Louise and Alice were teenagers when I was born, so they got to boss me around a lot." She chuckled. "I deserved it. Like I said, if I could sneak away with a book, I did."

"What was your favorite book?" Calla asked.

Jane thought for a minute. "*The Borrowers*. It was about a family of tiny people who lived in the walls and floor of a big old home in England. They borrowed things from the family that lived there...and one day, they were discovered."

"That sounds interesting!" Calla sat up. "My first favorite book—well, it's the start of a series—is called *The Song of the Lioness*. It's by Tamora Pierce, and she wrote a whole bunch of books about a kingdom called Tortall. I have all of them. They're the best!"

"That does sound interesting," Jane said. She moved back to the cookie dough and began to roll and cut another batch. "Maybe I'll look into those."

"And I love *Sarah, Plain and Tall*, and *Number the Stars*." Calla talked on while she industriously painted a green Christmas tree and added red, blue, and yellow dots to simulate lights. "And *Misty of Chincoteague* and *Tuck Everlasting* and *Matilda*. Roald Dahl wrote that. He also wrote *James and the Giant Peach* and *Charlie and the Chocolate Factory* and a whole bunch of others. He's a really good writer."

"Goodness," Jane said. "And you must be a really good reader if you've gotten through all of those."

"My teacher says I'm an advanced reader," Calla said indifferently. "I just like to read."

"Do you like books about animals?" Jane asked. "I used to love a book called *The Black Stallion* by Walter Farley, I believe. It was about a boy who got shipwrecked, and only he and this scary wild horse survived. But the boy tamed the horse, and it became a great racehorse."

"I've read that," Calla said. "It's a good book. The author wrote a whole bunch more too, but I think the first one's the best. I love horses. I love all animals, really. When I grow up, I want to be a veterinarian."

"What a wonderful goal. Do you have pets now?" Jane asked. "We have a cat named Wendell, and I used to have a cat named Oliver when I was young."

"We have a dog," Calla said. "She's staying with a pet sitter this week. I miss her."

"What kind of dog is she?" Jane imagined a small ball of fluff or perhaps a beagle mix.

"She's a greyhound," Calla said. "She used to be a racing dog, but she lost a bunch of races and they were going to kill her, so this group that saves greyhounds rescued her, and then we got to adopt her."

Jane's heart instantly melted. "Oh, that's a wonderful story. You and your mom are special people."

"We gave her a second chance," Calla said. "That's what Mom says. When I grow up, I'm going to have a whole houseful of dogs, and they're all going to be dogs I save. I'm never going to buy a dog."

"That's a lovely idea." The oven timer went off then, interrupting their conversation, and Jane paused to get the second batch of cookies out of the oven and put in the third.

They worked companionably for a while longer, finishing the icing on all the cooled cookies. Jane pulled the fourth set of trays from the oven and set the cookies to cool. As she did so, she said, "I have to go to the basement and bring up my Christmas cacti."

"Your what?"

"My cacti. You know what a cactus is?" When Calla nodded, Jane went on. "The plural form is cacti. These are not the desert cacti I bet you're thinking of but something a little different."

Jane entered the storage room and opened the basement door. She flicked on the light switch, flooding the bare wooden stairs with welcome light. "Going down!" she called cheerfully.

Behind her, Calla giggled, trailing a hand along the stone wall on one side of the staircase. "Wow. This is, like, really old."

"It's been here as long as the house, so yeah, it's well over a hundred years old now," Jane said. "Watch your step. These stairs are steep." She also paid attention to the steps. The last thing she wanted to do was fall.

As they reached the hard-packed dirt floor, Calla looked around at the stone walls, the shelves filled with Jane's preserves, and the unruly tangle of antiques and detritus of many years' worth of discarded items. "There's a whole house worth of stuff down here," she observed.

The comment startled a chuckle out of Jane. "I think you're right," she said. She went to a shelf and reached for one of the small potted plants she'd placed there. "Here," she said, handing that one and a second one to Calla. "If you can carry those two, I can fit the rest of these in a box, and we'll take them upstairs."

"So why did you have them in the basement?" Calla asked when they reached the top of the stairs.

"I was forcing them," Jane told her.

Calla looked blank as she set her two pots on the counter beside the box Jane had carried up. "Forcing them to do what? And how do you force a plant?" She giggled. "They don't care if you take away dessert, right?"

Jane chuckled. "To force a plant means to do something special to make it bloom at a certain time," she explained. "They're Christmas gifts. I started them from cuttings and potted them up last year. About eight weeks ago, I put them down in the dark basement with a grow light that comes on for ten hours a day, and then they're in darkness the rest of the time. It's also chillier down there, and I didn't water them often. All those things together forced them to bloom. Look."

She pointed at the buds on each small plant. "Every single one has buds. I'm going to put them in a window that faces east so they get good light, and in another few days, they'll begin to open."

"Just in time for Christmas," Calla said, her eyes wide. "You're pretty smart."

Jane grinned. "And now you know how it's done. It just takes a little patience." She debated for a moment. Then she said, "I have a few extras, if you need gifts for your family members. Would you like some?"

Calla's brows drew together. "I'll take one for my mom, if that's okay. I didn't get my dad and my stepmom anything, and I bet they won't even notice."

"You think they won't notice?" Jane was careful only to reflect what Calla had said. It was a technique she'd learned from Alice, who had learned a lot about how to keep young teens talking about their troubles from her work with her church group.

Calla jerked one shoulder up in a defensive shrug. "They're so busy with their new baby they don't even know I'm alive."

Jane had to bite her tongue to keep from assuring her that wasn't true. First of all, she didn't know Calla's father and stepmother. But more importantly, she sensed that Calla simply needed a listening ear more than she needed a lecturing adult. Finally, she said, "It's hard when you feel left out, isn't it?"

Calla didn't respond.

Jane racked her brain, but she couldn't think of anything else to say that didn't sound like she was prying, so she gave up the effort. "Say," she said, "tomorrow a friend of ours is holding her annual Christmas open house. It's a crafting adventure. You and your mom would be welcome if you'd like to come along."

"What's a...a crafting adventure?" Calla's brow furrowed.

Jane smiled. "She sets up several different stations where you can make your own Christmas ornaments. Everything is provided, and there's someone at each station to help if you need it. Think you'd like that?"

Calla lifted one shoulder in a show of indifference, her mood shifting unexpectedly. "I don't know. But I'll tell Mom. I have to go now. She wants to go shopping in Lancaster this afternoon." She turned and walked out of the kitchen, leaving Jane feeling more than a little deflated.

Jane watched Calla go, both sad and frustrated by the way she'd lost the connection they'd been creating. She felt bad for Chris, dealing with her unpredictable daughter day after day on her own. That would put a damper on one's good nature, no matter how much one loved a child.

She placed the last of her cacti on the east-facing window-sill. When she finished, she got out her small watering can with the long curved spout and gave each one a healthy drink. Somewhere in there, she heard the front door open and close, and through the window, she caught sight of Chris and Calla getting into their rental car and heading out of the gravel park-ing area. Off to Lancaster, she presumed. She imagined they'd find lunch and dinner somewhere in the rest of their day.

The ringing of the telephone sounded, loud and shrill, and she crossed the kitchen to answer it. "Grace Chapel Inn, this is Jane. How may I help you?"

"Um, hello. My name is Erik Rosdahl. I think my family—er, my daughter—is staying there, and I was hoping to talk to her. Calla Rosdahl?" The voice was pleasant and courteous.

"Oh yes!" Jane felt adrenaline flood her system. It was an absurd reaction, but she was thrilled for Calla. "I mean, I'm so sorry. She is staying here, but she's out shopping this afternoon. Could I give her a message?"

There was an audible sigh. "Just tell her I called, and I miss her. I doubt she'd have talked to me anyway." The man paused. "Did she mention me? Or her new sister?"

"A little bit," Jane said. Which wasn't a lie. Although Chris had given her the details, Calla *had* mentioned her father, stepmother, and their new baby. "Congratulations on your new daughter. I understand you've had a bit of a rough road."

"Yes, but it could have been much worse," Erik said. "She just has to get big and strong enough to leave the hospital. Calla wasn't permitted to come into the NICU, so she hasn't met her yet. I'm really hoping we get some good news soon, and I can bring Calla to visit. That will give Chris a bit of a break too. She's been a trouper through all this." He chuckled. "Have you spent much time with Calla?"

"We made cookies together," Jane said. "And I took her and her mom to pick out a Christmas tree for her room."

"So you've gotten to know her a bit," her father said. "I suspect Calla hasn't been much fun for Chris to live with—she's not shy about letting us know when the world doesn't work as she thinks it should."

"I've gotten that impression," Jane said carefully. Erik sounded caring and concerned, and she was suddenly filled with hope that he had changed for good from the careless young man Chris had known a decade ago. After all, who didn't regret some of the choices they'd made as an older teen or very young adult? "What would you like me to tell Calla?"

"Just tell her I miss her like crazy," Erik said. "And that I don't know the exact date yet, but I promise I'll see her soon. I know she's going to be a wonderful big sister."

"I'll be sure to pass that on," Jane said. "Congratulations again. I hope you all are able to come home together very soon."

"You and me both," Erik said.

Chapter Five

C hris entered the dining room alone on Wednesday morning for breakfast.

Jane had pancake batter ready and waiting, and she flashed their guest a smile. "Good morning. We have chocolate chip pancakes and sausage for breakfast this morning, along with a citrus side dish and apple or orange juice. And of course, coffee, tea, or hot chocolate if you wish."

"It all sounds heavenly," Chris said with a warm smile. "Coffee, please."

"Will Calla be joining you?"

Chris nodded. "And I'm sure she'd love hot chocolate. She just had to finish the chapter in whatever it is she's reading at the moment."

"Did she get my message?" Jane asked. In the end, she'd just written down exactly what Erik Rosdahl had said and slipped it beneath the door of Chris's room. She'd considered putting it beneath Calla's door, but she was afraid Calla might throw it away or hide it, and she'd wanted to be sure Chris knew Erik had cared enough to call Calla.

"Yes," Chris said. "It was good of him to call," she admitted.

"He sounded genuinely worried about Calla's feelings," Jane said.

"I think he is," Chris mused. "I just wish he'd have spared a few minutes to come and see her in the past month, you know?"

Jane did know, but... "Didn't you say he lives over an hour away? How far is the hospital where the baby is?"

"She's at Women and Babies," Chris said, naming a hospital in Lancaster County. "He lives northwest of there, while we live southeast of Lancaster." She fell silent.

Jane wanted to say more, but she sensed she'd given Chris something to think about, so she resisted the urge and returned to the kitchen. It only took a few moments to heat up the griddle, and soon she was pulling the sausages from the warm oven and using the spatula to slide stacks of golden-brown chocolate chip pancakes onto plates. As she carried the loaded plates into the dining room, Calla entered and slid into a seat next to her mother.

"Calla tells me you're going to an ornament-making party today, and you were kind enough to invite us," Chris said to Jane. "Are you sure your friend won't mind?"

Jane grinned. "Not at all. She throws a shindig every year. The more, the merrier."

"That sounds like fun," Chris said. "Would you like to go, Calla?"

The young girl shrugged. "I guess." She studiously applied butter to her pancakes, making sure every millimeter was covered.

"Great," Jane said, stepping into the awkward conversational breach that Calla's lack of enthusiasm had created. "I'll be ready to go in an hour. I'll meet you in the foyer."

Jane cleared the table in the dining room and then reset a fresh place for their late-rising single guest. She placed three croissants beneath a bell jar cover, refreshed the ice in the ice bucket in which she'd set the pitcher of orange juice, and left him a note that the coffee had been made fresh at nine. Next, she cleaned up the kitchen and pulled a tub of her homemade vegetable soup and a packet of pink applesauce from the freezer to thaw for lunch. She would make some buttermilk biscuits to serve with it, she decided. Louise liked those, and Alice wasn't working today, so she'd be around for lunch as well.

Then she went upstairs to shower and change into a clean pair of slim corduroy pants and a burgundy sweater with a cowl neck.

By the time she ran down the steps again, Chris and Calla were waiting in the front hallway, already bundled in their coats. Jane pulled on her own parka and opened the door. "Let's go make some ornaments!"

It was a short drive through Acorn Hill to Florence's huge red-brick home.

"Wow," Calla breathed as Jane parked along the street amid a plethora of other vehicles lining the curbs in what was arguably the nicest neighborhood in the community.

Florence had placed a massive evergreen wreath decorated with gold balls, pinecones, holly berries, and a large gold bow on the massive mahogany front door. Evergreen garland trimmed the doorway with matching gold bows at the top on each side. At each of the large windows upstairs and down, there was an evergreen swag with a gold bow centered on the windowsill.

A large blue spruce near the wide driveway had been covered with artificial white poinsettia blooms and more gold bows.

"Florence likes gold, and she likes to decorate," Jane said with a grin as she turned off the ignition. "Wait until you see the inside. She adds more every year."

They trooped up the flagstone walkway to the front door. Jane rang the bell, and a moment later, Florence threw open the door. "Welcome to my Christmas Craft Open House!" she said, a gleam of almost manic excitement in her voice. "Hello, Jane. And oh, you've brought friends. How lovely. Please come in. Ronald?" She gestured without ever turning away from her guests, and her husband came forward with a pained smile and outstretched arms, acting the part of butler. "You may give him your coats," Florence said regally.

Jane winked at Ronald as she handed him her coat. "Thanks," she said. "This is Chris Rosdahl and her daughter, Calla. They're guests at the inn, and I thought they'd enjoy your crafts."

Florence threw her arms wide. "Come in, come in." She wore white pants and a matching white sweater with gold reindeer on it. All the white lent her a distinct resemblance to a plump snowman. Her hair was carefully coiffed and her makeup artfully—and heavily—applied. "There's a Christmas tree in every room," she said happily. "Each one has a theme, and in each room, there's an ornament craft that echoes the theme of the tree." She urged them toward the formal living room. "You may start in here and work your way through the dining room, the kitchen, the library, and the music room."

Ronald, walking away with their coats, rolled his eyes, and Jane had to suppress a chuckle. "The library," she knew, was the Simpsons' den, where Ronald enjoyed watching football, and the "music room" was across the hall from the formal living room. Its main claim to fame was a baby grand piano which neither Simpson had any idea how to play. Florence, however, kept it carefully tuned. Louise had played it on occasion and bemoaned the waste of such a gorgeous instrument.

"Mom, look at this!" Calla had rushed ahead into the formal living room Florence had indicated. A tall and lovely Fraser fir covered with angel ornaments of all shapes and sizes and accented with white flower lights and sparkling iridescent hand-blown glass balls dominated the space before the heavy brocade draperies with the gold rope ties that framed the front window. A large angel in a shimmering gown with real feathered wings extended in a graceful arc perched atop the tree. "Are we making angels here?" Calla asked.

"We are indeed. And who might you be?" The voice belonged to Jane's aunt, Ethel Buckley, who was one of Florence's close friends and who had helped with this event since her move to Acorn Hill more than a decade ago. Ethel wore a bright red sweater with Christmas lights embroidered in a meandering pattern across it with red-and-green checked slacks and green shoes. The sweater clashed with the orange-red shade of her tinted hair, and the green Christmas-bulb earrings danced merrily as she hugged Jane and met the Rosdahls.

Soon, Chris and Calla were engaged in making an angel ornament with heavily embossed white craft paper, silver wired ribbon for the wings, and a pearl for the head through which a thin silk ribbon loop passed to place it on a tree.

Following Florence's directions, they moved next to the dining room, where an artificial tree was heavily laden with Florence's collection of holiday bell ornaments from all over the world. The craft to complement the decor was a bell made from an upside-down miniature clay flowerpot decorated with paint, sprinkled with glitter, and embellished with tiny glued-on snowflakes. A ribbon was knotted and passed through the water hole in the top for a hanger.

The morning passed quickly. Florence had tables loaded with a variety of Christmas cookies she and her friends had baked, and hot chocolate and mulled cider were served. Jane moved through the rooms with Chris and Calla, taking part in making each decoration offered.

In addition to angels and bells, they made doves of felt with glittering wings, Christmas balls covered with beads that caught the light, Christmas cookies made of baked clay that were painted, and jolly Santa faces made of sparkly craft paper layered one piece atop another.

If there was an overall theme, Jane decided, it was "shiny." Sparkle. Glitter. Gleam. Florence was attracted by anything shiny. Judging by Calla's rapt expression as she surveyed the crafts she and her mother had carefully placed in the basket Jane had brought along for that purpose, Florence wasn't the only crow in the crowd.

"That was fun!" Calla skipped ahead of Chris and Jane as they returned to their car shortly before lunchtime. "I wish we could do that every year."

"It was fun," her mother agreed, carefully not addressing the wish. "That's a very generous thing for Mrs. Simpson to do. And you say she does it annually?"

Jane nodded. "And it's always different. Florence gets as much pleasure out of hosting it as those of us who attend do out of making all the crafts."

"Should we have paid her?" Chris wondered.

"Oh no. She'd have been mortally offended," Jane assured her.

"I'm going to put all of ours on our tree," Calla announced.

"And I'm doing the same with mine on our tree in the living room," Jane assured her.

A family was coming down the sidewalk toward them, parents with two children roughly Calla's age behind them.

"Hi, Jane," the mother called. "Coming from Florence's open house?"

"We are," Jane said. "She's outdone herself with wonderful crafts this year." She indicated her companions. "Tim and Carol Matthews, meet Chris Rosdahl and her daughter, Calla, who are visiting the inn this week. Calla, Charlie and Sissy go to our church and are close to your age, I bet."

"Hello," the Matthews children chorused politely.

"Hi," Calla said flatly.

"Our mom and dad bring us to this every year," Sissy said. "Isn't it fun?"

"Sometimes it's a bore," Charlie said, contradicting his sister.

"Only when you spill all the glitter and Dad makes you clean it all up," Sissy retorted.

"And on that happy note," their father said, "I think we'll leave you ladies to enjoy your memories of a fun morning." He rolled his eyes, but he grinned as he hooked an arm around Sissy's neck and ruffled her hair as he spoke, and the family walked on.

Both Rosdahls were very, very quiet as they climbed into the car, and Jane couldn't help but wonder if seeing an intact nuclear family like the Matthews was painful for them. Did Calla's dad tease her and ruffle her hair like that? He certainly couldn't spend as much time with her as Charlie and Sissy's dad did with them, being present in their lives every day as Tim was, but Jane had gotten the impression during the phone call yesterday that he cared deeply for his daughter.

The moment they entered Grace Chapel Inn, Calla dashed upstairs to decorate the tree in her room. Chris accompanied her but soon came back down with a laptop.

"May I join you?" She indicated the burgundy sofa in the living room, where Jane was deciding where to place the ornaments she had made.

"Sure thing." Jane stood in the middle of the room and surveyed the tree. Something wasn't quite right. She moved the little angel ornament one branch down and stood back. That was better.

On the sofa, Chris opened her laptop and tapped a few keys.

Jane hung the bell, admiring the snowflakes that covered its surface and caught the light. Then she hung the Santa face and the other two ornaments before she stretched up on her tiptoes to put the little dove up high dead center beneath the large ribbon bow that served as the topper for the tree. "Does that look okay?" she asked over her shoulder.

Chris looked up from her laptop, studied the ornament Jane indicated for a moment, and then said, "It's perfect. What a lovely morning. Thank you so much for including us."

"I was glad you were able to join me," Jane said honestly.

"Oh my." Chris's exclamation caught Jane's attention, and she looked over at her guest just as Chris turned her laptop around. "This is my ex's baby. She looks like Calla!"

Jane walked over and studied the picture on the monitor. The baby looked unbelievably tiny, swaddled in the ubiquitous white receiving blanket with pink and blue stripes that all hospitals seemed to use for newborns. She wore a pink and white knitted cap and was nestled in a woman's arms, presumably Calla's stepmother's. She had an oxygen cannula taped in place across her little face. "Oh wow, she's really little," Jane said in awe. Then she said, "I thought you said you hadn't looked at the pictures."

Chris's cheeks reddened. "I think I've been a little selfish," she said. "I need to encourage Calla to bond with this baby, and I can't do that if I won't even look at pictures of her."

Jane nodded. "That's a wise point of view."

"You should see the pictures from right after she was first born," Chris said. "She didn't resemble Calla at all then. The first pictures Erik sent were of her in the incubator, and she looked like a little alien. She's gained like two-and-a-half pounds since then. And reading all his emails in detail, it sounds like they may let her come home soon. I put all the pictures in a file in chronological order for Calla so she can see her sister's progress." Chris clicked on a file and began to show Jane pictures of the newborn infant with tubes and wires everywhere, of her in an incubator, scrawny little stick arms and legs flung wide, of her eyes covered with miniature goggles, of her beaming mother holding her cradled against her chest. "Claudia got to hold her for the first time when she was nine days old," Chris said. She clicked the mouse again, pulling up another picture. "And Erik when she was two weeks." She shook her head. "I can't imagine it. Calla was a healthy almost-eight-pounder with a head full of red curls, and she seemed fragile to me."

"Does the baby have hair like Calla's?" Jane asked.

"She hardly has any," Chris said, "but what she does have has a reddish cast to it. That color and the curls come from Erik's mother, so it's very possible." She continued to gaze at the picture for a moment. "He's lucky," she said softly.

"Lucky to have another child?"

Chris nodded, and Jane noticed that she was blinking rapidly. "I would have liked that. But my opportunities to meet someone are few and far between, being Calla's primary guardian and all."

"She lives with you most of the time?"

Chris nodded. "He takes her every other weekend now, and we share holidays."

"Do you wish he would take her more?"

"Not really, even though it might make my life easier. And it wouldn't work with school very well anyway." Chris shook her head. "He cheated on me when she was little and made a lot of poor choices that didn't make him a great dad. I wasn't inclined to let him see her at all, but the courts decided he should have supervised visitation every other week. After my anger cooled and I went to counseling, I made an effort to set aside my bitterness and offered him more time with her. The current setup is what he chose. They took her on vacation for two weeks last summer, and that's the first he's ever done that. Since he met and married Claudia, he's been a way better dad. But now that this baby has had all these problems and Calla's been unable to be a part of anything , she's feeling so angry and left out I'm not even sure she's going to be willing to go to his house when he asks."

The two women looked up as Calla entered the room. "I hung all my ornaments," she said proudly, seemingly happier than she'd been when they'd arrived home. "How about you?"

"I did too," Jane reported, "and now I've got to go get some lunch started. Do you two have plans, or would you like to eat with my sisters and me?"

"Thank you, but we'll go out," Chris said. "I thought I might take Calla to Longwood Gardens today. If we stay until dark, we can see their Christmas light display."

"Oh you should," Jane said enthusiastically. "It's absolutely amazing. I don't go every year, but it seems they add something new each time I do."

"I want to go see it," Calla said, crossing to her mother's side and slouching against her with her head on Chris's shoulder. "Can we leave now?"

Her mother nodded. "But first, look at this. Your father sent another picture of your new sister. She's not in the NICU anymore. They moved her to a—"

"I don't care!" Calla shot to her feet as if she'd been stuck with a pin. "Stop talking about that baby. Leave me alone!" The last words were a shout as she spun and sprinted from the room, coppery curls flying. A moment later, the sound of her feet pounding up the steps echoed through the old house, and then a door slammed.

Chapter Six

Chris sat frozen for a moment, looking stricken in the wake of Calla's stormy departure.

"What on earth...?" Louise stuck her head into the room, then saw Chris and hastily withdrew.

Chris expelled a long breath then shook her head and rose. "I'm so sorry. I haven't pressed her much the past few days, and I thought maybe she would be a little curious."

"It's all right," Jane said. "This is a difficult time for Calla."

Chris nodded. "And then some." She closed the laptop and trudged from the room, and soon Jane heard her footsteps slowly mounting the stairs.

Jane took the basket in which her ornaments had been laid and headed back to the kitchen.

Louise was there, just beginning to set the table. "I take it the noise I heard was the daughter?"

Jane turned the oven on to preheat. "Calla. She's having a really hard time adjusting to her father's new baby. Or, rather," she said, not willing to give the wrong impression, "she's having a hard time missing her father's attention. The baby was premature, and he's been tied up and not able to visit." She got out a bowl and began to mix up the biscuits, cutting them with a glass before placing them on a baking sheet and popping them into the oven. While the biscuits baked, she dumped the tub of soup, now thawed, into a saucepan and began to warm it on the stove.

Louise opened the applesauce and divided it into three bowls. "I hope she doesn't disturb our other guests."

Jane grimaced at her eldest sister's faintly censorious tone. "She's a very unhappy child struggling with feeling unloved by a parent, Louise. Be kind."

"I am being kind," Louise protested. "But our other two guests will be arriving this afternoon, and it's not fair to them to have a child stomping around slamming doors."

"A fact I imagine her mother is probably explaining to her right now," Jane returned evenly.

The back door swung open, and Alice stepped into the kitchen from the porch. She'd been out taking a walk with her good friend Vera Humbert, as she tried to do several times a week. She glanced from Jane to Louise, and her eyebrows rose. "Trouble at the ranch?" she asked mildly.

Jane shook her head. "Not really. Our youngest guest became a little upset a while ago and—"

"And treated us all to a display of temper," Louise cut in. "I merely pointed out that we have other guests to consider."

Alice regarded them both with a smile. "I suspect her mother will point that out to her as well."

"That's what I said!" Jane exclaimed.

"However," Alice went on, "we may need to address it if it continues. We can't have our guests subjected to an upset young girl."

"And that's what I said." Louise looked pointedly at Jane.

"They're going out for the rest of the day," Jane said, a little miffed at Alice now, "so it won't be an issue for a little while, at least."

The sisters sat down to their lunch, after which Jane cleaned up the kitchen while Alice and Louise greeted the couple who had booked the Sunset Room. They arrived two hours earlier than expected and were pleasant and unassuming. They left shortly after checking in to visit and have dinner with family in the area.

On Thursday, with three days to go until Christmas, Jane walked into her bedroom to see Wendell, their gray tabby cat, up on the windowsill chewing one of her plants.

"Wendell!" Her gasp of horrified surprise startled the feline, who took one panicked look at her outraged face and leaped down. Unfortunately, he knocked over one of the plants, spilling soil and water all over the floor as he streaked away.

Jane went after him, cornering him downstairs in the dining room. She hefted his bulk into her arms, stroking his head to show him she wasn't really mad. "You know you're not supposed to be up at the plants, buddy," she reminded him.

"Why are you chasing him?"

A voice behind Jane startled her, and she set down the cat and turned.

Calla stood in the doorway behind her. "What happened?"

"Wendell happened," Jane said ruefully. "Give me a moment to clean up the mess he made, and then I'll get breakfast ready. Is your mom coming down too?"

Calla shrugged. "She might still be sleeping. I didn't check."

So the pair were still at odds after yesterday's unfortunate incident, Jane deduced. She winced inwardly, wishing there was something she could do to help the unhappy child. But she might have to settle for simply feeding her and trying to be a friend while they were in residence.

Jane pulled some rags from the pantry and returned to her room, Calla trailing her. As she began to mop up the floor, Calla knelt beside her, grabbed a rag, and wiped up the spilled water that had splashed on the wall.

"Thanks," Jane said. "Did you enjoy your visit to Longwood Gardens?"

"Yeah." But Calla spoke without much enthusiasm. "There sure are a lot of lights."

"There are," Jane agreed. "Did you have a favorite display?"

Calla thought for a moment. "I really loved that they have so many different colors of lights. The trees with the blue lights are really pretty. But down around the one lake they had a boardwalk, and in the woods all around it there were these glowing orb things that slowly changed colors. I really loved those."

"Oh, I know just where you were," Jane said, rising. "I've seen those, and I agree. They're hard to look away from." She smiled as they left her room and walked down the stairs to the kitchen. "I won't get there this year, but maybe next year I can go back. Did you know they have over a half million lights all over the property?"

"Wow," Calla said. "I guess I believe that. There sure were a lot."

Footsteps approached the kitchen from the foyer. Jane glanced up, half expecting to see one of her sisters, but it was Chris who appeared in the doorway. "There you are," she said to Calla. "Please don't sneak out of your room without letting me know."

"I only came downstairs," Calla said.

Chris held out a cell phone. "Your father's on the phone. He'd really like to speak with you."

Calla froze, and Jane saw a look of naked longing flash across her face before the expressionless mask fell into place again. "Tell him I can't talk right now. I'm helping Jane clean up."

Chris shook her head, continuing to extend the phone. "Calla, he never calls my phone. You know he really wants to hear your voice. Tell him yourself."

"No." Calla shrank into herself, turning away from her mother.

Chris heaved an exasperated sigh. She lifted the phone to her ear and said, "Erik? Could you hear that? Calla refuses to take the phone."

"Mom!" It was a cry of outrage. "You didn't have to say that."

Chris, still on the phone, ignored her daughter. "Yes, I'll tell her. Bye." She ended the call. "I'm not lying for you," she said to Calla. "Your dad says he'd like you to call him back when you want to talk."

Calla huffed, but she didn't speak, and after a moment, Chris turned and left the room.

"French toast for breakfast," Jane called after her. "It'll be ready about nine."

"Thank you." Chris's footsteps could be heard mounting the steps.

A moment later, Calla looked over at Jane. "You know about my dad's new baby."

Jane nodded. "Yes."

Calla fell silent again. But after another moment, she blurted, "He never comes to see me anymore. He's so busy with that baby. All he does is send pictures that my mom tries to make me look at, like yesterday." She made a sound of disgust from the back of her throat. "I don't want to look at that stupid baby."

How was she supposed to reply to that? Jane could hear the suppressed anguish beneath Calla's poor attempt at aloof indifference.

Before she could formulate a diplomatic response, Calla muttered, "He doesn't care about me anymore."

Now that, Jane realized, she did have an answer for—in the form of a question. "If he doesn't care about you anymore, why is he sending you pictures and emails and calling to talk to you?"

Calla hunched her shoulders, staring at the floor. "He didn't get me at Thanksgiving like he was supposed to. And he said he didn't know if I could come after Christmas."

Jane stared at the slight figure radiating misery and angst. She sighed. "I bet your dad feels terrible about that."

And then Jane had an idea. If Calla wouldn't look at pictures of her sister, maybe she'd be curious enough to look at generic babies. She finished rinsing the rags she'd used to clean up and tossed them into a basket in the pantry to be washed later.

"You know," she said conversationally to Calla, "I don't really know much about premature babies. I think I'll go do a little research so I can imagine what your new sister is like." She turned and left the room.

In the office, she booted up the computer and googled PREMATURE BABIES. Calla trailed along behind her and hovered in the doorway.

"You're welcome to join me," Jane said, striving for an offhand tone of voice as she first went to the March of Dimes site. She began to read silently, aware that Calla had come to stand at the corner of the desk.

"Anything interesting?" Calla asked, echoing Jane's tone.

Jane shrugged. "It says there are four stages of prematurity. Do you know how many weeks early your sister was born?"

Calla shrugged. "Like eleven, I think."

"Okay," Jane said. "So she was born around twenty-nine weeks' gestation."

"What's ges-gestation?"

Jane thought for a moment. "The stages of how the baby develops from the beginning up until it's born. A normal baby is born after about forty weeks' gestation, so one born at twenty-nine weeks is less developed. A lot less developed, actually." She pointed at the screen. "This says they are taken care of in the NICU, which stands for Neonatal Intensive Care Unit." She pronounced the acronym as a word: "Nik-yoo."

"NICU," Calla said. "My grandma was in intensive care when she had a heart attack."

Jane nodded. "Very similar, except this is just for premature babies."

"What do they do with them?"

Jane scrolled down the page. "They feed them, usually through special tubes, and they weigh them to be sure they are gaining. They keep them warm in incubators, check their breathing and heart rates with the help of monitors, and give medicines if the baby needs them. They're trained to watch for certain medical problems that premature babies often have. Would you like to look at some pictures?" Jane held her breath, afraid she might have pushed too hard.

But Calla nodded.

Jane scrolled back to the top of her search results and clicked on IMAGES, and instantly the screen filled with babies. Tiny babies. Babies in incubators. Babies with wires and tubes and monitors attached to many parts of their fragile-looking little bodies.

"Jeepers." Calla leaned closer to the screen. "They're tiny. Look at that one!" She pointed to a picture of a mother's index finger with an infant's miniscule fingers curled lightly over it. "And that one," of an adult hand cradling two itsy-bitsy feet. Another picture showed a father's wedding ring on the upper arm of his preemie child.

"They really are itty-bitty," Jane said. "That's why they have to stay in the NICU for a long time until they develop enough to come home."

"My dad's baby was born after Halloween," Calla said.

Jane nodded. "And now it's almost Christmas, so I bet she's getting close to being big and strong enough to come home."

"I didn't get to see her when she was born," Calla said. "They wouldn't let kids come in the NICU, because they were afraid of the flu." Her voice was aggrieved.

Jane nodded. "I guess the flu could probably kill a pree-mie. They have to be very careful."

"But I'm not sick. I never even got the flu," protested Calla.

Jane couldn't help grinning. "And I guess you could tell in your crystal ball you weren't carrying any flu germs."

Calla grinned too. "Okay, I get it. They can't take any chances."

"That's right," Jane said. "Can you imagine what the flu would do to a teeny little thing like that?" She pointed at the screen.

"Dad told Mom he could hardly get Claudia to go home long enough to sleep and shower. Did my dad have to stay there all the time too?" Calla sounded genuinely curious rather than resentful for the first time.

"Not all the time," Jane said. "I wouldn't think. But see here, it says they encourage parents to practice 'kangaroo care' for at least one uninterrupted hour a day for the first three months of life."

"What's kangaroo care?"

"The baby wears only a diaper and is placed on the bare chest of the mother, father, grandparent, sister, or other caregiver and snuggled close. It says you should do this with premature and very young infants as much as possible to stimulate brain development and other health benefits. So I imagine your dad has helped with that so that your step-mom could get some rest, which is really important for new moms. And also, I imagine he has a job that he had to go to?"

Calla nodded. "He's an engineer for a software company."

"So he might have had some time off, but he maybe risked losing his job if he didn't go back after a short time, I bet. And he probably has insurance which he needs for the baby's care."

"Mine too," Calla said. "My health care is through his job."

Calla was silent for a moment, studying the pictures of moms, dads, and even what looked like a grandma or two practicing kangaroo care with babies. Then she laughed, pointing at a photo in which a woman was reading a book with a baby snuggled beneath a blanket on her chest. "Hey, I could read and do that at the same time!"

Jane chuckled too. "I bet you could. And I bet your stepmom and dad would be thrilled to have a third person to help out."

Calla was silent. Jane returned her attention to the screen, going back to the images she'd first pulled up of the tiny infants.

"That one fits in one hand," Calla marveled, pointing. "How can they be that small and still be alive?"

Calla clearly had no real concept, Jane realized, of what her father and Claudia had been going through. How could she? She had refused to look at any of the pictures Chris had shown Jane of Calla's tiny baby sister with multiple tubes in an incubator or of the gloved and gowned parents who finally got to hold the little one after the first days.

"She's growing," Jane said, "and if this information is correct, she'll probably be able to come home pretty soon." She wanted to add, *So if you want to hold her, you'd better get over to your dad's*, but she bit her tongue firmly.

Then another thought came to her. "What would you have liked your dad to do when the baby was born so early?" she asked. "For you, I mean."

Calla hesitated. Shrugged. "Claudia gave me a picture album that says BIG SISTER on it so I'll have a place just for pictures of me and the baby together."

Jane melted a little. Claudia sounded like a good person. "I'm sorry you didn't get to go to their house at Thanksgiving."

"Dad was at the hospital," Calla said. "He told Mom they ate in the hospital cafeteria and didn't even have a real Thanksgiving. In an email, you know. 'Cause they don't talk much."

A sensitive spot for a sensitive child, Jane realized. "Ah. So what else could he have done?"

Calla shrugged again, a defensive twitch of her shoulders. "He and Claudia sent me a book about being a big sister when she was born. But I don't feel like one."

"So even though he was busy with a new baby, he sent you something."

Calla frowned. "Yeah."

"But I guess you really haven't seen or heard from him since then," Jane mused, knowing her words were false.

"He emails," Calla reminded her. "And he calls, but..." Her voice trailed away. "I guess he can't really go too far away when she's that little," she finally said.

"It would be scary," Jane agreed. "I imagine he'd want to be close in case something happened." Calla appeared to finally be realizing that she was, in essence, forcing her father to choose between her and a new baby in uncertain health.

"Do you think she could die?" Calla sounded very subdued.

"Oh honey, I don't know for sure, but I don't think so," Jane said. "The first couple weeks were probably really scary for your dad and stepmom, but it sounds like things are going as well as they could be. Your mom told me a little bit about it earlier. Your little sister is receiving excellent care. It's just that she's still very, very little and fragile, and that's why she's been in an intensive care unit where they can watch her all the time." She extended an arm, and Calla approached, allowing Jane to draw her into the curve of her arm as the child perched on the arm of her chair. "There are really good doctors and nurses now who are specially trained to work with premature babies, and most of them survive and do just fine."

Chapter Seven

On Thursday evening, Jane asked Alice if she, Chris, and Calla could accompany Alice's ANGELs on their annual Christmas caroling tour. Calla was about the same age as some of the younger ANGELs, and Jane thought they all might enjoy it. Although the responsibility for the group was Alice's, Louise often went along to lead the group in their carol singing, and Jane felt certain she would welcome them.

Calla was excited about going caroling, but as they joined the group milling about outside Grace Chapel Inn, she quietly walked along between Jane and her mother, glancing around at all the girls giggling and greeting each other, but making no attempt to interact with them. Louise had walked along with them but then broke off to join the adult singers who would be helping to lead the girls.

Alice's gaze met Jane's, and Jane could see that her sister had sized up the situation accurately.

"Linsey?" Alice beckoned to a girl who looked to be one of the younger ANGELs. Jane knew the girls were generally between eleven and fourteen, so this girl was probably not much older than Calla. "This is our friend Calla who's visiting for Christmas. Calla, this is Linsey Arlow. She just joined our group."

"Hi." Linsey smiled at Calla. "Want to come meet some of the other girls?"

"Sure." Calla sounded anything but certain, but she went willingly with Linsey and soon was absorbed into the chattering mass of girls.

Under Alice's direction, the group walked from the church to a number of nearby homes where elderly members of the congregation who rarely got out of their homes lived. The families of those folks had been alerted to watch for the carolers, and at home after home, doors were flung wide or window curtains opened to show white-haired residents beaming and clapping as the carolers shared the good tidings of the Christmas season.

The fourth house at which they stopped was the home of Martha Bevins, an older member of the congregation who had recently broken a hip. Although she was already up and walking with a walker, she was still homebound much of the time. As the ANGELs and their chaperones began to sing "Silent Night," Martha maneuvered her walker onto her front porch, her husband hovering behind her like a protective nanny.

As the sweet soprano voices sang the familiar hymn, Jane could not help but think of Christ's birth in a whole new light. She'd been immersed in talk of babies, of how fragile the tiny lives were. Giving birth in a stable, wrapping the baby in ragged lengths of cloth and laying Him in an animals' feed trough filled with straw suddenly became very real and, if Jane was honest, rather appalling. What enormous trust Mary must have placed in God to have gone through such an ordeal as a first-time mother, Jane realized. She wondered how a very young, probably uneducated woman of extremely modest means could have faced her fate with such equanimity.

What unwavering faith, Jane thought in awe, as the song's final strains filled the air. She must have truly believed in the promise God had made to her.

"...*Jesus, Lord, at Thy birth,*
Jesus, Lord, at Thy birth."

On Friday morning, Jane made a new recipe for breakfast. First, she made pizza dough and cut it into six-inch circles. She placed them on baking trays lined with parchment, used her thumbs to create a slight border around each one, and sprinkled them with cornmeal.

Next she turned her attention to a skillet in which she heated spinach leaves in olive oil until they just began to wilt around the edges. Removing the skillet from the heat, she combined the spinach with Parmesan cheese, sour cream, minced garlic, sea salt, and a pinch of black pepper, and then she spread the spinach mixture over each of her dough circles and popped the trays into the oven for five minutes.

Calla came into the kitchen close to eight, just as the timer dinged.

"Good morning," Jane said with a smile as she pulled the baking sheets from the oven.

"Morning," Calla returned. "Yum. What's for breakfast?"

"Breakfast pizzas," Jane said cheerily. She decided maybe it wasn't the best idea to tell a ten-year-old they had spinach in them, and she grinned to herself as Calla made appreciative lip-smacking noises at the sight of the baked crusts.

"What are you planning to do today?" Jane asked as she broke two extra-large eggs into the center of each circle of dough. She stuck the trays back into the oven to bake until the egg whites were set and the yellows were still runny.

Calla shrugged. "I don't know. Mom talked about going to Hershey for the day."

"Oh, I bet that would be fun," Jane said. "They decorate the park, and some of the rides stay open. I don't think it's supposed to be super-cold today, so it probably would be a good day for it."

"They have rides open in the winter?" Calla looked surprised.

"They do," Jane said with a grin. "And if you stay until it gets dark, you'll get to see all the lights come on, and there's a light show set to music."

"Good morning. That's nice to hear." Chris came into the kitchen.

"Good morning," Jane said. She checked the timer she'd reset. "Breakfast in five."

"Perfect," said Chris. "Any other Hershey Park tips we should know about? I thought we'd leave around ten thirty and do the Chocolate World tour before we go to the park."

"Oh, you absolutely should," Jane said. She thought for a moment. "Make sure you see Santa's reindeer. And there's a wonderful little stand called Simply Chocolate near the bumper cars that sells terrific goodies. They sell a cookie decorating kit that you can use right there while you eat if you like."

"How do you know all that?" Calla sounded suspicious.

Jane grinned. "I went along with the church youth group last year as a chaperone." As she carried orange juice and fruit cups into the dining room, she told them, "ZooAmerica is part of the park, so you can visit the zoo while you're there too. And before you come home, you should do the driving tour of the Hershey Sweet Lights display. They have over six hundred animated light displays that are absolutely fantastic!"

Chris looked at Calla and grinned. "Sounds like we'd better eat a good breakfast. We're going to be packing a lot into this day."

Jane's timer signaled that it was time to take the breakfast pizzas from the oven. Hurrying back to the kitchen, she pulled out the trays and sprinkled additional Parmesan over each pizza. Alice and Louise had come into the kitchen and were assembling their own breakfast as Jane carried the pizza platter to the dining room table. Their other three guests had joined them this morning, and after greeting everyone and serving coffee and tea, Jane withdrew to the kitchen to eat with her sisters.

Louise offered to clean up the kitchen afterward, and Alice had to get ready for a shift at the hospital. Jane headed upstairs to find Chris and Calla. She'd had an idea.

She knocked on Chris's door and smiled when Chris opened it. "Did you two bring Christmas stockings with you? I know you won't be rushing off to visit family on Christmas Day, and I'd like to help you make it as much like your normal celebration as possible."

Chris shook her head. "I didn't even think about it, and I'm annoyed with myself, because at home we always hang our stockings on Christmas Eve. I did get a few little things to put in them, thinking maybe I could buy some today."

"Well," Jane said, "I was thinking of making some, and if Calla would like, she can help me before you leave this morning."

Chris's eyes widened in astonished delight. "Really? That would be wonderful! You know, Jane, you should charge for your services. You're far more than just a hostess. You're an event planner, a crafts coordinator, and a baking instructor all rolled into one!"

Jane laughed as Calla followed her from the room. "We'll be down in the library," she told Chris.

"I made a bookmark to put in Mom's stocking," Calla said. "I brought it along, but then I figured I'd just have to give it to her the way it is. This will be so much better!"

Jane had placed a box of craft supplies on the library table that occupied one end of the room. Together, she and Calla pulled out felt, a hot glue gun, scissors, glitter glue, shiny beads, sequins, and more from the box.

"I have an idea," Calla said. "I'll make Mom's, and you can make mine."

"Sounds like a good plan." Jane held up the pattern for the stocking. "First we need to pin this to the felt and cut around it. What color do you want your stockings to be?"

"White for Mom's," Calla said. "I'm going to put a Christmas tree on it. And red for mine, please."

"All right. I'm going to give you an angel on yours. Sound okay?"

"Sounds pretty!" Calla said enthusiastically.

The pair set to work, wielding pins, scissors, hot glue, and decorations.

Midway through the process, Calla's mother came to the door of the library. "This looks industrious," she remarked.

"Don't look at mine!" Calla said, shielding her work with her body.

Chris turned away. "All right." She held up several papers she was carrying in one hand. "I only came to borrow Jane for a minute." Turning to Jane, she said, "I have a couple of pictures I printed out of Calla's little sister. After we talked yesterday, I thought you'd like to see the newest ones."

"I'd love to," Jane said. She moved to Chris's side, aware that Calla had gone very still at her end of the table.

"Oh, this is adorable," Jane said, as Chris handed her the first picture. "Where on earth did they find a hat that tiny?"

"Erik's mother probably made it," Chris said. "She knits all the time. She made something similar when Calla was born." The hat in question was pale pink with a pink flower attached slightly off center.

"My grandma's a really good knitter," Calla announced. "She made me a sweater for school. All my friends wanted one."

"She's growing," Jane said. "She looks different from those first pictures I saw. Her little cheeks have filled out, and her eyes are bright. Oh, look at this." She almost cooed as Chris handed her a picture of the infant nestled in her father's arms. She was looking up at him as if he was the most wonderful thing she'd ever seen. "What's her name?" Jane asked, realizing that she'd never heard it mentioned.

"Camellia Rae," Chris said.

Calla, Jane was aware, was concentrating fiercely on her work. But she hadn't gotten angry and left the room, which was a victory in Jane's mind.

Handing the pictures back to Chris with a smile, Jane thought it was time to change the subject while things were going well. "Thank you for sharing those. Earlier, you said Christmas stockings were one of your traditions. Are there others you'd like to observe?"

"We go to church on Christmas Eve," Chris told her. "How about you?"

"Oh yes," Jane said. "You're welcome to attend Grace Chapel with us. Our father was the pastor there for thirty years. After church, we always came home and got out milk and cookies for Santa and carrots for the reindeer, and then he'd read the Christmas story from Luke. We still do that every year. And on Christmas Day, we open gifts together in the morning and then at midday, we have a feast and invite any friends and neighbors who don't have other plans. If you'd like to join us, you'll know my aunt, Ethel, who was at the craft open house, and maybe a few others."

"That sounds lovely," Chris said. "Calla, would you like to join them?"

"Yes, please. That sounds nice," Calla said, still concentrating on the stocking she was making.

Jane got back to work on hers, and before long, the stockings were finished.

"Can we hang them?" Calla asked eagerly.

Jane grinned. "Sure. Let me find two extra stocking hooks, and you go get your mom so she can see them."

They met in the parlor, where Louise's, Alice's, and Jane's stockings were already hanging. Jane produced two clear acrylic hangers shaped like large letter *C*'s, weighted at the top so they would hang right from a mantel.

Calla and Chris each slipped their stockings onto the hangers as Jane moved the three sisters' stockings over so that all five could be evenly spaced above the fireplace. She rearranged the greenery and lights lying across the top of the mantel to disguise the hooks.

Calla clapped her hands as they stepped back, surveying the festive scene. "It looks wonderful!"

"Indeed it does," Jane said, happy with her idea.

"I'm going to go clean up our things," Calla announced. She turned and left the parlor, and they could hear her moving along the hallway back to the library.

"Thank you," Jane called after her.

Chris shook her head, grinning. "I may need to kidnap you to come home with us, Jane. You've had such a positive influence on her."

Jane smiled. "I wish you lived close. She's delightful. She's almost old enough to be one of Alice's ANGELs too, which I know she'd enjoy."

Chris nodded. "At home she participates in a club for gifted kids and sings in the school choir and plays soccer. She's a social child, usually, although since Thanksgiving these unpredictable moods have been getting in the way of that. But I'm taking it as a positive sign that I was able to show you those pictures earlier without her having a meltdown. If only her father would find the time to visit. I think that's what she really needs—reassurance from him directly."

Jane adjusted some more of the greenery over the mantel. "This is a terribly stressful time for all of you," she said diplomatically.

Chris sighed. "Her dad has been much better in the past two years, and I'm hoping this is just a temporary glitch. I imagine I'd be a basket case too if that was my baby attached to all those monitors and I had to leave the hospital without her."

"That would be difficult," Jane affirmed quietly. After their conversation the previous day, she was glad Chris was able to see a different perspective.

"I'm not a very nice person," the younger woman confessed. "Part of me resents the time Erik has given to this new baby because of how it's upset Calla, even though I know having a preemie must be a frightening experience, and I'd want to be there all the time too if I was in his place."

"But you'd never forget about Calla."

"I'd never forget about Calla." She nodded. "And it made me angry, because I thought he had. Except now I have to admit he really hasn't. Other than visiting, which would have meant he'd have had to be away from the hospital for most of a day, he's been surprisingly attentive. He's sent Calla gifts, emailed her pictures at least once a day, tried to call. So I can't say he's been ignoring her. In fact, I suspect he feels really guilty about not seeing her. We don't really talk, so I don't know that for a fact, but..."

Jane also remembered the awkwardness that had grown between her former husband and her as they'd lost the closeness they'd once had and become nothing more than strangers with a slight acquaintance. "It's a hard thing, having a marriage fail," she mused. "I had no children, so when my ex and I grew apart, there was no reason for us to ever see each other again. I think it must be so much more difficult when you share children, having to see and speak to this person who once was your best friend in the whole world, the person you told your darkest fears and your greatest triumphs to, and who shared everything with you."

Chris sighed. "That's it in a nutshell. Aside from all the other feelings, the loss of the person who was once your safety net and your confidante is really hard. Sometimes I want to share things about Calla—not big, important things, just some little funny or cute or touching thing—and I have no one to tell. That's the hardest thing about sharing a child with an ex, I believe. And since you're forced to see them and speak to them occasionally, that's salt in the divorce wound that makes it harder to heal. I try to avoid it at all costs."

Jane shook her head. "I would not enjoy having to speak with or see my ex regularly again. But if I had children, I might feel it was important to put a good face on for the child's sake. Maybe."

Chris made a face. "You're right, and you're very nice not to lecture me about it. I haven't been thinking about what's best for Calla."

Jane didn't think she needed to comment on the subject anymore. She gestured toward the hallway. "Shall we go help Calla?"

Chris nodded. "Thanks again for the stockings. We always hang stockings at home, and I just forgot about bringing them. All her gifts are in the trunk of my car, and I'm going to put them under the tree you so thoughtfully helped us find."

Chapter Eight

Christmas Eve was one of Jane's favorite days of the year. She rose early on Saturday morning to make her pumpkin pies for their Christmas feast, and once those were in the oven, she started on an apple pie. It wasn't just any old apple pie though. A friend from culinary school had gifted her a recipe from her own grandmother for a cranberry-apple pie with a tasty almond-laced crust.

When she turned down the oven temperature for the pumpkin pies, she placed the apple pie in the oven as well. Then she turned her attention to her final pie, a tasty pecan she'd often baked when she was a chef in California. Pecan pie wasn't the popular dessert staple in Pennsylvania that it was across the South, but people loved it, and she made it at least once a year.

The pumpkin pies and the cranberry-apple pie finished baking just about the time she finished placing the last of the pecans in concentric circles to decorate the top of the pie. Placing it in the oven, she turned to greet Alice, who had just walked into the kitchen, yawning.

"Yum," Alice said. "Too bad we can't have that for breakfast."

Jane laughed. "Sorry. But I was planning to make waffles with blueberry compote and lemon ricotta cream."

To her surprise, Alice's eyebrows rose doubtfully. "Blueberry and lemon? Sounds rather pucker-y to me."

Jane laughed. "Trust me, you'll love them. Want me to fire up the waffle iron now?"

"You're feeding our guests at nine, right?" Alice asked. She glanced at the clock, which read a few minutes after eight. "I don't want you to have to make two breakfasts. Besides, I could use your help with my ANGELs project first, if you're game."

"Sure. What project?"

Alice pointed to a stack of miniature red plastic cups stacked on the counter. "You know that big spider plant in my room that's loaded with babies? I've clipped off some of them, and I want to give them to the ANGELs as Christmas gifts. I'm going to plant them in these cups and tie a pretty ribbon around each one."

"What a lovely idea," Jane said. "We had the same idea this year."

"You were my inspiration," Alice said. "You've been tending those little Christmas cacti for weeks now."

While Alice went upstairs to get the spider plant cuttings, Jane set out eleven of the little red cups. According to Alice, there were eleven girls currently in the group.

When Alice returned carrying a wide vase with a bunch of baby spider plants crammed into it, keeping their roots wet in the water, she said, "Let's make an even dozen. I thought I'd give one to our young guest too."

Jane smiled. "Nice idea."

"She seemed to enjoy herself last night," Alice said.

Jane nodded. "Her mother said she sings in a choir, so I imagine she felt at home."

Just then, the object of their conversation came rushing into the room, red curls bouncing. "Hi! It's Christmas Eve. Hey, what are you doing? Can I help?"

Alice laughed and put an affectionate arm around Calla's shoulders. "We could use your assistance. We're going to plant these spider plants in the little red cups and decorate them with pretty Christmas ribbon. They are gifts for my ANGELs, the girls we caroled with last night."

"That was fun," Calla said. "I wish we could do it again."

"Perhaps you and your mom will come back and celebrate Christmas with us again," Jane said, "and you can."

The three of them spooned potting soil from a large bucket into the little cups and gently planted a pretty green-and-white-striped spider plant in each before giving them a bit of water. "Not too much," Jane cautioned. "We don't want them swimming. That will rot the roots."

After all the spider plants were potted and the soil cleared away and cleaned up, the trio worked together to glue the ribbon around the top of each cup and tie it with a festive bow. Alice had glitter-encrusted Christmas ribbon in shades of silver, gold, and green that enhanced the little gifts. Finally, they placed them all in a wide, flat basket Jane used to gather produce from the gardens during the summer.

"I'll give these out at the Christmas Eve service tonight," Alice said. "I'm certain all the ANGELs will be there."

"I need to get breakfast started for the guests," Jane said.

"Can I help?" Calla asked.

"Sure." Jane grinned at her. "First, we should set the table, since this is a meal preparation that requires a lot of attention once we get started."

Together, they trooped into the dining room with flat-ware, cups and saucers, and small bread-and-butter plates.

They left the breakfast plates in the kitchen so Jane could prepare and serve each waffle meal individually.

Jane showed Calla how to set a proper place setting, with the fork at the left and the knife and spoon on the right. "The blade of the knife always goes toward the plate," Jane instructed, laying one down in proper position to show Calla. "Then the bread-and-butter plate goes above the forks, and the coffee cup and saucer is set to the right of your spoons."

"Are we having bread and butter along with the waffles?" Calla asked.

Jane laughed. "No, because the waffles are already all the bread we need. But the bread-and-butter plate can be used to place your serving of butter on so you can pass the butter dish to the next person and not need to ask for it back." She pointed. "You decide how much butter you think you're going to want on your waffles and place it here."

They returned to the kitchen for water and juice glasses, which Jane carried in on a tray. "The water glass is the larger one," Jane instructed. "That one goes right above the knife. The smaller one is for juice, and it is placed just to the right and down a tad from the water glass, sort of between the water glass and the coffee cup."

"I don't drink coffee," Calla said.

"In that case," Jane told her, "if you're ever in a nice restaurant, you just turn your coffee cup upside down on the saucer, and the server will remove it. But you may wish to keep it if you'd like, say, hot chocolate or tea." She went to the graceful mahogany buffet that stood against one wall and opened a drawer, withdrawing five cloth napkins for the guests' place settings. "Here. I'll show you a pretty way to fold a napkin."

"Jane?"

"Yes?"

"After breakfast, would you look at pictures of my baby sister with me?"

Jane's hands stilled on the napkins. "Sure."

"I mean," Calla rushed on, "since we looked at those other babies yesterday, I kind of want to see how she looked when she was born. If she had tubes and stuff, you know?"

"I get it," Jane said. She wanted to clasp her hands above her head and shake them like a prize fighter, but she quelled the urge to celebrate. Looking at pictures was a start, but it certainly wasn't acceptance. "So this is called a napkin ring." She forced herself to continue the impromptu lesson and not make a big deal of Calla's request. "I'll show you how to fold the napkin into pleats, pull it halfway through the ring, and then lay it on the plate and fan out the top and bottom."

After the table was set, they returned to the kitchen. Jane showed Calla how to zest lemon and whisk it with ricotta cheese and other ingredients. After that was placed in the refrigerator, Calla helped her simmer blueberries in water and honey until the mixture thickened and they could add a little lemon juice.

"Now we make the waffles," Jane said.

Calla helped her measure dry ingredients in one bowl and wet ones in another. They mixed the two well, and then combined them.

"It needs to rest for fifteen minutes," Jane told her young assistant. "We'll heat up the waffle iron, and then we should have just enough time to put water, juice, and butter on the table before we whip up these fabulous waffles."

"This is fun," Calla said. "Maybe I'll be a chef on the side when I grow up."

"On the side?" Jane queried.

Calla nodded. "Because I want to be a veterinarian, remember?"

"Oh, right," Jane said. "You could always just cook for fun, like a hobby. I imagine being a veterinarian will keep you pretty busy."

"Or I could do both part-time," Calla said, her eyes dreamy.

Jane smiled to herself, thinking of how wonderful it was to be a child with all your dreams still intact and all your options ahead of you. "All right, part-time chef," she said. "Let's finish in the dining room and then get cracking on our waffles."

When they returned to the kitchen, Jane turned the oven on low, and they filled the waffle iron repeatedly, cooking a golden-brown mound of waffles.

"Mom's in the dining room, and so are the other people," Calla reported. "I told them we'd have breakfast on the table momentarily."

Amused, Jane nodded. "Momentarily sounds about right. Lay out those five plates in a row, please."

Calla scurried to line up the plates, and Jane placed two waffles on each one. She topped each with the blueberry compote and a dollop of lemon ricotta and instructed Calla to sprinkle a garnish of lemon zest over each.

"There!" Jane said. "These are works of art. You bring two and I'll bring two, and then you can come back for your own."

Calla picked up two of the plates. "I'll serve my mom."

The guests were suitably impressed by Calla's explanation of how they'd made breakfast together. Jane smiled as she left the little redhead regaling them with the details.

Back in the kitchen, Jane found Louise pouring coffee while Alice made herself a cup of Earl Grey tea with a slice of lemon. "I've still got enough waffles for us if you'd like some," Jane told them.

Alice smiled. "I was hoping you'd say that. I caught a glimpse of those plates you carried in. What a gorgeous meal."

Jane quickly assembled three more plates for her sisters and herself, and they enjoyed their own blueberry compote and lemon ricotta waffles before Louise departed to practice the music for the Christmas Eve service and Alice headed for a shift at the hospital.

After breakfast, Calla had the promised hot chocolate, and then she moved right back into assistant mode, helping to clear the table and load the dishwasher. Between them, they had the kitchen spick-and-span again in no time.

"Want to look at pictures now?" Calla asked indifferently, although she was practically squirming with impatience by the time the last pot had been washed and set in the drainer to dry.

"I'd love to," Jane said honestly.

"Let me tell my mom we need her computer." Calla dashed from the room.

A few moments later, Chris appeared with her laptop cradled in one arm. "Calla says you two are going to look at some of the baby's pictures," she said to Jane, an inquiring look in her eyes.

Jane nodded. "Would you like to join us?"

"Only if it's okay with Calla," Chris said. "Let's go in the dining room."

Calla headed for the door into the dining room. "Sure. Yesterday, me and Jane looked at a bunch of pictures of premature babies, and I want to see if ours looks like them. Mom, did you know they have to get food through tubes in their noses?" She shook her head in disbelief. "I wonder why they don't drown. Doesn't air go through your nose into your lungs?"

"It does," Jane said, as Chris set the laptop on the mahogany table, and the three of them drew up chairs close together.

"But in the back of your throat, there's also a tube called the esophagus that your food goes down to get to your stomach. So that's where a nasal feeding tube is placed."

"Wow. Weird," Calla whispered. She turned to her mother. "Did my sister have one of those?"

Chris nodded. "For a while. But now she's big enough to drink milk on her own." She turned on the laptop and tapped the touchpad several times until she opened the folder in her Pictures folder labeled Calla's sister.

The screen immediately began to populate photos. One row, two rows, and more and more.

"There's a lot of pictures!" Calla said.

Chris nodded. "Your dad didn't want you to miss anything, so he sent a lot of pictures. Would you like to start at the very beginning?"

Calla glanced at Jane. "Well, yeah, I guess. Just so we can see how much she looks like those other pictures, right?"

"Right," Jane said, but inside, she was doing a happy dance again.

In the beginning, the baby looked so tiny and fragile it made Jane's heart hurt, even though she'd seen some of the pictures once already and thought she was prepared. Her parents, prevented from holding her by the need to keep her in the warm, humid air of the incubator, were reduced to sticking their hands through ports in the side where they could do little but touch her tiny fingers.

But as the days passed, pictures showed them learning how to weigh her, how to change the doll-size disposable diapers she wore, how to adjust the wires and monitors that became dislodged as she was repositioned.

On the ninth day there was a photograph that brought tears to Jane's eyes of a beaming young mother carefully cradling the tiny infant. Jane could only imagine how that moment felt after so many minutes and hours of waiting. "Look," she said, pointing at the baby's tiny head, which was uncovered in one photo later that week. "She's definitely got reddish hair like you, Calla."

Calla rolled her eyes, clearly trying to look cool and unconcerned. "She's gonna get called 'carrottop.'"

Soon another week had passed, and there were photos of Erik holding his daughter for the first time, smiling widely. In one hand, he held up a sticky note with something written on it.

"What's that say?" Calla asked.

Chris zoomed in on the image, pulling the little piece of paper into higher focus.

We miss you, Calla was followed by a large heart. *Wish you could be here too.*

"Oh, that's a keeper," Jane said without thinking.

Calla didn't say a word. She reached out and tapped the screen to return the image to normal size and then moved on to the next photo.

Chapter Nine

Only a few days ago, Jane reflected, Calla would have reacted angrily to the sight of her father holding up a note saying he missed her. Then again, only a few days ago, she would have refused to so much as glance at such a picture, so progress had been made. But judging from the unhappy look on Calla's face as they continued to scroll through the photos, it was far from a complete transition.

"What's that picture?" Calla finally asked. They had looked at pictures of bath time, of Erik reading a book to Camellia, who was still in an incubator, of him and Claudia practicing kangaroo care in a large rocker beside her incubator, and more.

"That's one of the regular baby cribs they use in the hospital," Chris told Calla. "It has clear sides and is attached to the top of a set of drawers on wheels with a place for diapers, extra blankets, baby clothes, and things like that. You were in one when you were a baby. About five weeks ago they decided she was big enough to come out of the incubator and sleep in there."

"Whoa." Calla's rusty-red eyebrows shot up. "So why couldn't she just come home then?"

"She had to stay in the incubator until she could regulate her own temperature, meaning her body would cool down without a heat source. But even once that happened, she still wasn't taking all her feedings by mouth. She weighs about four pounds in this picture, a whole pound bigger than when she was born. She has eight kangaroo care times every day, every three hours around the clock. I believe your stepmother is committed to being there for all but the midnight, three a.m., and six a.m. times, and your dad goes every morning before work and every evening when he gets off."

"Oh my goodness," Jane said. "That's an exhausting schedule."

Chris nodded. "I can't imagine it. She's seven weeks old today, so they've been running back and forth to the hospital now for about fifty days. Hopefully, that won't last much longer."

"But she's still wearing a monitor thingy even though she's in a normal bed." Calla pointed to the wires snaking out from beneath the little outfit the infant wore.

Chris nodded. "She was still having times when she would stop breathing on her own. I think she still is."

"How do you know so much about her?" Calla asked her mother.

Chris shrugged. "Your father sends pictures almost every day, and he usually writes a little update. I put all the written notes in a separate file for you, in case you ever want to read about how Camellia grew during those early days. I remember most of it pretty well right now."

"Camellia's a stupid name," Calla said. "Why did they choose such a weird name?"

"Calla Renee!" Her mother was frowning. "That's a terrible thing to say."

"Wait." Jane's attention had been caught by the name. "Calla, it's a flower name, just like yours."

"A calla's a lily," Calla said. "A camellia is a lily too?"

"Not a lily but a beautiful flower that grows on a large bush," Jane said. "And what's more, your dad and step-mother chose to remember you in *two* ways when they named your sister."

"We both have flower names. What's the other one?" Calla asked, her brow wrinkling in thought.

"What's your middle name?" Jane asked.

"Renee."

"What's her middle name?"

"Rae."

"Oh my goodness." Chris put a hand to her mouth. "Calla, I didn't even realize it. Jane's right. Camellia Rae is named for you! She—"

"She has my initials," Calla said. She paused for a moment. "Why did they do that?"

Chris smiled. "Because they love you so much they wanted to honor you by giving you a sibling who shares your initials, maybe?"

Jane wanted to hug the younger woman.

For once, Calla didn't look mutinous. She didn't look wary or annoyed or any of the ways she usually did when they began talking about her little sister. "Can we look at the rest of the pictures?" she asked quietly.

Chris obligingly returned to the pictures. "So here she is three weeks ago. They moved her out of the NICU to what they call an intermediate special care nursery. She's getting stronger every day, and this morning your father's update said they think she'll be released from the hospital very soon." She pointed to the final picture, of Camellia strapped into a car seat. "This is called the Car Seat Challenge. The baby has to be strapped into a car seat for ninety minutes, and her heart rate and breathing function can't drop during that whole time. Once that happens, she'll be scheduled for release."

"When did they do that?" Calla demanded.

"Your dad just sent that picture this morning," her mother told her.

"Did she pass?"

"I don't know."

Calla was silent, eyes still on the last photo. Finally, she said, "Mom, may I use your phone to call Dad?"

"Of course," Chris said. "It's upstairs on the nightstand beside my bed."

Without another word, Calla turned and rushed from the room. A moment later, they heard her footsteps pounding up the stairs.

Chris looked at Jane. "I believe you may be an angel in disguise."

Jane laughed. "If you say that to my sisters, they'll set you straight. I was mostly the bane of their existence when they were teenagers and I was a bratty, much younger child."

"I don't care," Chris said. "You're certainly my angel. I was beginning to think Camellia's birth had ruined Calla's life forever. I felt like there was nothing I could do to make her feel any less hurt, and it was bringing up all my old bitterness toward Erik." She paused. "I believe it's time to let that go."

Jane reached an arm around the younger woman's shoulders and hugged her gently. "All part of the service at Grace Chapel Inn," she said lightly, ignoring the way Chris was blinking furiously. She rose and slid her chair beneath the table. "I've got some preparation to make for tomorrow's dinner. We'll have several guests joining us, and you and Calla are more than welcome to eat with us as well. We'll be attending church in the morning, so I plan to have the meal ready around two. Oh, and there's also a candlelight Christmas Eve service tonight. I'd love for you to join us for that."

"Thank you," Chris said. "We didn't make any specific plans yet for this evening, but we were hoping to attend church. What time does the service begin?"

"Seven thirty," Jane said, "but the special music starts around seven, so we'll be leaving to get seats at six thirty. It will be standing room only by seven."

"Gracious me," Chris said. "We'll be ready."

Just then, a clattering on the stairs alerted them to Calla's return. "Mom!" she shouted, dashing into the dining room and sliding to a halt. "Guess what?" Jane noticed she held her mother's phone in her hand. "Camellia passed her car seat test, and she's supposed to go home the day after tomorrow. Dad wants me to come visit then. Can I go?"

Chris was smiling at her daughter. "Of course you can."

Calla put the phone back to her ear. "Mom says yes." Then she added to her mother, "But I might not want to stay long if the baby cries a lot."

Obviously startled, Chris said, "I had no idea your father was still on the phone."

"He wants to talk to you." Calla held out the phone. "Here." She handed the phone to her mother. "Hey, Jane, remember when you said I could have some of those Christmas cactus thingies you grew in the basement?"

"I do," Jane said, drawing Calla into the kitchen to give Chris a little privacy.

"Merry Christmas a day early," she heard Chris say into the phone. "I'm glad to hear things are going well."

Jane smiled to herself as she answered Calla's question. "The offer still stands. How many do you need?"

"Two. One for my mom, and I guess I'd better take one for my dad and stepmom. And the baby, although she's too little to care. Do I have to take her a gift, do you think?"

"That might be a thoughtful, big sisterly idea," Jane said.

"What do you think she'd like? She's too little for almost everything."

"Babies don't see very well after they're first born, and since Camellia's going to come home before the real date she was supposed to be born, I bet it's going to take a little while for her vision to get better. I went to a baby shower not long ago where someone gave the mother-to-be a set of square cards with black-and-white patterns on them to show to her baby. What if you made something like that? We could put Velcro on the back and make a ribbon with Velcro on it so it could be attached to the side of a crib or something, and if you made a few extra cards, you'd be able to switch them out so Camellia would have different patterns to look at."

"I like that idea!" Calla said. "But I don't have any paper or anything."

Jane grinned. "Don't worry. I am the queen of craft stuff. I have some white poster board you can paint your black patterns on, and I have Velcro and ribbon. Couldn't be easier."

Jane got Calla set up at the kitchen table with six-inch poster board squares they cut out, black paint, and a sturdy paintbrush. A few minutes later, Chris stuck her head into the kitchen and beckoned to Jane. "Could you come here for a moment?"

Jane walked into the dining room and let the door swing shut behind her. "What's up?"

"Could the Christmas meal tomorrow stretch to one more guest?"

"Absolutely. Anyone I know?"

Chris shook her head. "Know of, but you haven't met him yet. Erik would like to join us. It's going to be a surprise for Calla. What's she up to in there anyway?"

"She's making a present for Camellia." Calla's father was coming. Jane was thrilled for the child. "So your ex is coming here?"

Chris nodded. "Claudia's parents are in town and are going to be helping at the hospital tomorrow, so she and Erik agreed he needed to come see Calla. Then Camellia's supposed to be released from the hospital on the twenty-sixth, and Erik would like Calla to leave here tomorrow with him, stay overnight, and go with them to bring Camellia home the next day. Then I'll drive up there and pick her up on the twenty-seventh, so she'll get to spend a little time with them. I'm sorry," she said. "I know we were planning on staying through New Year's, but this will mean so much to Calla. I can't say no."

"Goodness." Jane sank into one of the chairs at the table. "What a flurry of last-minute planning. That's really nice of them to include her at such a crucial time."

"It was really nice of you to take the time to show her what the journey a preemie goes through is like," Chris said. "I didn't even think about trying to explain to her how frightened they must have been those first few weeks. I just kept trying to force her to accept a new reality. But I think when you showed her the pictures of premature babies and talked about what happens with them, it became much more real to her, and she was able to see that her dad wasn't just ignoring her because he wanted to, you know?"

"I'm very thankful that it seems to have helped," Jane said. She'd felt drawn to Calla, led to share information with her. Certainly, Jane thought, there had been a higher power guiding her choices.

"Thank you," Chris said softly, "for helping to heal my daughter's bruised heart."

"You're welcome," Jane said simply, wondering if Chris realized how much her own heart had healed since she'd arrived a few days ago.

Jane served thick grilled cheese sandwiches and homemade tomato soup for supper, to which she invited Chris and Calla. All three of their other guests had family plans and had been gone much of the day, but the Rosdahls would be attending church with the sisters. It was only fitting that they break bread with them before the service.

Jane fed Wendell as soon as supper was cleaned up and then hurried upstairs to change into a soft green wool sweater and black trousers. She draped a black and green woven scarf around her neck and dashed back downstairs to join Alice, Louise, Chris, and Calla for the short walk to the church.

"So you're the church organist," Chris said to Louise as they walked.

"I am," Louise said. "But there are a large number of other people involved in the music ministry at Grace Chapel. I think you'll be pleasantly surprised tonight."

At the church, Louise parted ways with them. Alice, Jane, Chris, and Calla made their way into the sanctuary, where the greeters handed them bulletins and white candles set in white plastic holders for the candlelight portion of the service. Alice led the way to about halfway up the aisle and slipped into a pew, with the others following along behind her. Jane allowed Chris and Calla to enter the pew before her so that she would be sitting closest to the aisle down the center.

Calla looked around with interest as the pews around them quickly filled up. Jane and Alice smiled and greeted friends and introduced the Rosdahls, and Alice took time to distribute the little spider plant gifts from the basket she had brought along to her ANGELs.

"Hi, Calla," said Linsey, the girl Calla had met during the caroling outing. "Merry almost-Christmas."

"Hi, Linsey." Calla beamed. She gestured at the little spider plant in the festive red cup that Alice had given Lindsey. "Do you like your gift? I helped make them."

"It's pretty. Think Santa will find you at Grace Chapel Inn?" Linsey teased. "I bet you'll have a fun Christmas."

"It's already been a lot of fun," Calla confirmed. She sat back in the pew as Linsey moved on with her parents.

The special music before the service began a short time later. First, a handbell choir played "Carol of the Bells" followed by "Go, Tell It on the Mountain," and finally, a lovely Christmas medley. The handbell ringers ranged in age from teens through adults. The bells had been a gift to the church some years before, and with the dedicated instruction of the Grace Chapel choir director, the group had tackled increasingly sophisticated music. Last year a bequest in a church member's will had allowed them to purchase a fourth octave, and several more ringers had joined the group.

Jane noticed that Calla appeared riveted during the ringing of the bells. As the choir members let the final note vibrate and slowly fade away, Calla blinked as if coming out of a trance. While the ringers silently filed into the two front pews and Louise launched into the processional hymn, "O Come, All Ye Faithful," Jane leaned over and whispered, "They were great, weren't they?"

"Uh-huh." Calla nodded, her eyes shining.

The choir processed to the opening hymn, resplendent in their navy robes with the subtle shine of metallic trim, and the service began. It featured a traditional reading of the

Christmas story from the scriptures, interspersed with beloved carols.

Jane savored every moment, memories of Christmas Eves past warming her heart. How fortunate she was to have had the heritage of her childhood to fall back on when things went wrong in her marriage. She suspected that Chris had not had the same experience. Was it too much to hope that this Christmas could play a pivotal role in the Rosdahls' spiritual life?

Chapter Ten

Communion was served, and Jane nodded to Calla that she could take a piece of the soft, chewy bread when the plate came to them. During communion, Louise played soft arrangements of a wide array of Christmas hymns that the congregation could sing along to except for the moments when the bread and cup were consecrated and consumed.

Finally, the moment came for Jane's favorite part of the service. The communion assistants and ushers strode forward to the front of the church, where the acolytes waited with their candle lighters. While the congregation sang "Silent Night," half the assistants received light from the acolytes by holding up their candles to the candle lighters until the wicks caught the flame.

At a signal from the pastor, the assistants fanned out. Those with light strode down the center aisle, while those without went to the outside aisles along the windows, stationing themselves every three rows from front to back.

The overhead lights dimmed. The candlelight was passed from person to person along each row from the middle to the outside. Within a few minutes, everyone in the congregation held a lit candle.

The pastor held his flaming taper and, while the congregation continued singing softly, repeated the familiar Bible verse from the eighth chapter of John. "'I am the light of the world. Whoever follows me will never walk in darkness, but will have the light of life.'"

And as the hymn moved into the third and final verse, each person raised his or her candle high.

Beside her, Jane heard Calla suck in a gasp of awe. As the candles were raised, the amount of candlelight in the darkened church suddenly increased and spilled forth, illuminating the worshippers celebrating the birth of the Savior.

As the last notes of the hymn died away, the lights came blazing back on, and everyone extinguished the candles.

Reverend Thompson said, "May the light of this Child light your way forever. May the blessings which broke through the darkness on this night be yours always. May you always have cause to sing praises, give thanks, and celebrate the true Light of the world, our Savior, Jesus Christ."

"Amen," responded the congregation.

Reading from the final page of the bulletin, the pastor said, "Go in joy! Fear the darkness no more!"

"Thanks be to God!" responded the congregation.

Louise played the joyous first chords of "Joy to the World," and the congregation burst into the exuberant final song.

As the service ended and Louise began to play the postlude, Jane had to swallow a surge of emotion as Calla turned, eyes shining, and said, "That was awesome!"

Chris smiled over her daughter's head. "It was. Thank you so much for including us in your Christmas traditions. This was the most beautiful church service I've ever been to."

Then she grimaced. "Although I haven't been to church at all in a long time."

"Mom," Calla said, "when we get home again, can we find a church like this, with handbells and stuff for girls my age and music and everything?"

Her mother smiled. "It won't be exactly like Grace Chapel, but we can look for a church we both like and where there are a lot of kids your age." Again, she looked at Jane. "Time for some positive changes in my life. Finding a community of believers would be an excellent first step."

Jane, Alice, and the Rosdahls were swamped with friends and fellow worshippers stopping to offer holiday wishes as they made their way to the front of the sanctuary to meet Louise, who needed to put away her music and hang up her choir robe before leaving. Then the five of them trooped back out into the darkness for the walk home.

Calla looked up. "Wow! Look! There are a ton of stars out."

Everyone paused and looked up. The air was cold and crisp, the night clear. Above them, the heavens sparkled with a host of twinkling lights.

"Can you imagine what it would have been like to see a great white star blazing against a sky like this?" Chris asked in a hushed tone.

It was a rhetorical question, and no one felt the need to answer, not even Calla. After a moment's contemplation, they continued on their way to the inn.

"Now we all get out of our church clothes and into our jammies," Jane told Chris and Calla, as they entered the house.

"When we were young," Alice said, "our father made hot cocoa while we put on our pajamas, and then we all sat around the fire while he read the second chapter of Luke to us."

"What's the second chapter of Luke?" Calla asked.

"The Gospel according to Luke contains the traditional Christmas story," Alice told Calla. "Tonight at church you heard little bits and pieces from all four of the different Gospel writers. What we're going to read will sound familiar because you heard it at church earlier."

"Could I read it?" Calla asked.

"Oh Calla, our hostesses probably have their own Christmas tradition," her mother protested. "We're guests—"

Louise held up a hand, stilling Chris's words. "Calla, we would love to have you read the story of Jesus's birth. Thank you for offering."

Jane shot her eldest sister a grateful smile. That was the perfect thing to say. "Why don't we all get into our pajamas?" she suggested. "I'll make hot chocolate, and we'll break out the Christmas cookies and listen to Calla read the story of Christ's birth."

Everyone scattered then, reconvening in the living room around the big family tree the sisters had decorated weeks earlier.

Jane had put on comfy flannel pajama pants, a matching knit shirt, and a big fuzzy robe she'd owned for years. She'd whipped up a large pot of steaming hot chocolate, a cup of tea for Louise, and a fancy platter of all the types of Christmas cookies from the cookie exchange, as well as some nuts, a nutcracker, and a plate of cheese, crackers, carrots, and sliced apples.

Chris scrambled up from the couch when she saw Jane come through the door with the laden tray. "Oh my goodness, can I help you?"

"Let's just clear off the coffee table," Jane said, "and make it Snack Central."

Chris and Alice did her bidding, and soon the five of them were lounging on the couch, the overstuffed chairs, and in Jane's mother's rocker, watching the leaping flames in the fireplace as they ate the treats Jane had put together. Moments later, Wendell wandered in and hopped up in Alice's lap, kneading his paws gently on her thigh and purring.

"This is nice," Calla said dreamily, her gaze on the lighted tree.

"It is, isn't it?" Jane replied, propping her feet on the footstool in front of the rocker she'd chosen. She blew on her cup of hot chocolate. "Let's play 'What if.'"

"What's that?" Calla asked, looking around as if she expected to see a board game materialize in front of her.

"Think about the skills you have, the things you're good at, the things you enjoy doing for others," Jane said. "What if…you could choose one gift to give to the world, one thing that you could do or make happen? What would it be? Money is no object, but it has to be something you could actually achieve if you set your mind to it."

"Gracious," Alice said. "That is an ambitious notion."

"Money's no object, you say?" Louise confirmed.

"Correct," Jane said. "If you had unlimited funds and time and all the help you needed, what would you do to better the world?"

"Oh, I know mine," Alice said.

"Something to do with young people," Louise said immediately.

"No," Alice said. "But now that you mention it, I could incorporate that too. Two of my favorite things are working with the ANGELs and rescuing animals in need. What if I could establish a network of young people to volunteer in animal shelters to help socialize shelter pets so they would be more likely to get homes?"

Jane clapped. "That's a lovely idea, Alice. Anyone else?"

"I like to read," Calla said. "And I think reading is one of the most important things in the world. Everyone should have the chance to learn to read. So I guess that would be mine. What if I set up groups all over the world to help people learn to read?"

Chris stared at her daughter, shaking her head in wonder as Jane clapped again. "That's brilliant, Calla. What a great idea!"

"Mine would, of course, have a musical theme," Louise said after quiet descended again. "Research shows us that music training is the equivalent of learning another language and can actually make it easier for people to learn additional languages. What if I arranged for every child in the world to have formal music lessons?"

"You'd be one busy lady," Jane said, grinning as she clapped. "That's also a terrific idea."

Chris cleared her throat. "I'm not musical, and I've never spent much time around animals. But I like to sew. What if I set up organizations all over the world to teach women to sew, so they could help make clothing for their families and maybe even sell things to bring in money?"

This time, everyone clapped along with Jane.

"That's a great idea," Alice said. "Oh if only we could make these reality."

"Your turn, little sister," Louise said to Jane.

Jane turned to Chris and Calla. "Something you probably don't know about me, since it's the dead of winter, is that I like to garden. When I moved back here, one of the things I did was restore our mother's garden. I grow flowers, vegetables, and herbs. I think teaching people to grow things so they can feed their families would be a wonderful gift to the world. So what if I sent master gardeners all over the world to teach people how to garden? People in cities could grow things on their rooftops and in parks if they didn't have green spaces of their own, and people in super-dry areas would need help learning irrigation methods to water their crops. It would be a big project."

"Feeding the hungry," Alice said softly, "would be a noble calling." And this time Calla led the clapping.

"Well," Jane said, leaning forward and snagging a cookie, "that was fun. The world would certainly be a better place if each of us were able to realize our dreams, wouldn't it?"

"It would indeed." Louise indicated the coffee table, where Jane had placed a Bible in preparation for their Christmas reading. "Calla, it is time for our reader to share the Christmas story."

Calla was sitting on the sofa with her mother. She slid forward and picked up the thick volume. Jane had marked the start of the story. "Where do I start?"

"The second chapter," Jane told her. "Verses one through twenty."

Calla opened the book and scanned the page for a moment. Then she took a breath, and in a surprisingly firm voice, she began to read. "Chapter Two. The Birth of Jesus. In those days Caesar Augustus issued a decree…"

As the child read, the room was still, focused on her words. Alice had her eyes closed, a small smile playing over her lips as she listened. Louise was nodding approvingly, while Chris's eyes held a sheen of tears, and she beamed with pride.

Jane looked at Calla. Her red curls were unbound and unruly, her face solemn as she read the Christmas story aloud. "…and she gave birth to her firstborn, a son. She wrapped him in cloths and placed him in a manger, because there was no guest room available for them."

Calla glanced up then, her eyes bright as she caught Jane's regard, and she smiled, a sweet, childish expression that made Jane's heart turn over in her chest.

She thought of how unhappy Calla had been only a few short days ago, and she sent up a silent prayer of thanks that she had been given the privilege of helping the young family, both mother and child, to regain their happiness. Chris finally seemed to have released the resentment she'd carried, while Calla felt surer of her place in her father's family and was returning to the happy, extroverted girl her mother described.

As Jane continued to listen to the clear treble voice of their youngest guest, initially so difficult and defiant, retelling the familiar story Jane's father had read throughout her childhood and adolescence, a feeling of warmth and peace stole through her. Miracles did indeed occur in the world. The proof of it was sitting right before her.

About the Authors

Beth Adams lives in Brooklyn, New York, with her husband and two young daughters. When she's not writing, she spends her time cleaning up after two devious cats and trying to find time to read mysteries.

Melody Carlson is one of the most prolific novelists of our time. With more than 200 books published and sales topping 7.5 million, Melody writes primarily for women and teens. She's won numerous honors and awards, including The Rita, Gold Medallion, Carol Award, and Romantic Times Lifetime Achievement Award. Her novel *All Summer Long* premiered as a Hallmark movie in August 2019. She currently has several other projects under consideration/optioned for film, including a teen film which will soon go into production. Melody resides in Central Oregon with her husband and Labrador retriever. They enjoy camping and house renovations.

Anne Marie Rodgers has written over twenty inspirational and inspirational mystery novels for Guideposts Books and over five dozen books in her publishing career, including a number of bestsellers and award winners. Anne Marie is deeply committed to giving a voice to the world's animals who cannot speak for themselves. She has worked in emergency veterinary care and volunteered with wildlife rehabilitation, canine training and foster care, service dog puppy raising, and neonatal orphaned kitten rescue. She currently works in administration for a day veterinary practice. Anne Marie and her husband delight in their family, which includes three grandchildren, another on the way, and a varying number of furry family members. In 2019, they adopted a blind, diabetic Labrador retriever who refuses to believe he is handicapped.

A Note from the Editors

We hope you enjoyed this volume of Tales from Grace Chapel Inn series, created by the Books and Inspirational Media Division of Guideposts. We are a nonprofit organization that touches millions of lives every day through products and services that inspire, encourage, help you grow in your faith, and celebrate God's love in every aspect of your daily life.

Thank you for making a difference with your purchase of this book, which helps fund our many outreach programs to military personnel, prisons, hospitals, nursing homes, and educational institutions. To learn more, visit GuidepostsFoundation.org.

We also maintain many useful and uplifting online resources. Visit Guideposts.org to read true stories of hope and inspiration, access OurPrayer network, sign up for free newsletters, download free e-books, join our Facebook community, and follow our stimulating blogs.

To learn about other Guideposts publications, including the bestselling devotional *Daily Guideposts*, go to ShopGuideposts.org, call (800) 932-2145, or write to Guideposts, PO Box 5815, Harlan, Iowa 51593.